Four Corners

Four Corners

Ruth Clapsaddle-Counts

Pentland Press, Inc.
England • USA • Scotland

PUBLISHED BY PENTLAND PRESS, INC.
5124 Bur Oak Circle, Raleigh, North Carolina 27612
United States of America
919-782-0281

ISBN 1-57197-079-7
Library of Congress Catalog Card Number 97-069231

Printed in the United States of America

Author's Acknowledgements

The author wishes to gratefully acknowledge the following professionals who have intoxicated her with the romance of American archaeology in the Southwest: David Snow, Curator of the Palace of the Governors in Sante Fe; Tim Maxwell, Eric Blinman, Chuck Hannaford, and Steve Lakotas of the Office of Archaeological Studies of the Museum of New Mexico; rock art expert Polly Schaasfma and her husband, Curt, of the Culture Lab of Anthropology in Sante Fe; Florence Lister and her late husband, Bob, of Mancos, Colorado; the dean of Chaco Canyon, Alden C. Hayes and his wife, Karen, of Portal, Arizona; Stephen H. Lekson and his wife, Kathy, both of the University of Colorado; William Lipe of Washington State University; John Rick of Stanford; Mark Varien of the University of Arizona; Stuart Struever, founder of Crow Canyon Archaeological Center in Cortez, Colorado. He and his wife, Marti, are champions of our ancestral Puebloans, more popularly known as the Anasazi; Professor John Waters of the University of Georgia for his philosophy of historic preservation; Dan Murphy, storyteller par excellence, formerly with the National Park Service; Jerry Rogers, former Keeper of the National Register of Historic Places and now with the National Park Service, Sante Fe district; Bud Warren of the Maine Maritime Museum in Bath; Carl M. Sara in Washington, D.C., the American expert on maglev trains; Phil Stewart, Director of the Cherry Blossom Ten Mile Run in Washington.

— Ruth Clapsaddle-Counts

Sante Fe, New Mexico, 1998

Chapter One

"Here's a book, Daddy. See, it's all about archaeology."

Emily had selected a little storybook from the rotating kiosk of juvenile literature in the Dulles International Airport news shop. Holding up the colorfully illustrated cover to show him, she told her father, "It's written for older kids twelve to fifteen, but I bet I could read it to you while we wait for Grandfather's flight from Athens."

Worthington Rhodes beamed at his daughter as he straightened the collar on her sailor suit. He adjusted her sailor hat atop her curly blonde hair and playfully touched his forefinger to her nose. "Good idea, Emily. The book may provide a question or two for you to ask your grandfather when he arrives. Three hours late already, and now they've posted another delay on the monitor." He reached into his hip pocket.

"Put your wallet away, Daddy. Mommy gave me my allowance, so I'll pay." Emily, sounding and acting very grown-up, rummaged a five dollar bill from her over-the-shoulder pouch bag. As she waited in the checkout line, she began to leaf through the title pages and into the first chapter.

The type was large and Emily was holding the book far enough away so that her father didn't need his reading glasses to see the text and the illustrations. He didn't want to think about his father's profession, let alone read about it, but Emily was pointing to the book's definition of the Greek word "archaeology," and he couldn't help but read, "To talk about ancient things." She turned to the next page where archaeologists were described as, "Scientists who excavate ruins, digging in the dirt to find out what happened years ago."

"My grandfather's an archaeologist," Emily said to the cash register clerk, pronouncing the multiple-syllable word without difficulty as she submitted the book with its bar code to the electronic scanner. "He's coming to visit me today."

"How old are you?" the clerk asked, looking down and smiling at Emily, welcoming the conversational embellishment to her routine of retail sales.

"Nine and a half." Emily smiled, revealing braces on her teeth. "But this book's going to be a piece of cake for me. I can tell from the sentences. Subject, verb. Subject, verb. And no long words except 'archaeology.'"

"Watch out for the mummies," the clerk warned, handing Emily her change.

Emily laughed and waved a good-bye. Moving out into the towering concourse of the terminal with its adult hustle and bustle, Emily clutched her book in one hand and waited for the familiar grasp of her father taking her other hand.

"We'll find a quiet place where we can wait for your grandfather," Worthington said, his hand squeezing hers a bit too tightly. Family, he thought as they walked, dodging the onrush of people laden with baggage, three generations of their extended family were about to gather today in this airport. He mulled over the word family as if he were defining it for the first time. His nuclear family, a loving environment for nurturing his children, was about to be polluted by a noxious grandfather. Maybe Emily could purify the atmosphere.

Freeing her hand from his, Emily pointed upward at the monitor. "There's Grandfather's plane—number 4-9-0."

Worthington started to answer his daughter but was interrupted by a firm hand on his shoulder and a greeting. "Mr. Rhodes, how nice to see you. I thought you were into bullet trains, not airplanes." The man's laugh was polite, respectful. Worthington felt the strong, experienced handshake, meant to be remembered in the voting booth.

"Senator," Worthington replied, "you're right. Fast maglev trains are the answer to our country's transportation needs for the next millennium."

"And high time, too. We can no longer play second fiddle to the French and their TGV. Besides, I've come to believe that Congress's appropriations for all those freeways was tax money unwisely spent. The *Windjammer* will be much more energy efficient. This your daughter?"

"Yes. Emily, meet Senator Carl Schurz from Missouri. He was a doubter at first, but now he's highballing it with us all the way, aren't you, Senator."

"No question about it." Senator Schurz was quick to nod, displaying his familiar campaign smile. "Your transcontinental bullet train will create construction jobs for my constituents and supply contracts for my Missouri industries, now that defense contracts are on the wane—that is, if funding is approved by the Lower House." This time his laugh was demeaning. Addressing Emily, he explained, "In our governmental scheme, the chairman of the House Appropriations Committee has the power. He's almost as important as we one hundred who have been elected to the Upper House, the great United States Senate."

"I'm confident Congressman Roybal will continue to support the *Windjammer*," Worthington said. "His electorate needs work, too."

"Your big train is going to be good for the country, isn't that right, Daddy? That's what Mommy says."

Worthington smiled and hugged Emily. "Two more at home like her," he said proudly. "Her older sister's playing soccer this afternoon and her younger brother's in a school play. A father can't be everywhere at once."

"You have a wonderful family, Mr. Rhodes. Children are our hope for the future. But I must run. I'm off on a fact-finding mission to Cannes on the French Riviera. European Community, tariffs, trade, NATO—those sorts of issues, you know. Nice to meet you, Emily."

She waved after the senator. "Daddy, do you suppose he will visit those caves in France with the animal paintings? The ones Grandfather wrote to me about."

"You'll have to remind your grandfather that he promised to take you to the Lascaux caves some day. But I think the senator's going to Cannes to play in the sand. Come on, there's a quiet reading place for us over there." Father and daughter found two seats side by side. "Okay, Emily, you read a page or two and tell me the story in your own words. I'll keep my eye on the arrival screen."

Emily began reading. Out loud she asked, "Do you know my book's definition of archaeology?"

"Yes, I looked at the first page over your shoulder while we were in the cashier line. You should recite the definition for your grandfather. You'll impress him."

Worthington couldn't help himself, for as Emily turned the pages, he thought back to his first encounter with archaeology. He calculated that twenty-one years and nine months had passed since that episode in Greece. His photographic memory projected the humiliating scene onto a screen as high as the Dulles concourse. His father was making fun of him, and the other men down in the excavation, all looking up, were pointing at him as if he were a fool. He was standing in the hot Mediterranean sun on the edge of their dig. How out of place he must have looked, for his father and the other men were bare chested, sweaty, dusty, unshaven for days, and he, wanting so much to make a favorable impression on his father, was dressed in his only suit.

At age eighteen, jet-lagged from the overnight flight from Boston to Athens, he'd come straight-away by bus to the dig site at Delphi, planning to tell his father about his dream of becoming a pop singer and to explain that he had no interest in going to college to become an archaeologist. He had so wanted to sit with his father in a taverna, if only for a few moments, and talk man to man about his future. He had so hoped this distant father of his, a man whom he barely knew, would give him a paternal blessing.

He remembered that his father had not even climbed up out of the dig to greet him. Instead, in a patronizing voice, his father had demanded to know why he had shown up in Greece, unannounced. With the eyes of the entire dig crew upon him, he had experienced a numbing case of stage fright. All he could do was to blurt out how his high school friends and his Uncle Bill believed that some day he would become famous.

His father had laughed, and then the others, as if on cue from their leader, joined in the merriment at his embarrassed expense. Vividly he recalled his father yelling up at him, "You want to do what?" When the laughter from the other men had died down, his father had lectured him. "We're searching for scientific truth here, lad, the truth about the world's greatest civilization. You, as my son and my father's grandson, are destined to join our search. Music! Bah! This wondrous civilization will sing all the tunes you need to know. The monumental achievements of my ancient Greeks in literature, theater, architecture, any of the arts, including democracy, have yet to be surpassed. Everything of any merit was said and done in city-states like this one here." His father had pointed to his dusty dig. "For the sake of science, we must learn all we can from these great people. From out of the past these people are trying to communicate their wisdom to us. Now you go back to Maine and do as I told you in my letter. Call my colleague, Dr. Elliot. He'll admit you to Northwestern. I guarantee it." His father and the men had turned their backs on him, intent only on their trowels, their shovels, their whisk brooms, and their fine-mesh sifting screens.

As if in a trance, he had turned away and walked back into Delphi where he waited hours in the hot summer sun for the return bus to Athens, alternately crying his heart out and perspiring with rage. Finally he had gone into a taverna and ordered a beer. The rage within him rising along with the foam in the mug, he had promptly driven his fist into the first human target that presented itself—the bartender's laughing jaw.

Brought back to his senses by the man's stubbled face thrust into his, and the man's large, sinewy hands gripping his suit jacket, he'd broken loose using all his strength and fled outside into a rear passageway, running at full speed toward the bus stop and escaping onto the departing vehicle.

During the long, slow bus ride and on the flight back to Boston, he realized he had passed through some sort of a rite of passage to manhood. His Aunt Hattie was right, a college education was the real ticket to stardom. By the time the plane landed, he had put aside his childhood dreams of becoming a singer; he would go to college. But he vowed that he'd never go to Northwestern and study archaeology. He'd go to Bowdoin and stay close to the only family he knew, his Uncle Bill and Aunt Hattie.

Later, in college, seeking answers about all of society, its past and its future, he had asked himself, could his father have been right about the superiority of those long-ago Greeks? Nothing new in literature since Homer's *Illiad*? Nothing new in art since the *Charioteer of Delphi*? Nothing new in theater since *Oedipus Rex*? Nothing new in architecture since the Parthenon? Nothing new in transportation since the chariot? Nonsense! He would focus his life's work on proving his father wrong, at least about one aspect of ancient Greek life—transportation.

Abruptly the giant screen of emotional memories in the Dulles concourse went blank as Worthington was brought back to the present by his daughter's voice.

"Listen to this," Emily exclaimed. "My book says there were many important inventions in the ancient world. People had the wheel in Grandfather's Greece."

"Yes, I know."

Emily flipped the page. "And the . . ." She stumbled a bit over the next word. ". . . Toltecs, down in Mexico, had the wheel, too, but used it only for their toys." She pointed to one of the drawings. "See, here's a picture of a Toltec toy dog who has wheels instead of legs."

"The funny puppy's equipped to win any dog race." Worthington laughed. "Just look at the expression on his face. He's smiling."

Emily laughed along with her father. "Daddy, why didn't the Toltecs have real wheels like the Greeks?"

"There's a good question for your grandfather."

"But what do you think, Daddy?"

Worthington ran his hand through his thinning hair. "Well, I suppose they didn't have any roads."

"My book says the prehistory peoples in the Southwest had roads. The . . ." She paused as she followed the syllables of the next word. ". . . An-a-saz-i. They built roads in the Four Corners."

"They're the ancient ones your grandfather is coming to study during his sabbatical. When he called from Greece, he told your mommy it was time for him to explore a fresh perspective."

Emily nodded. "Mommy said he's going to go on a dig. But what's a prospective?"

"No, the word prospective might be used in conjunction with motherhood. For example, when a woman is expecting a baby, she is a 'prospective mother.' But I said, 'per-spec-tive.' My word means a viewpoint with depth. You're in the process of learning about archaeology from reading your new book. And you'll gather more information from talking with your grandfather. You'll develop a new perspective on the subject, and from it form your own view-point."

"You mean, I'll be able to explain archaeology to Elizabeth?"

"Yes, your assignment will be to make the subject interesting enough to keep your older sister's attention."

"Maybe she already knows about archaeology."

"Even if she does, she doesn't know your perspective on the subject, does she?"

"Well, no, I guess not."

"Go on." Worthington gestured at the book. "See if there's any more to the story about the wheel in our American Southwest."

"OK, I'll read to myself and give you my report." Emily read several pages while Worthington walked to the airline counter and inquired about the flight from Athens.

"We're expecting flight 490 in half an hour," the attendant replied to his question.

"For sure this time?"

The attendant forced a smile and nodded.

From behind him a voice inquired, "Mr. Rhodes, waiting for the Athens flight, too?"

"Why hello, Ms. Trinket. Yes, my father's on it. And you?"

"I ducked out of the White House, telling the President I'd only be an hour or so for a quick trip to Dulles to welcome my mother back from Delphi. She planned the itinerary for her archaeological study trip to Greece around your father's latest book."

"He'll be happy to hear from another of his readers."

"I hope my mother will be in a better mood than I suspect the President is with the plane's four hour delay. As she would put it, the Chief must be having a 'conniption fit' about my absence." Ms. Trinket explained, "He needs me to field those dogged questions from the press corps."

"You brought your laptop computer with you, I see."

She nodded. "Working on his speech for tomorrow. He's going to mention your *Windjammer* project."

"Favorably, I hope."

"Of course. The President believes you are demonstrating leadership on a national scale with your transportation plan for the next century."

"It's been very helpful to have his support from early on. Come, meet my daughter."

Ms. Trinket bent over and shook Emily's little hand. "My, what a nice child. She has your blue eyes, Mr. Rhodes."

"I'm a young lady," Emily said. "And I'm going to be an archaeologist."

"You just now decide that?" Worthington laughed.

Emily nodded. "It's this book. Look here, Ms. Trinket, it's about this Toltec man. He was a genius. He made toys and then he said . . ."

"Emily, Ms. Trinket has to work on a speech for the President."

"It's all right, Mr. Rhodes. Go on, Emily."

Emily held up her book, pages open. "In A.D. 1100, this Toltec engineer was thrown out of his hometown, Chichen Itza on the Yucatan Peninsula, because the priests and elders thought his ideas were too radical. So they sent him far away on a trade expedition to the American Southwest. They were hoping he would never return. But in case he did come back, he would bring turquoise to decorate their silver jewelry."

Ms. Trinket toyed with her necklace.

"So what happened to this genius?" Worthington asked.

"He took all his men with him and they marched for weeks across the deserts of northern Mexico and southern New Mexico and finally came to where the Anasazi lived." This time she pronounced the name without hesitation.

"Emily, what leads you to believe he was a genius?" Ms. Trinket asked.

"Oh, you missed the first part. He invented the wheel."

"But they didn't have horses to pull wheeled carts," Ms. Trinket said. "There weren't any horses here until Columbus arrived."

Emily folded the book over and showed her an illustration of an Anasazi dog. "Maybe they trained their dogs to pull the carts."

"Emily, does your book tell how these American natives greeted this Toltec when he arrived with his splendid invention?" Worthington asked.

"His name was Ixtill Eight. Isn't that a funny name? The Anasazi killed him," Emily said matter-of-factly. "Here's a picture. See, it shows them clubbing him over the head. He's holding the wheel."

Ms. Trinket drew back from the book, her hand flying to her mouth. "But why are they beating him to death?" She looked at Worthington for an explanation.

"My book says the Anasazi didn't want any new ideas coming into their lives," Emily continued. "They were content with the way things were."

"That's pretty brutal behavior, don't you think?" Worthington said to his daughter.

"Such killings have happened in modern times to our leaders," Ms. Trinket said weakly.

"Oh, I see what you mean." Worthington spoke the word slowly, "Assassination." He looked at Emily. "Does your book offer any further explanation?"

Emily turned the page. "No, that's the end of the story, Daddy."

"But where's the moral?" Ms. Trinket asked.

"There isn't any." Worthington frowned. "It's a warning from out of the past: don't be the person out there on the edge advocating a new idea for society." He braced himself against the airline counter for support.

Chapter Two

"Here he comes now!" Emily squealed with delight. "Grandfather! Grandfather Dusty!"

Worthington tried to smile at his father, but the expression failed. He quickly turned his attention to Emily. "Now you can give your grandfather that big hug."

Emily jumped up and down with excitement. The tall man reached down and scooped her up in his arms.

"You've grown a big beard," she exclaimed as she ran her fingers through his graying whiskers trying to find a smile hidden beneath.

Worthington reached out and shook his father's hand. "Welcome to Washington, sir. I guess eminent archaeologists are expected to have a beard."

"And wear a rumpled hat," Emily said, still up in her grandfather's arms, her own hat askew. She pulled the leather hat from his head, revealing a bald, suntanned head.

Dusty laughed. "Emily, put my hat back on. I'm expected to wear an old hat, carry a trowel at the ready, grow a beard, and have a need for a manicure and a laundromat. I guess that's why they call me 'Dusty.'"

"But have you given up smoking yet?" Worthington asked as he adjusted Emily's sailor hat.

"Yes, I have. But I'll tell you, on that flight I was ready to light one up. We had a highjacking scare outside Athens and had to turn back. That's why my plane was so late."

"Good heavens," Worthington exclaimed. "What happened?"

"Some fanatical Greek kept yelling about the government not fulfilling its basic obligations to the people."

"Basic obligations?" Worthington repeated the phrase out loud in a reflective tone.

"I can understand him wanting to make the point that basic obligations must be honored," Dusty said, "but the fellow was crazy in his outburst, slurring his words, and gesturing wildly. Maybe he was on something, I don't know. The copilot, a very brave man indeed, came back to try to calm him down, and made a quick move, grabbing the highjacker's arm, while the steward, who was coming up from behind, tackled the man in the aisle right next to my seat. Several crew members and I pinned him down while the copilot grabbed his weapon. We tied the bandit into a seat, and the pilot turned the big plane around and flew back to Athens where the authorities took the man into custody. As it turned out, his gun was only a toy."

Emily's eyes were wide. "Weren't you scared, Grandfather?"

Not this man, Worthington thought to himself. With all his bravado he would never admit to any sign of weakness. But where was Dusty in honoring his own basic obligations? The fact is, his father had sent him off to Maine into the care of Uncle Bill and Aunt Hattie for what turned out to be his entire upbringing. Having pawned off his only child, Dusty was free to escape to Greece. There, unencumbered by family obligations, he could emulate his own revered father by playing the role of the great expatriate American archaeologist, treasuring centuries-old, dust-covered artifacts. Only cracked vases, crumbling statues, and buildings-in-ruins decorated his family tree.

One of Worthington's first recollections was wondering why he was the only little boy in Maine who had no father, no mother. It was Uncle Bill who told him that his mother had died in childbirth. He'd come to know his mother only through those faded photographs Aunt Hattie had shown him. And his father—the insensitive lout—when he did return to this country to see his publisher and launch a new book, never even mentioned her. The callous old goat talked only about each new excavation into the earth as if it were his true love, only to be replaced a year or two later with another dig, and then another. Eventually he'd had intercourse with what had seemed to Worthington to be all of Greek antiquity.

But he, Worthington, hadn't turned away from his obligations to his wife Sara, to Elizabeth, to Emily, to Danny, and to all of society. No sir! He was going to save America, tie the nation together once again with high-speed surface transportation in the same way the young country's travel, commerce, and culture had been united more than a century ago by the early railroad giants—the Huntingtons, the Vanderbilts, the Leland Stanfords. His *Windjammer*, his country, his family—yes, they were his basic obligations, and he was honoring them all.

Worthington looked at his watch. "Let's get the Volvo. I think I should drive you straight away to the reception. I'll call Sara from the car phone and tell her we're not coming to the house, and explain your flight delay. You can say hello to Elizabeth if she's home."

"And Danny?"

"He may be home by now, as well, that is if our *au pair* has picked him up, or Sara may have driven Elizabeth straight from her soccer game to see the second act of Danny's school play."

"What if you had more than three?"

Worthington laughed. "Then we'd need a third car and a second nanny. There are so many activities and events scheduled for kids these days. Some days I wish I could be a full-time father."

"In my day, raising kids required only a full-time mother."

As they drove along the expressway, Emily asked her grandfather, "Do you have a cellular phone in your dig?"

Dusty chuckled. "No, our excavation site is so remote no one will deliver pizza."

Emily reached into the front seat, extracted the car phone from its cradle on the console and punched in her home number. She said to her mother, "Grandfather Dusty's plane was kidnapped, but he's here now. Do you wish to speak to him? I bought a book on archaeology at the airport. I'm going to ask Grandfather Dusty some perceptive questions."

She handed the phone to her grandfather, who quickly reassured Sara he was all right. Then he spoke to Elizabeth and finally to little Danny. With pride in his voice, Dusty touted his grandson to Worthington. "Danny told me he had the starring role in his school play. He was Thomas Edison."

"Yes, the play is an original story about technology and new inventions," Worthington replied. "The idea was that if Edison were alive today, he would invent personal computers, orbiting satellites, space stations on the moon, compact disks, et cetera."

"All the kids in Danny's class had their chance to say what Edison would invent, and Danny told about Daddy's super-fast maniac train."

"That's magnetic, Emily," Worthington corrected. "I saw the rehearsal. Danny was really good as the famous inventor, considering he's only seven."

Looking directly at Worthington, Dusty admonished him, "See, you, too, could have succeeded in science. The skill runs in our family."

"I want to be an archaeologist," Emily said. "Is that a science, Grandfather?"

"You bet it is," Dusty said emphatically. "The science of archaeology is like a young woman about to blossom. And, if your father had taken my direction, there could have been three generations of Rhodes as archaeologists. And now, with you and Danny, there'd be a fourth to follow."

"Was your daddy an archaeologist, too?" Emily asked.

Worthington started to reply, "Yes he was, Emily, he was . . ."

"Back at the turn of the century," Dusty interrupted, "he was one of the early pioneers in the discipline."

Worthington tightened his grip on the steering wheel and thought to himself it wouldn't have been even two generations if Aunt Hattie and Uncle Bill up in Maine hadn't agreed to take care of me so he could run away to Greece. Remembering his summer vacations, Worthington pictured himself and Uncle Bill aboard Uncle Bill's homemade lobster boat back before the awful accident. He'd never forget those bright early mornings, the sun rising over the Atlantic, the clouds on the horizon billowing like so many sails of distant clipper ships. Then, later in the day, after they had harvested the last of the lobster catch from the traps, Uncle Bill would do magic tricks with that deck of cards he always carried with him as the boat sped homeward through the waves toward their picturesque little harbor for the night. How the other lobstermen admired Uncle Bill. Deservedly so, because he had organized the co-op for marketing their catches. He might be described as a lovable showman, perhaps even a promoter of sorts. Worthington thought how he sorely missed the man's warmth and affection. Uncle Bill was killed at sea. He took his slow, twenty-nine foot boat out one winter day when small craft advisories were posted. He regarded himself as invincible because he was able to do almost any magic trick. As such, he didn't believe in radios and barely understood radar. A fog came up. He became confused, lost his way, and headed out to sea instead of back toward the harbor. One of those big oil tankers, plying the coastal waters, literally ran over his frail little lobster boat.

Picking up on her grandfather's word, Emily said, "I know about pioneers. They're the settlers who went west."

"Yes, Emily," Worthington said, "but we mustn't let ourselves limit pioneering to geographical frontiers. There are also pioneers who open up new lines of thought or activities or develop new technology."

Worthington thought back about his own boyhood quest for career goals. One day when he was a few years older than Emily, and before he entertained the idea of becoming a pop star, he and Uncle Bill were out on the water together. He had confided to his uncle, "I want to learn about our history of shipbuilding in the ports along our Maine coast—trace the industry back to the clipper ships, the windjammers, the yachts, study the plans for all those grand wooden boats built at Bath, Wiscasset, and Waldoboro. And then I want to advance our nautical technology into the future. I see several techniques that I think will increase both the speed and capacity of our lobster boats. And I'll bet I can win that Fourth of July race for you, Uncle Bill. Perhaps just as important, I have ideas for improving the unloading facilities in our little harbors."

But holding up his hand and shaking his head no, Uncle Bill had advised, "You make an impact on the land, son. The sea is populated with mystery and danger, but the land is clear sailing, and it's yours to conquer."

Dusty interrupted Worthington's recollections. "I don't remember the bridges across the Potomac being toll."

"It's quite recent," Worthington explained. "The Department of Transportation has imposed a toll on all interstate highways and bridges where federal money has been spent for construction. Officially it's the 'Responsibility Tax,' the RT, meant to raise money to rebuild our nation's infrastructure, but the media has dubbed it the 'Rat race Tax.' The tolls are another source of funding for my bullet train."

"Another government tax," Dusty said sarcastically.

"It's a relatively painless user fee, the same toll you pay when you enter a national park or monument. Some call it a 'sin tax' for burning up all that gasoline and producing those polluting emissions. You'd be surprised, Father, how many millions of dollars we raise every day across the country."

"Here, I'll pay the toll." Dusty looked back at his granddaughter. "Emily, have you picked out your college yet? I just might have a little more money in my wallet for your tuition."

"Put your wallet away, sir." Winking at Emily, Worthington quipped, "Mommy gave me my bridge allowance this morning."

He wanted to warn Emily to be careful, for tied to the old man's generous offer were a lot of strings. Dusty would dictate to her her course of study. He would take away all her options and set her on a course he'd design. He'd try to live her life for her. And when she'd say she wanted to do something else, Dusty would belittle her ideas.

"Thank you very much, Grandfather Dusty, but Mommy gives me an allowance, too, and I'm saving part of it for my college education."

Worthington smiled with satisfaction. He wouldn't have to worry about Emily looking out for herself.

"I suppose you will want to go to your father's college," Dusty said to Emily. "But remember, they don't offer an archaeological program for you to study. You should go to the college I recommended for your father."

"Sir, she's only nine and a half years old. Let's get her through grammar school first." Worthington slowed for the toll booth. He tried to keep his voice calm. "All three kids may not want to become archaeologists. Sara said just last night that Emily should go into teaching, Elizabeth social work, and Danny sports."

"No, Daddy, I want to be an archaeologist. Danny says he wants to be a race car driver. And Elizabeth says she's going to the Olympics."

Worthington looked at his father. "Bowdoin College has an excellent reputation. I made a lot of friends there. In fact, half the New England congressional delegation went there. We Bowdoin graduates enjoy camaraderie. Besides, their degree program in liberal arts is world renowned."

Dusty snorted. "Arts are amorphous—about as far from science and facts as you can get."

Worthington glanced at his father before returning his attention to the traffic. So I broke the chain, he thought. That's tough, because I'm perfectly happy doing what I'm doing. I had no desire to be an archaeologist. I'm not cut out for scientific research, laboratory work, or conducting an isolated dig in the dirt in some faraway place, having to live week after week without contact with people like some Basque sheepherder. It's great he's happy, successful and so well respected in his field, but he and I are two different people, the same way my kids are three separate individual young people. What they do or don't do with their lives is up to them. Why subject my family to these kinds of pressures just to keep up some irrelevant tradition?

"You miss the point, son."

"Which is?"

"Genes. You're ignoring them."

The old debate of heredity versus environment, Worthington thought. With me it was Uncle Bill's determination in rising at three in the morning, day after day, and driving his pickup truck to the dock and boarding his old, wide lobster boat before sunrise for yet another trip out on the water—hard work, the Yankee ethic. To hell with genes, it's environment that really shapes our personalities.

Dusty looked at Worthington and held up his index finger. "Science is what's important in this world. Not trying to build some high-speed train. You're frittering away your life on cocktail parties and influence peddling, trying to promote this political project of yours. Now, tell me, where is the ultimate truth in any of your shenanigans?"

"The truth?"

"Yes. You know what your problem is? You've never sought out the scientific truth about our world, ourselves, our culture. You're bungling your life away on frivolous matters."

Emily's lips quivered. She started to cry. Tears came, one glistening on her cheek. She looked at the beard. "My daddy knows everyone in Washington. Even the President. We just talked to his speech writer. She's putting Daddy into the President's speech tomorrow. Isn't that right, Daddy?" She rubbed her eyes.

"Don't cry, Emily. Grandfather Dusty just got a little heated about things."

Emily looked into her grandfather's eyes. "Everybody in my school thinks my daddy is an important man."

"I'm sorry I yelled at your daddy, Emily. Maybe you wish the highjacker had shot me."

"That's enough, sir."

As they drove across the Potomac River bridge and entered the nation's capital, Dusty grumbled under his breath and cleared his throat several times. "Maybe it was a good thing my plane was late. Now you and Emily can come with me to Dr. Ardmore's reception and talk. You'll see how she pursues the truth. She's a good scientist."

"Do you want to stay, Emily?"

"Will she autograph my book?"

"Only authors sign their books," Worthington explained.

"Rubbish, Dr. Ardmore will be happy to write a message in your book," Dusty assured her, adding, "I'll personally guarantee it."

As he drove the Volvo onto the brick pavement at the entrance to the Four Seasons Hotel in Georgetown, Worthington wondered how his uncle and his father, two brothers, could be so different. Bill was sociable, fun loving, easy to talk to, and easy to like. But Dusty was just the opposite, always bragging about how he could guarantee the actions of other people. Worthington checked himself. He knew he must cover up his animosity toward his father for Emily's sake.

He told his father that he and Emily would join him. The evening's reception would be a diversion from having to listen to his father expound on his Greek world. And since he himself was preparing for a series of cross-country promotional talks about his *Windjammer*, maybe he could pick up a presentation technique or two from Dr. Ardmore. She had certainly held her own at the initial *Windjammer* hearing before Congressman Roybal's committee. Her good humor under the pressure of all those inane questions had really impressed him.

Worthington gave the keys to the valet and asked where Dr. Ardmore's reception was being held.

"All those fat cats are down in the Hellenic Salon off the Grand Ballroom," was the valet's reply.

"Be respectful of benefactors, young man," Dusty said sharply. "They fund important scientific research."

As Worthington got out of the car and took Emily's hand, she looked up into his eyes. He spoke to her in the intimate voice of a loving father. "Emily, you can grow up to be whatever you want. I've lived my life with this resolve, and you must also trust in your own dreams."

Chapter Three

Stuart Wales, Executive Director of the Institute and Living Museum of Archaeology, the powerful nonprofit known as ILMA, had justified the expense to the chairman of his board, Quentin Ford IV, by pointing out how appropriate the Hellenic Salon of the Four Seasons Hotel would be for Dr. Ardmore's reception and her presentation. The banquet room's decorative theme of the Greek ruins of Delphi, he told his chairman, would underscore their purpose of fundraising for archaeological preservation, as well as set the stage for recruiting volunteers for ILMA's forthcoming dig in the American Southwest. To clinch his argument, Stuart had shown Ford the room. He pointed to the wall murals depicting Delphi's partially reconstructed temple of Apollo, its restored treasury building, the city's hillside theater, and the long, narrow athletic stadium. The perceptive muralist had surrounded these magnificent edifices with row upon row of building blocks and sections of columns, each marked with inventory numbers, awaiting the day when Delphi, the center of the world to the ancient Greeks, would be reassembled to welcome a modern-day oracle.

Ford had been readily convinced, and handed Stuart a check. "If I can give a million to that Indian museum in Indiana, I can spend a few thousand to throw Georgetown's most prestigious reception of the year."

At this evening's event, the decorative ruins of this old world site were outdone by the display dominating the food table. Not by the food, but by the magnificent ice sculpture centerpiece—an icy replica of the tiered, multi-storied twelfth-century Taos Pueblo. Miniature pole ladders crafted from sticks of white aspen, tilting against the ice, showed how access was gained to roof tops and upper level entrances. A scale-model yellow and red zia flag flew from atop this New Mexico landmark frozen in time. Tiny windows, offering a peek inside, suggested that the American Southwest pueblo, while strikingly different in appearance, might be equally as captivating as the classical Greek temple.

The culinary offering was unique, too: quesadillas, sopaipillas with their sweet honey, the popular corn dish posole, blue corn chips in replicated Mimbres pottery bowls, tiny side dishes offering a choice of green or red chile salsa, corn tortillas with Anasazi beans, Indian fry bread with liberal sprinkles of confectioner's sugar, a vegetable tray accented with jalapeño peppers, and a fruit tray highlighted with sectioned prickly pears.

A trio of musicians dressed in tuxedos—a pianist whose white hair jounced with his musical energy, a Benny Goodman clarinetist clone, and a violinist lost in his expressions—provided an entertaining prelude to the evening's program. Their musical arrangements afforded each an opportunity to accentuate his special talent.

Suddenly the music stopped, a signal for guests to conclude their snacking and move toward the chairs arranged for Dr. Ardmore's presentation. But there was always one last bite and one last sip. Those gathered at one end of the table lingered one last moment, continuing their conversation with a man who, even without his baseball glove and bat, was recognized by all as Alexander Parish, the former star third baseman of the Washington Sluggers.

"Gosh," he exclaimed, "I'm so excited about my name being on the roster for Dr. Ardmore's next dig."

"You'll get a framed ILMA degree certificate to add to your trophy display," an admirer commented.

"Yes, archaeology is my second love. Besides, you can't be monogamous when there are so many fields to play in." Alexander read the man's name tag and added, "Isn't that right, George?" He looked down at George's female companion. "Of course, I donate a little money, too, as I am sure you do, Mrs. Ah . . . ah . . ."

"Oh indeed," she purred, her gaze glued to his television face. "But please call me Martha."

George was quick to bring up his favorite subject. "I'm interested in what you have to say about those mysterious ball courts in Arizona that Dr. Ardmore describes as large, oval-shaped earthen depressions. How do you think they played the game, and what were the rules?"

"They threw the rule book away, and . . ." Alexander smiled at Martha. ". . . made up the game as they went along."

George was intent on pursuing his pet subject. "Dr. Ardmore says the object was to throw a hard rubber ball through a ring mounted high up on a wall. I'll bet your friend Nolan Ryan would have trouble pitching through that ring, given its angle and height."

"Aw, he'd do it with a spit ball."

Those around Alexander laughed.

"One version I've heard says the losing team literally lost their heads," another patron quipped.

More laughter.

"But Dr. Ardmore said it was the Hohokam people, not the Anasazi, who played in that league," George said, intent on showing up Alexander's skimpy knowledge of the subject. "And she traces the sport to Mesoamerica."

Martha looked up at Alexander. "I just know we'll find their rule book on our dig. Maybe you'll be the one to unearth it." She swept away the last remaining cheese and chicken quesadilla. "Wouldn't such a find be appropriate for you as a baseball celebrity?"

"You and I will have to search for it together," Alexander whispered to her.

George glared. "We're all going to be digging in Anasazi land, not the Hohokam territory." He turned to Martha. "But no matter where we go, dear, we'll still need direction from Dr. Ardmore in order to know where to dig. I'm referring to the computer analysis of each site, as well as aerial surveys. Satellite mapping of archaeological sites has become a science as exact as my oil exploration business in Texas. In fact, archaeology's turning into a game of surveillance."

"Looks like we've a spy coming into our midst," said a woman whose nametag identified her as MRS. HENRY D'CAMP, BOARD MEMBER. She nodded toward the tall man with the little girl in a sailor suit approaching the buffet.

"Try something new," Worthington suggested as he placed the last sopaipilla on a paper plate and handed Emily the pillow-shaped puffed pastry. He pointed to the honey pot. Emily eagerly plunged the dipper while her father held a napkin, just in case.

George whispered to the foursome around Alexander, "What's Worthington Rhodes doing here? I thought he was intent on his *Windjammer* train erasing the Four Corners."

"Just think," Martha speculated to the others, "if all that 'Rat race' money could be put to use restoring our quaint old buildings in Houston and revitalizing other city centers around the country."

"And financing more archaeological excavations," Mrs. D' Camp added. "I'm writing my congressman about it, you can be sure."

Martha nodded her approval. "Let's find our seats, George. Dr. Ardmore is about to begin."

◆　◆　◆　◆

Upon entering the banquet room, Dusty Rhodes made a bee-line for the well-stocked bar.

A hand reached out, grasping his. "Why, if it isn't the well-known author, Archibald Stonelock Rhodes," Stuart Wales declared. "We're honored you've come all the way from Greece to participate with Dr. Ardmore in ILMA's field seminar."

"Anna's reputation has traveled across the ocean. Besides, your institute deserves my support."

"Let me pour you a glass of New Mexico wine and introduce you to some of our aficionados of archaeology." The executive director tapped the sleeve of the woman beside him. "Brenda Turner has traveled a long way, too—from Colorado. She writes a column called 'Anasazi Update' for her weekly newspaper in Cortez."

"Pleased to meet you, Ms. Turner. It is Ms., isn't it? I don't see any ring on your third finger, left hand."

"Have you taken yours off for the night, Mr. Rhodes?"

Stuart moved between Dusty and Brenda and filled a black man's empty glass. "Dusty, I want you to meet our mayor, His Honor Jedson Beyer."

"Mayor."

"Here for a busman's holiday, Mr. Rhodes? Or maybe you are pursuing a different recreation?"

Stuart quickly intervened. "Mayor Beyer is going to say a few words of welcome to get us started this evening."

"You're calling the 'all-aboard' tonight," Dusty suggested.

"No, that was my father's job. He was your Uncle Tom Pullman Porter. This evening I'm going to enlighten our audience with a story about an African-American who made the most momentous archaeological discovery concerning American prehis-tory."

Dusty started to comment, but Stuart interrupted by introduc-ing the man joining them at the bar. "I'd like you to meet Quentin Ford IV, ILMA's Chairman of the Board."

Ford spotted Worthington Rhodes. His face red with anger, the chairman growled at Stuart, "What the hell is he doing here?"

Stuart turned around to see the man about whom Ford was upset.

Mayor Beyer saw Worthington grasp Emily's hand and lead her to a front row seat. He replied to Ford, "Why, that's Worthington Rhodes, the man who is the brainchild behind our nation's new bullet train." Looking at Dusty, he asked, "Any relation, Mr. Rhodes?"

Dusty nodded. "That's my granddaughter holding the book about archaeology."

Everyone's attention focused on Emily.

"She's a honey, isn't she, Mr. Ford," Stuart said.

Ford's expression changed from exasperation to cunning. He put his hand on his lieutenant's back. "Stuart, you're in training for another of those crazy foot races, so run over there, fix our train man a drink and change his perspective. Convince him he should put his Washington political power to work on a good cause—preserving his country's prehistoric sites for his children and his children's children instead of bulldozing the past in the name of what he calls 'progress.'"

Before Stuart could take a step, the piano player brought his keyboard to life, the clarinetist picked up the tempo, and the violinist joined them in a crescendo of musical introduction. The conversational buzz in the room faded, and everyone's attention turned toward the stage. There stood Anna Ardmore, dressed in khaki shorts and matching short sleeve jacket, turquoise bracelets on her suntanned arms and a safari hat shadowing her eyes. Her shoulder-length hair was the tone of golden copper. In her hand she held a feathered arrow, which she touched to the brim of her hat, giving a salute to benefactors of ILMA and their guests.

"She's the Delphi Oracle," Stuart said.

"She's Artemis, the virgin goddess of the hunt," Dusty said under his beard.

"Steady, men. Remember, she's a good draw." Ford winked. "I never knew whether it was her reputation as a scientist or her good looks. Either way our patrons are quick to pull out their checkbooks when she makes her heartfelt plea for understanding and preserving our valuable American prehistory. A nonprofit can't do much without a lot of money flowing in. Pays for the salaries of our staff . . ." He eyed Stuart. ". . . and printing and mailing all those brochures on expensive recycled paper."

"And this wine and cheese, as well." Brenda Turner raised her glass toward Dr. Ardmore in a toast.

"She could get elected to any office," Mayor Beyer said.

Alexander Parish ogled her. "She could coach me any day."

Dusty gave Anna a slight wave.

Anna smiled, recognizing him. She bounded down the three steps and embraced Dusty. With her lips close to his ear, she whispered, "I'm so excited you've come half way around the world to see me tonight. I can hardly wait until we're alone." Drawing back, Anna smiled at Stuart, placed her hand on Quentin Ford's arm, looked up at Alexander and smiled, and said a "how nice to see you again" to Mayor Beyer.

Emily slowly walked over to her grandfather and pulled on his sleeve, placing her book in his hand. "Grandfather Dusty, will you please ask the beautiful lady to sign my book?"

Anna looked down and smiled sweetly at Emily. "I'm Anna Ardmore. And what is your name?"

"Emily," she answered, returning Anna's smile. "Grandfather Dusty says you're an archaeologist."

"Yes." Anna eyed Dusty. "I study old things."

"I want to be an archaeologist some day."

"Good, we need more women in the field."

Emily pointed to her book. "My book says this Toltec genius invented the wheel and brought it to the Anasazi."

Overhearing, Stuart told her, "My sweet, there is no scientific evidence of the Anasazi ever having the wheel. It's true that the Indians of the Americas gave the Europeans snowshoes, the toboggan, corn and potatoes, and other things as well, but it was the Spanish who brought both the wheel and the horse to the Americas."

Anna bent down to be face to face with Emily. "Let me dedicate your book to your future career. We women have a big job ahead of us." As she closed the storybook and handed it back to Emily, Anna looked up and made eye contact with Worthington.

"Anna, it's time for us to get started," Stuart said to her as he looked at his watch.

Dusty took Emily's hand and together they sat next to Worthington.

Stuart escorted Anna and the mayor onto the stage and tapped on the microphone, gaining the audience's attention. Introducing Jedson Beyer, he indicated the mayor would deliver a brief welcome on behalf of the nation's capital.

"Thank you, Stuart," the mayor began. "Dr. Ardmore, members of the board, patrons, and ladies and gentlemen. It is fitting that we assemble here in Washington in our tribute to Dr. Ardmore and her quest for the real story of the American Anasazi of our great

Southwest. For it has always been the influential people of the East who focused the nation's attention on the American West. Artists from the Hudson River School went west after the Civil War to paint the magnificent landscapes. Followed by the cowboy artists, Remington, Russell . . . .

"It didn't take the owners of the Santa Fe Railroad long to see the value of art in encouraging travel. The art works of the Taos School, which were reproduced in tourist brochures, inspired everyone's imagination by capturing the romance of the West. In conjunction with the railroad, Fred Harvey opened hotels and restaurants. And he invited the Indians to display and sell their rugs, blankets, pottery, kachina dolls, and feathered fetishes. In White motorbuses, prim Harvey Girls guided tours to remote native villages and prehistoric ruins, affording Easterners the first glimpse into America's own ancient civilization.

"And then we have the Rockefellers who funded Native American research, supported the reservation schools, and were a tremendous influence in inaugurating the modern-day Indian Market in Santa Fe. And, of course, as I am sure you are aware, it was Mary Cabot Wheelwright of Massachusetts, who early on collected Indian crafts and whose personal collection launched one of the nation's most prestigious museums in Santa Fe. Men and women of vision indeed.

"Yes, my friends, this evening we are walking in the footsteps of these farsighted benefactors. And those of you who venture forth with Anna Ardmore on her excavation may well tingle with the excitement of discovery, for you will be with a leader who is on the cusp of research delving into the lives of the Anasazi."

He paused, and assured of his audience's attention, added, "You all know, of course, what 'Anasazi' means." He waited a moment for emphasis. "It's a Navajo word that translates as 'they who are not us.'"

The mayor smiled and waited for his picture to be taken by an ILMA staffer. "Oh, by the way, I must tell you the story of George McJunkie, the African-American cowboy who a half-century ago discovered the projectile point near Clovis, New Mexico that turned North American archaeology upside down. For you see, the arrowhead was imbedded in the skeleton of a mastodon that had been extinct for ten thousand years. And prior to 1950, it was accepted belief among scholars that there were no people on our continent before the birth of Christ. So, what you may discover out there in the wilderness on this summer's field seminar could again rattle the rigid cage of archaeological thought."

Stuart Wales hadn't expected the mayor to be such a showman, setting the stage for Anna. He admitted he couldn't have done better himself.

After applause, Stuart thanked the mayor and introduced Anna, condensing her extensive curriculum vitae, "You all know Anna Ardmore as ILMA's most celebrated spokeswoman. She is internationally recognized for her studies of the Anasazi and her advocacy in preserving their many ruins. Dr. Ardmore has a degree in ethnology from the University of New Mexico, a master's in anthropology from Stanford, and a Ph.D. in archaeology from the University of Kansas. She currently holds the Rockefeller Chair of American Prehistory at the University of the Southwest. A scholar and a scientist, she has the skill to communicate to all ages her excitement with the discipline. Among her publications, which include numerous articles in scholarly journals, are three volumes tracing the prehistory settlement of North America and the heritage of today's Southwest pueblos. Her best known work is her learned treatise on Native American children growing up in the pueblos, entitled, *Children of the Past*. Please join me in welcoming Dr. Anna Ardmore."

Anna received a standing ovation. Illuminated by the spotlight, Anna's intensity, her dedication, and her reputation enchanted the guests. Those seminarists who were planning to join Anna's archaeological excavation took out notebooks, ready to record her words. Others listened so intently that Quentin Ford IV felt certain they would be writing healthy checks to ILMA before the evening ended.

Worthington couldn't take his eyes off Anna. As he listened to her presentation, he became intrigued with how Anna charmed her audience. Everyone, including himself, responded as if they were receiving a personal message. Her hand gestures, her body movements, her technique of caressing the language, her emotional arguments on behalf of her people fascinated him.

"Our culture, our civilization, learns from its predecessors. And there you have the argument for, and the beauty of, preservation of our heritage and the study of the past." Winking at Emily, Anna went on, "Otherwise each new generation would have to reinvent the wheel."

There was, Worthington thought to himself, nothing quite so alluring—yes, sexy—as an intelligent, mature woman carrying out her role of advocacy for her cause. But it was how she ended her talk that thrilled him the most.

"Had they not left the Four Corners around A.D. 1300, the Anasazi people, with their culture and their advanced architecture, might still be thriving today. So come with me to those deserted water and wind-carved monuments of red rock rising above an endless, rolling sea of mesas and arroyos. Search with me among those desert varnished tableaux for buried answers to all our questions. Our assignment will be to stop, look and listen."

Chapter Four

Four Corners: a Coast and Geodetic Survey point where four converging edges meet. Geographically speaking, the point where four American Southwest states come together, touching ever so ethereally. Anna Ardmore's Four Corners. In anticipation of returning there, she could see the landscape, smell the sage, feel the warm, sandy soil, sense the spiritual presence of her ancient people who would never have divided their Mother Earth at such an arbitrary point.

Anna looked at herself in the mirror in the women's lounge and began to refresh her makeup. As she outlined her lips with a pencil brush, she thought about the public and private boundaries of a person's life. Twisting the tube of lipstick, she exposed the gloss. Using firm strokes, she applied the color. Pressing her lips together, she unlocked the private corners of her own life. Being an attractive woman in a man's field had brought opportunities for flings while bivouacked on those long, isolated digs. Her colleagues, once even a graduate student, were anxious to liven up those campfire evenings. She'd had her pick, but she'd made certain it had been her decision, not theirs. With her being the instigator, her relationships had been all the more intriguing to her.

At one point in her life she had become concerned she was too liberal with her sexual advances, and so she had sought counsel from the university psychiatrist. Lying on the red leather couch in his office, she'd told him of her many escapades. Responding, he had asked her to think about how women, especially attractive women, should uphold society's behavioral standards, honoring those basic obligations of settling down, getting married, and raising children.

She had replied that these were each separate decisions for a woman. Personally, she would never marry, and she would never have a baby. She told him her career was of paramount importance to her, so she viewed sex not for procreation, but for recreation. Wanting to save her, he had lectured her. When that didn't work, he grabbed her, kissed her—forcing his tongue into her mouth—told her she was irresistible, and then proposed marriage. She had broken loose, jumped up off his therapy bed, and fled the scene, reassuring herself for weeks thereafter that she was not the one with a problem. The result of this incident was that she came to savor her freedom even more.

Anna applied mascara to her eyelashes and stared into the reflection of her eyes, wondering what she would see if she looked deep into the eyes of Worthington Rhodes, who everyone said was bent on destroying the remains of the Anasazi world. Would she behold the private biosphere of her adversary? Yes, clearly he and she were adversaries, competitors for control of the Four Corners—he, with his technologically correct scheme to create an entirely new national transportation system which could well break the smile of the Anasazi, and she, with her archaeologically correct hopes and dreams for preservation of the area's thousands of prehistory sites. In another world, she would be physically attracted to this charismatic trailblazer, but here and now, she knew she must suppress her sexual instincts and focus her efforts on blocking this pathfinder if she was to win out over him and save the Four Corners.

The public lives of modern-day leaders like Worthington Rhodes were seen in the newspapers, the magazines, and on television. But Anna wanted to look behind this societal mirror—to see beyond the outward forces shaping the actions of these men, not only identify the pressures put upon them by special interest groups, their colleagues, and the media, but also recognize their inward motivations and the pressures they placed upon themselves.

If she could excavate this private dimension of Worthington, she could use this information to achieve her own preservation goals. Seeing the darling little girl by his side earlier this evening, Anna speculated about Worthington's domestic life, his marriage, his family priorities. Onto that mental picture she superimposed a plot to compromise this devoted father, this champion of new technology. To begin with, she would use Dusty to learn more about Worthington's off-camera life. Parents, after all, she was sure, knew their offspring better than anyone. She'd play up to Dusty to gain insight into her adversary. Yes, the night ahead was her private space in which to act.

A few minutes earlier, as the audience in the banquet room had thinned out, she had seen Dusty smile at Emily and heard him say to his son, "Worthington, you take Emily on home. It surely must be past her bedtime. Dr. Ardmore has some questions for me. She and I will have a light supper. Food on the plane, you know, doesn't satisfy a real man's appetite."

Worthington had nodded, bid his father a "good evening" and taken Emily's hand to leave.

Standing beside Quentin Ford IV, Anna and Dusty had watched father and daughter depart. Almost to himself, Ford had muttered, "How could a such a man, such a nice family man, pose such a terrible threat to our American heritage?"

Dusty had asked, "Mr. Ford, aren't you getting a bit carried away?"

"No, it is his bulldozers that will carry us away." Ford had then donned his tailored topcoat, put his hat on his head, pulling the front tip of the brim down with a sharp tug, revealing his hostility. As he left he had said, "Something must be done."

"Quentin's right, Dusty," she had said, touching his sleeve with her fingertips. "Something has to be done about your son."

Dusty then looked at her and said, "Would you like a drink before dinner?"

She had smiled and said, "Yes, that would be very nice. Let me freshen up a bit first."

Now, outside the women's lounge, having made certain the brim of her safari hat was no more than a quarter inch above her eyebrows, she rejoined Dusty, took his hand, and led him into a quiet corner of the hotel bar. The decor of the Quorum Room featured an arrangement of framed caricatures of well-known legislators, past and present.

"Fitting for Washington," Dusty remarked, gesturing around the room. "You see, here on the left, these ludicrous distortions of the truth dramatize the Senate down through the years." He gestured toward the pictures on their right. "And over there we have the cartoon characters who've made up the House of Representatives."

"The artist is simply trying to give us another dimension of our members of Congress, but frankly, I think it would be more fun to have photographed them in the buff, hiding nothing."

"Not even a fig leaf covering up their private parts, like how the Christians garnished those beautiful Greek sculptures?" Dusty asked.

"Yes, that was a real mistake. Artistically speaking."

The waitress arrived. Dusty ordered a Chivas Regal neat and Anna a glass of Portuguese Madeira.

"Say, have you heard about the latest bit of research from Greece?" Dusty asked with a lecherous grin.

Anticipating an off-color joke, Anna thought to herself, humor him. She opened her lips questioningly and waited.

"Well, one of my female associates, while exploring this cave on the Peloponnesus, uncovered a series of third century B.C. drawings showing Spartan warriors with erect penises. She became so intrigued with the question of length that she devoted all her time to further scientific research, pouring through the literature of ancient Greece and compiling data from museum pottery collections."

Anna knew what she was supposed to ask, and so she fluttered her eyelashes. "And what were her conclusions?"

"That the typical length when fully erect that is, the median length as computed from her statistical sample was . . . ah . . ." he hesitated, and then blurted, "twelve-point-zero-seven centimeters."

"Well, Professor Dusty, one of my graduate students conducted a similar study a year or so ago. He surveyed the Anasazi rock art and tabulated thousands of images of the flute player known as 'Kokopelli' who was always shown with a full erection. My student used this data for his doctoral thesis. I've committed his exact findings to memory."

Dusty leaned forward.

Anna held up both hands, separating them, palms facing, indicating the measurement. "Anasazi males have got your Greeks beat. Our length was thirteen-point-three-four centimeters."

Dusty downed his scotch and motioned for the waitress. "Honey, bring us some menus. It looks like we've taken over this corner of the Quorum. And bring us a bottle of white wine."

"Any kind other than that awful Greek retsina," Anna instructed.

Dusty laughed heartily and told the waitress, "She's right. We're into the French stuff tonight. *Cherchez la femme* and all that." A loud belch interrupted his laugh.

Anna watched the waitress' reaction to Dusty's vulgar manners and saw her roll her eyes. As the waitress turned and walked away, Anna pondered how she was going to extract information about

Worthington. Fathers always liked to brag about their sons. And in so doing, Dusty might inadvertently reveal dark family secrets, allowing her a peek at the skeletons in their closet.

Dusty interrupted her thoughts. "Where's that cute waitress? I've got the appetite of an adolescent boy."

Anna saw her chance. "Do you think you could curb your son's appetite for land grabbing?"

"You bet. I've told him already what I think about this train thing, and I'm sure I can talk some sense into him. In fact, I'll guarantee it."

Anna smiled. "But I still can't figure out how he could possibly devise such a project, ignoring the havoc he's going to wreak on the land. After all, his father being such a prominent archaeologist . . . ." She leaned across the table, closer to Dusty. "Do you suppose he has other appetites?"

"I don't want to talk about him. Let's not ruin our evening together."

"But I want to know what you think."

Dusty looked upset. The waitress brought their wine, uncorked the bottle, poured a little in his glass. He tasted the wine, waited for her to fill the glass, and then took a large gulp. He looked at the menu and quickly ordered a hamburger rare with everything, French fries and onion rings. "It's been a long time," he said. "They can't fix a decent hamburger in Greece. And their buns . . . ."

"I'll have the poached salmon and a Greek salad in honor of my very handsome companion for the evening."

Dusty drank the rest of his wine and promptly poured himself a second glass.

Anna thought about her next move, and was happy their dinners arrived. The break allowed her time to consider her options while Dusty voraciously devoured his hamburger. She could abort the plan to find out about the private side of Worthington. She could continue to stroke Dusty's ego in the hope he would inadvertently reveal a hush-hush family thing. Or she could lead him on, beguile him into thinking she was going to take him to bed if he would tell her more.

"Maybe this is too personal a question," Anna began, "and tell me if I'm out of bounds, but why didn't you remarry after you lost your wife all those years ago?"

"Anna, are you proposing to me?"

"I might be able to come up with an interesting proposal for tonight, that is, if you'll be perfectly honest with me."

"Well, I haven't been celibate all these years, if that's what you want to know. What man would say no to those dark-eyed Grecian beauties?"

"Your son might, but then again you may know otherwise."

"Oh, he's straight as an arrow, but if I think about it, I'm sure I could come up with an interesting story about him. In fact, I'll guarantee it. Now, let's talk about your proposal for tonight."

Anna raised her eyebrows. "In that case, let me ask you another question. Have you ever used video on your digs?"

"No, I haven't. And I don't have a cellular phone out in the field to call for pizza delivery either. That's the same answer I gave Emily."

"I'll bet there's another thing you've never done."

"What's that?"

"Seen yourself on video." Anna smiled. "I've often wished we could film our ancient people."

"Go back in a time warp?"

"Yes, so to speak. But now we have to be content with video-taping our excavations."

"I guess you're really into camcorders."

"Yes, I learned about visual recording from Margaret Mead, the first anthropologist to take pictures of her subjects. Had the technology been available to her, I'm certain she would have captured the moments on videotape. And now I can. You should think about doing it. Exposes lots of techniques. I'll show you how you would appear if I were some future archaeologist reaching back in time, photographing your actions . . . your body . . . your antics. Come on, my prominent Greek archaeologist, let's have some fun."

Dusty rapidly paid the check and followed Anna into the elevator. Inside her room, Anna attached her camcorder to the tripod, extended its legs, and pointed its lens toward the king-size bed which the chambermaid had turned down for the evening.

"Is that piece of candy for me?" Dusty asked, pointing to the after-dinner mint placed on the pillow.

"Only if you're good," Anna said as she stood by the bed and unbuttoned her khaki jacket and slipped out of her khaki shorts. "The rules of our aboriginal ball game are that both players must stay in view of the camera at all times or . . ."

"Or what?"

"Off with their head."

Dusty sailed his rumpled old hat through the air.

"Now you've got it right. I'm sure the camera wants more."

Hastily removing his navy wool pullover sweater, Dusty moved quickly to her side, stepping out of his trousers, revealing torn boxer shorts and a protruding bulge.

"Take it slow," she said, "I've plenty of film."

"And a tape measure?"

"Calibrated in centimeters."

Dusty tried to take her in his arms.

Anna spun away. "I want you to lie back on the bed so the camera can get a horizontal angle."

As Dusty readily complied, Anna reached into her bag and extracted two long strands of woven yucca fibers along with two narrow strips of rabbit fur.

Looking slightly alarmed, Dusty asked, "What are . . ."

"Shh," Anna admonished. She took one of his wrists and strapped the rabbit fur around it, looping the yucca rope several times, tying the other end to the headboard of the bed. She repeated the action on his other wrist.

He managed to ask, "Why not real rope?"

"We're archaeologists. We must emulate the subjects we study." She moved on top of him. Anna positioned herself so that, straddling him, she controlled the pressure on her clitoris, timing her body movements to synchronize with her escalating sexual energy. She closed her eyes and rocked with her thrilling rhythm, building, always building to the crescendo of her shuddering climax.

Dusty was startled by the strength of Anna's outcry. His Greek huntress had completely overpowered him.

"Before I untie you, tell me your story about Worthington."

"Damn it, Anna, give a man a chance to catch his breath."

"Quit your bellyaching, and keep your end of our bargain."

Dusty saw another chance to get even with Worthington for ending what should have been a three-generation family tradition of archaeologists. "Well, okay, here's what happened, I gave him money to go to college to study archaeology, but what did he do instead? He chose that liberal arts college up there in the wilds of Maine. Can you imagine going to college to study liberal arts? Why, I even tried to blackmail him into going to Northwestern to study under the tutelage of Dr. Elliot."

"You were blackmailing an eighteen-year-old boy?"

"Well, why not? He wanted to study liberal arts. I threatened to tell the admissions officer at Bowdoin about what he did to his Uncle Bill. My frivolous son, you see, was responsible for my brother's death."

"How, for heaven's sake?"

"He removed the radio and radar equipment from his uncle's lobster boat without telling him—said later he was fixing it. Bill took the boat out, the weather turned foul, and my poor brother lost his way in the fog. His small craft was crushed by a giant oil tanker."

"That's tragic. But I don't see . . ."

"It was a deliberate act on Worthington's part."

Anna's skeptical look caused Dusty to say, "You don't believe me? Ask my sister-in-law, Worthington's Aunt Hattie, Bill's poor old widow. She'll tell you the real story."

The real story, Anna concluded then and there, was that Dusty was probably talking through his rumpled hat.

Chapter Five

Standing on the sidewalk outside his office building on Massachusetts Avenue, Worthington Rhodes squared his broad shoulders, tilted his head back and looked up at the antique exterior. He marveled at how construction workers had preserved the face of the 1890s Greek Revival structure, while the original building behind had been demolished, and in its place a new skyscraper erected, its lower floors scaled to mesh with the window pattern of the old building, while its upper levels crowned new heights. A professor of architecture at Georgetown University had described the process as "facadism," whereby new construction with its nexus of electrical wiring, computerized temperature controls, materials of plastic, aluminum, tempered glass, and synthetic fabrics advanced the building to state-of-the-art efficiency while preserving its historic aura.

Sometimes at the beginning of a day in which a crucial meeting was scheduled, Worthington would pause and conduct this visual examination before crossing the building's threshold and entering his public world. He remembered reading about how the very first skyscraper, built in Washington, D.C. more than a hundred years ago, utilized the then-new construction methods: steel "I" beams that formed a load-bearing frame allowing the building to rise higher than its neighbors; a cage powered by electricity that enabled people to rise and descend vertically; and new communication instruments that permitted a person on the top floor to talk across town without having to scurry down flights of stairs and wait for a streetcar to transport him and his voice to another location. But the building's height had alarmed everyone. In the 1880s no one had seen an office building rise fifteen stories. Many thought this first high rise would surely blow over in a strong wind or crumple under its own weight and fall down upon them. Moreover, to their dismay the structure had risen higher than their beloved obelisk, the Washington Monument. So the people roiled against this manifestation of progress and set height limitations for perpetuity.

Early on, Worthington had concluded that if change was to be accepted it must be tied to the national backbone of heritage and tradition. Adhering to that axiom, he had nostalgically dedicated the *Windjammer* to the nation's glorious transportation past—the primary reason he had been successful in steering legislation through Congress for the research, design, and testing phases.

Now the time had come to ask Congress for funds to begin construction of the first transcontinental leg of the project. Yes, if he were to run into opposition for the *Windjammer*, he would quote his maritime hero, "I have not yet begun to fight."

He entered his office building and rose rapidly in the high-speed elevator, thinking that no matter how advanced the technology, no matter how beneficial for the future of the country, he must continue to present his *Windjammer* in terms of visual and verbal bytes tied to the nation's past.

"Congressman Roybal is here for your meeting, Mr. Rhodes," Charlene advised, poking her head into his office.

"Orlando DeBaca Roybal," Worthington said softly to himself, and then more loudly, "Chairman of the House Appropriations Committee. The city planner who developed a flair for politics."

"Twenty-five years ago," Charlene commented. "He has seniority, been in Congress for what would be a career for most of us."

"And I understand he still likes to draw those colorful planning maps of cities. He and my son Danny should share their crayons." Worthington adjusted his tie. "Well, Charlene, the time has come to make another of my pitches. How many more times will I be called upon?"

His assistant smiled admiringly at him. "Presentation of new ideas is your forte, sir." She paused. "Shall I show the congressman into the conference room?"

"No, he'll be expecting me to personally escort him."

To Worthington's surprise, Congressman Roybal was accompanied by a woman. An Indian woman. Charlene hadn't mentioned her, so Worthington tried to act as if she were expected while at the same time wondering who she was. There were so many personnel changes in Washington these days one couldn't keep up, yet he was upset he hadn't been briefed about someone accompanying the congressman.

"Meet my new press secretary, Silver Bell in the Night," Congressman Roybal said with pride. "She hails from the Taos Pueblo. She'll be preparing my press releases, so she wanted to learn about this project of yours first hand."

Silver Bell in the Night didn't smile, her handshake was unyielding, and Worthington worried that the look in her dark eyes was one of disapproval. Hoping to lighten the moment, he smiled and invited them into the visual presentation room. "Our dog-and-pony show on America's future transportation system is about to start."

Looking around the room, the congressman identified the art deco posters depicting famous trains of the 1930s. "*Twentieth Century Limited, Santa Fe Chief,* and my favorite, the colorful, streamlined *Burlington Zephyr.*"

Charlene delivered coffee and Danish pastries.

"We have donuts, too, Congressman," Worthington offered, "if you prefer."

"Ah, yes, jelly, if possible," Roybal replied.

Worthington nodded to Charlene. His assistant left and promptly returned with a tray full of donuts.

Silver Bell in the Night sat in silence as Worthington focused his attention on the congressman. "It's good of you to come to our offices, given your busy schedule," he began. "Moreover, this opportunity allows me to personally thank you and your committee for funding the *Windjammer's* research and development."

Roybal smiled. "Yes, I've always supported your project. I've reminded my colleagues it's a national priority for America to have the world's most advanced rail transportation system."

Worthington looked at Silver Bell in the Night and smiled. "There's a good quote for your press release."

Leaning forward, the congressman added, "So we can beat those nips, frogs, and krauts at their own game."

"You may want to edit out that last part," Worthington suggested to the press aide. He returned his attention to Congressman Roybal. "Your representing a sparsely populated mountain state and supporting us has made an impact on House members from the East Coast and California where traffic congestion is strangling people's lives. All of us at the *Windjammer* are grateful. And now that our prototype engine has been proven and our first test route has been certified by the Federal Railroad Commission, we're ready to let construction contracts. Hundreds of equipment manufacturers—several in your district, in fact—are poised to move forward." Worthington leaned closer to the congressman. "Did you and your family enjoy the ride on our test run to Disneyland?"

Roybal nodded. "My family was thrilled. Your bullet train covered the distance from LAX in minutes. Little Theresa, my youngest—I have eight, you know—was more excited about our train ride than the hug she received from Mickey Mouse."

Worthington laughed. "And we're right on target with our second test route. It'll replace the Long Island Railroad's busiest corridor." He went on, caught up in his own enthusiasm. "Fitting, isn't it, since it was on Long Island at the Brookhaven Institute where the original American technology began. Dr. Gordon Danby and Dr. James Powell were caught one day in traffic gridlock and vowed to find a better method of transportation. Of course, the Germans and the Japanese built the first prototypes. And you may be interested to know the original concept of a no-flux guideway came from a Frenchman at the turn of the century."

"Maybe so, but American ingenuity will win the day," Roybal proclaimed.

"Let me show you how the *Windjammer* will unite our nation." Worthington punched a button. The room darkened, and the instrumental colors of Glenn Miller's *Chattanooga Choo Choo* filled the air. To Worthington's delight, Silver Bell in the Night smiled upon hearing the big band sound.

"All aboard," Worthington announced, returning her smile.

A pair of silver screens descended from the ceiling. The left one displayed a map of North America. A bright red beam appeared at New York City and began to move westward. The crimson artery pulsated passed Washington, D.C. and flowed steadily through the Appalachian Mountains toward the Mississippi River. Advancing straight as an arrow, the flaming beam crossed the Great Plains, dissected the Four Corners, bridged the Grand Canyon, and rolled into the Los Angeles metropolitan area.

"Our first transcontinental corridor," Worthington declared proudly, tapping the congressman's sleeve.

"I've never been much good at reading maps, Mr. Rhodes," the congressman replied, his interest focusing instead on a glazed donut with raspberry filling.

"Mr. Rhodes' railroad will not bring back the bison." Silver Bell in the Night's voice was soft and pensive.

Congressman Roybal looked askance at his press secretary. "We appropriated money to propagate your buffalo in Yellowstone, and now the ranchers are taking pot shots at them whenever they stick their furry heads across the park boundary." To Worthington he inquired, "Your engine got a cowcatcher?"

Worthington laughed. "Ah, we don't have to worry about stray cattle. Our right-of-way is fenced and two miles wide."

Silver Bell in the Night held her hand to her mouth and exclaimed, "Two miles!"

"With very good reason."

"But why must you blaze such a wide trail?"

"Well, Ms. Silver Bell in the Night . . ."

"Please call me Silver Bell," she said, smiling politely. "In Washington, everyone abbreviates."

"Well, Silver Bell, we want our project to be future-proof. We will be providing for the transportation needs of an economically expanding continent for centuries to come, and we will be saving costs of future land acquisition. In the past, we've simply widened and paved old animal trails."

"Those buffalo, deer, and antelope traces followed by my ancestors of the not-so-distant past."

"But, Silver Bell, we have to move on. You'll recall that even our first transcontinental railroads were inadequate from the beginning."

"Yes," Roybal said. "Congress paid those railroad barons a per mile fee, encouraging them to weave their tracks into patterns as crazy as those in a Navajo rug."

Silver Bell stood, walked to the window, and looked down on Massachusetts Avenue.

Worthington watched her. "I bet you wish you were back in your home country where people don't abbreviate."

"And respect our 'crazy' legends."

"Ah, sorry, Silver Bell," Congressman Roybal said. "I didn't mean . . ."

"That's all right, Congressman, we're here to learn about Mr. Rhodes' project. Let's allow him to continue." The press aide returned to her seat and took out her notepad, clicking her ballpoint pen repeatedly.

Worthington went on. "We did a little better with our interstate highway system in the 1950s, but even then political pressures dictated the routes. So, when Congress appropriated funds to the states to do the initial survey work for the *Windjammer*, they stipulated that the route must be a straight line."

The background music changed to the guitar of Arlo Guthrie. The second screen displayed a photograph of a sleek wide train. On the side of the bullet-shaped engine was the *Windjammer* logo of full-blown red sails against a sky-blue background. With a rich baritone voice, Worthington joined Arlo Guthrie in singing the chorus:

Good mornin', America, how are you?
Say, don't you know me? I'm your native son . . .
I'm the train they call the City of New Orleans.
I'll be gone 500 miles when the day is done.

"Make that three thousand miles, not five hundred," Worthington corrected. "Actually, our train will require less than a day to cross the entire continent."

"A miracle," Congressman Roybal exclaimed.

"Plus, as a passenger, you'll be witness to the beautiful American countryside and gain an appreciation of the breadth and beauty of our great nation. In traveling by plane, each of us is like a missile launched from one mammoth airport terminal to the next, zipping along at 35,000 feet, seeing only clouds, before we once again find ourselves walking through another tunnel-like jetway. We've turned into a nation of air terminals and rental car agencies. We miss the amber waves of grain, the bucolic farms, the tractors plowing the rich soil, the hills and dales, the apple blossoms, the spring wildflowers, the little children waving. Our *Windjammer* passengers will gain a hands-on view of the real America."

"But Mr. Rhodes," Silver Bell interjected, "your straight route will knife through Indian lands, trespassing on sacred sites of the Southern Utes in Colorado and New Mexico and the Navajo Nation in Arizona. Have you sought permission from their tribal governors?"

"Congress will deal with the Indians," Roybal said. "In the past we've always been able to amend our treaties."

Silver Bell scribbled a rush of words, repeatedly applying exclamation marks on her notepad.

"You may want to make note of our public hearings in cities across the country." Worthington handed her his itinerary. "In addition, I've been invited to the Indian Powwow in Gallup, New Mexico." He turned to Roybal. "Now, Congressman, you'll be interested in this next slide."

The colorful interiors of a passenger coach filled the screen. Emulating a luxury yacht, each private compartment sparkled with red leather seating, polished wood trim, and thick carpets. Up to date with communication equipment, the mahogany desks housed built-in television sets, modems, fax machines, and telephones. The adjoining toilet and shower room contained a white porcelain bidet. At the public end of the coach was an open area with blue upholstered chairs, a library, and a serve-yourself wet bar. In a mirrored alcove, exercise equipment included a stair-step, a treadmill, and a rowing machine.

"I could get in shape while traveling," the congressman said, patting his belly as he bit into another donut.

"Environmentalists will be pleased that our train is pollution-free, levitated and propelled by electromagnetism, moving along silently four inches above its guideway—that's our terminology for the track—no diesel smoke or toxic emissions." Worthington lowered his voice to a confidential whisper. "With it's aerodynamic shape, we've been able to reduce the noise level to what our engineers describe as the pink and white categories."

"Those levels that are not annoying," Roybal remarked, looking to Worthington for confirmation.

"Yes, like a breeze billowing in the sails."

"The reason for the name." Roybal repeated, "the *Windjammer*." He nodded his head, congratulating himself on his in-depth knowledge.

"Our engineers have made passenger comfort a priority. The vertical suspension of the coach body consists of a secondary suspension system with sixteen level-controlled pneumatic springs suspended pendulum fashion acting as vertical guides in the levitating frame."

Roybal yawned.

Worthington pressed on. "And our gauge is double-wide—three meters—allowing for much wider coaches."

"How wide is that? In feet and inches, I mean," the congressman wanted to know.

"Equivalent to a ten foot gauge in terms of today's railroads."

"And how far apart are the tracks of real trains?" the congressman asked.

"In this country, one-point-four-four meters—four feet, eight and half inches; in Russia, five feet; and Spain and Portugal, five feet, six inches; and in Japan . . ."

"I get the picture."

"Sorry, I got carried away. The point is," Worthington added proudly, "we'll accommodate ever so many more passengers per coach. Our train offers space to move around, and no confining seat belts."

Worthington pushed another button. Like star bursts from Fourth of July fireworks, turquoise beams extended from metropolitan areas.

"Look at all those commuter routes," the congressman exclaimed to Silver Bell. "We could thin out that damned traffic on the Beltway."

Worthington agreed.

"We conducted opinion surveys among commuters."

"What did they tell you?" Silver Bell asked, again readying her ballpoint pen and notepad.

"The number one reason people put up with commuting is privacy. Time alone helps them bridge the gap between family and work. We'll offer our commuters their own compartment, affording them the same privacy as they enjoy in their automobiles."

"And someone else will have to vacuum out the mess," Roybal said as he brushed the powdered sugar from his pant leg onto the floor.

"Now, Congressman, as to our freight modules, you'll notice the size." On cue, the screen showed mammoth freight cars bulging with cargo. "They're detachable from their wheeled platforms so they can be hoisted onto oceangoing container ships at our new deep water terminals."

"They'll have to enlarge the cargo ships," Roybal said, "to accommodate your big new freight cars."

"Astute observation, Congressman. In order for us to satisfy the world's commercial appetite, sustain our free market economy throughout the twenty-first and twenty-second centuries, the transporting of heretofore unheard of quantities of goods will be required.

"And, as I've said, we as a nation don't want to come back in twenty years and widen the right-of-way for more tracks, additional oil and gas pipelines, electrical transmission lines, more warehouses and loading docks, more stations and even more cities. So your committee will be asked to vote a right-of-way sufficient for the next two hundred years. The *Windjammer* project will indeed launch the next millennium."

Silver Bell hid her eyes with her hands.

"Are you all right, Ms. Bell?" Worthington asked.

"I'm reminded of the words of your poet, Henry David Thoreau: *We do not ride on the railroad; it rides on us.* One of my people's spiritual figures, Spider Woman, will counsel caution."

"Spider Woman?" Worthington arched his eyebrows.

Her dark eyes bore into his. "She's the spirit who, since the beginning of time, has guided us where to build our pueblos. We're her children. Even my mentor, Dr. Anna Ardmore, respects Spider Woman's domains."

Anna Ardmore again, Worthington thought to himself as Silver Bell continued, her voice firm, "But now, Mr. Rhodes, it is you who will create the cities of America, reshaping the lives of its people, including my people."

"New cities!" Roybal exclaimed. He rose from his seat as if he were cheering the Washington Sluggers. "You'll need someone to design them, plan them, won't you, Mr. Rhodes? You'll need somebody to draw . . ."

". . . new planning maps for the cities." Worthington finished the sentence.

"I do love to color those plans depicting green parks, brown treelined boulevards, blue residential neighborhoods, red industrial parks . . . ."

Worthington pushed another button. Bright orange beams burst forth from New York north to Boston and Montreal; south from Washington to Atlanta and Miami; north from Los Angeles to San Francisco, Seattle and Vancouver; and south from Dallas-Fort Worth to Monterrey and Mexico City. "A fitting transportation network for North America, now with our free trade agreement, don't you think, Congressman?"

"I voted for NAFTA," Roybal replied.

The music switched to *Atchison, Topeka and the Santa Fe.*

The congressman grew more excited as he sang along. "I can see the bright yellow engine number Forty-Nine. Rollin' down the tracks, all the way from Phil-a-delph-i-a." The congressman's voice was lyrical. "I can hear that whistle echoin' across the hills . . . with the wheels a-singin' westward ho . . . cross the Kansas plains all the way to New Mex-i-co."

Worthington applauded.

"I do like your music," the congressman said, "and your colorful displays."

"Don't forget our new city for the Four Corners."

"Within my district?"

"That's what we've been thinking, Congressman."

Congressman Roybal stood. "Mr. Rhodes, you do have a magnificent plan for the nation's future. I for one will . . ."

Silver Bell interrupted. "Congressman, you and I should review this important matter in the privacy of your office, don't you think?"

Worthington understood now why he was upset with his staff for not having prepared a deep background dossier on someone so obviously influential as Silver Bell in the Night.

Chapter Six

Though Quentin Ford IV was one of the wealthiest men in America, Anna was neither dazzled by his vast riches nor daunted by his prominent social status. Each respected the other for his and her passionate advocacy of American heritage and archaeology. Their unique relationship, Anna mused, was ninety-eight percent platonic. Only once had she seduced him into a sexual interlude in the back seat of his stretch limousine while his uniformed chauffeur—way up there in front—had driven them along the byways of the bucolic Virginia countryside.

As her taxi approached Quentin Ford IV's fine house on this Washington afternoon, Anna recalled Quentin's story about how his mansion had been built after the Civil War by one of the early railroad tycoons. But as time passed and the costs of upkeep soared, the palatial manor had fallen into disrepair. At the turn of the century, as the United States grew into a world power, foreign governments sought impressive headquarters for their ambassadors and proper places to host diplomatic banquets. And so, one by one, mansions in this Washington neighborhood had been restored to their nineteenth century opulence. Quentin Ford's grandfather, his millions amassed in his importing business, by then matching the treasury of many such countries, acquired and restored this Italianate residence to a grandeur equaling any embassy.

At the ornate double entry door, Anna was greeted, not by one of the servants, but by the benefactor himself, who accepted her hand and kissed her cheek. The brown and white striped feather in her hat band brushed across his face.

"A rough-legged hawk feather," Quentin identified.

"Robin Hood's favorite."

"Come to rob the rich?"

Anna laughed. "Just answering your urgent phone call."

"I wanted you to be the first to know how I am personally going to save our country."

They walked across the checkered black and white marble tiles of the foyer, ascended a grand staircase on which was centered a thick Persian Bijar runner, and entered his library. Shelf after walnut shelf, Quentin's book collection caressed the American spirit from his signed first editions to his folios of post-Civil War photographs of western frontier lore. A collection of Native American dance masks filled an alcove. A 1900 Ganado Navajo rug, its red and white pattern featuring a bold yellow thunderbolt and the ancient cosmic symbol of a swastika, was the library's focal point.

Anna picked out a signed first edition of *The Delight Makers* by Swiss-born Adolf F. Bandelier, written during his eight years living with the Cochiti Pueblo Indians in New Mexico. "My father read this novel to me when I was a child. Bandelier was the first literary advocate for my Anasazi."

"He was an early benefactor, as well," Quentin commented.

"I'm anxious to know what my favorite benefactor has on his mind."

"If Bandelier were alive today, he would have the same thoughts about doing in Worthington Rhodes as I have." Quentin filled two glasses with Amontillado sherry from a cut glass decanter, handing one to Anna. He waited for her to sip, and when she had, he downed his in one tilt of the etched glass. "There will be so much destruction from the *Windjammer* project that our national soul cannot be saved. We have only one option if we are to preserve our great nation. Otherwise, after more than two hundred years, I am afraid the final curtain will ring down on the America we have come to love and cherish." Quentin's expression turned to evangelic rage. "This devil project of Worthington Rhodes, as we both know, is going to devastate our country. Environmental evils of chemical pollution, toxic waste, even nuclear energy abuses pale in comparison."

"Quentin, I too am opposed to the *Windjammer*. I've testified before Congress. I've written letters to my local newspaper. I even had my essay printed on the Op-Ed page of the *New York Times* last week. And I rally my students and fellow faculty members to oppose this destructive program by writing to their congressmen."

"More, much more is needed, my dear Anna. You see, it is this one man who has single-handedly brought this sinful scheme along.

His pagan philosophy, his propaganda that touts jobs and technological progress has entrapped the White House, the media, the unions, the construction companies, Congress, and the legislators in those states that stand to benefit economically. They are all cleverly captured, shoved deep in his pocket and zippered tight. And when the next election rolls around, the people and the press will support any politician who votes the *Windjammer* into existence."

"But what about the cost?" Anna asked. "I've heard it will cost fifty million dollars a mile to build. Some say the effect will be to double, or is it to quadruple the national debt? Congress will have to vote a lot more money than those millions they appropriated for its research and development. And I understand the RT has raised only a fraction of the necessary dollars."

"Yes, at first blush Congress is being asked to bet even more than our peace dividend on the success of a new and unproven transportation system. But Worthington Rhodes has been very clever. His innovative financing techniques, you see, will reduce the government's actual out-of-pocket costs to a relatively few billion. The man's a visionary. Moreover, he has a practical side. He's thought of everything. He's created a quasi-government corporation for the *Windjammer*. He's sold stock to suppliers and construction companies and floated triple-A-rated bonds to investors.

"Another ingredient in our man's plan is to entice first class commuters to invest in their own private compartments. He's initiated a new type of real estate condominium ownership. Some analysts project revenue from these sales will more than pay for building the coaches. And as to freight—the same. I know, because my import business is being pressured into buying units in a freight module in order to assure we have rights to ship our goods."

"But where is he going to get the money, those billions you mentioned, to build the system itself?" Anna pressed.

"His new cities will need housing, shopping malls, doctor's offices and so on. Remember the first railroad boom more than a hundred years ago? Those railroad tycoons developed new cities on land they owned, sold lots to settlers, and built new factories. Worthington's doing the same. Developers are being told they must invest in the system. Construction companies are being pressured into tithing ten percent of their contracts back into the kitty."

"But what about forces beyond his control: world markets, world trade, world conflicts?"

"That's the problem, isn't it? If the *Windjammer* fails, a horrid financial debacle could bankrupt our government and push our capitalistic system to the brink of disaster. Maybe even over the edge.

Our society could find itself in tatters. People would soon lose faith and seek some other system to replace capitalism, like communism or socialism, or heaven knows what. We can't permit our country to take this kind of risk any more than we can allow Worthington to destroy our national heritage and our precious archaeological sites through wanton bulldozing."

"From the way you describe matters, Quentin, it sounds as if Worthington can't be stopped."

"I haven't said that."

"So what are you saying then?"

"The only way for us to save our country and preserve its heritage is to remove Worthington Rhodes."

"But, Quentin, if you're thinking of getting Worthington fired from his position as head of the *Windjammer*, remember what history tells us—if something happens to one leader, another will step forward."

"That's historical folklore. Look at how different history would have been if Hitler and Mussolini had been assassinated early on before they invaded those little countries of Europe and Africa. Had those assassinations been arranged, I'm convinced we'd have never suffered the devastation of World War II."

Anna frowned. "I'm afraid I don't quite see the parallel here with the *Windjammer*." She hesitated. "Surely you're not talking about . . . about some awful, dire action, are you?"

Quentin's face grew redder. "Look, our republic depends on perpetuating both capitalism and our national ethos. Plow asunder this great heritage of ours and you'll take away the soul of our country. Our people will quickly descend into a lawless state of anarchy. They will seek out only the satisfaction of selfish interests, their lives floundering like fish out of water, lacking guidelines, devoid of familiar cultural benchmarks. People will be like coastal ships at sea, adrift in an endless raging storm of confusion without lighthouses of tradition and heritage to guide them. Within a short time all of us will revert to raw animal instincts, our valued and time-honored principles of life, liberty and the pursuit of happiness debased like a currency deprived of its backing of gold or silver."

"Why don't you buy off Congressman Roybal? Without his support Congress won't vote for the *Windjammer*."

"I've tried money," Quentin told her. "But he's ignoring me. Worse, I feel certain he's going to support the *Windjammer* in the critical committee vote coming up. Hell, I even offered to make a deposit into a Swiss bank account so he wouldn't have to report it to the federal election authorities. But now I refuse to contribute any more dollars to his campaign. It's turned into a matter of principle with me. If the next congressional election were going to be held prior to the critical vote in the House, I'd financially support his opponent."

"He doesn't have an opponent, that is, one who's a serious threat. Hasn't for years. I know. I live in his district."

"You're right," Quentin agreed. "So there is really only one way for us to stop Worthington Rhodes."

Anna was growing panicky. "I've an idea. What about talking to Roybal's new press aide. Silver Bell in the Night is a former student of mine."

Quentin snorted. "Surely you don't expect an Indian maiden to influence the course of the mighty United States of America's House of Representatives—no matter how smart she is."

"Quentin, stop! I don't want to hear any more."

"You do realize how many sites . . ." He pointed to a drawing of the Four Corners on a deer skin stretched on an easel. A straight red line ran diagonally across it. "This line dissects Chimney Rock, Mesa Verde, Goodman Point, as well as uncounted, untouched, and unnamed sites in the Southern Ute Reservation. Don't you want to preserve these Anasazi ruins, their legends, their sacred places . . . as well as our state and national parks and historic monuments, not only in the Southwest but all those others that find themselves in the *Windjammer*'s destructive path across the country?"

"Yes, of course, Quentin, I'm on your side. You know that. But you can't . . . I mean, you mustn't . . . We're not dissident nobles caught up in some palace intrigue vying for the crown back in the sixteenth century. We're in America. Today. These are modern times. Not Shakespearean England. Why, it's practically the twenty-first century."

"But we must be realistic. We must do what we must."

"Quentin, please wait. I'll think of something. Give me some time . . ."

Quentin shook his head. "The vote in the House is coming up. Whatever idea you might come up with would have to be quick." He paused. "Trust me. No one will ever know. I'll make the arrangements. I know certain people . . . and how these matters are carried out." He enunciated the word slowly, "Discreetly . . . very discreetly. You need never know another thing about it." Quentin lowered his voice, hoping to soothe her. "My purpose this afternoon is simply to reassure you everything will be taken care of. You can proceed with your dig, knowing you'll not be disturbed by surveyors and bulldozers bearing down on you."

Anna cringed. "But Quentin, please, please give me forty-eight hours to come up with an alternative to your plan. I beg you."

He hesitated. Slowly he smiled, and finally nodded. "Well, all right. For you, my dear Anna." Gently he took her hand in his. "But not a minute more."

◆　◆　◆　◆

During the taxi ride back to her Georgetown hotel, Anna knew she must come up with some plan to save Worthington's life and at the same time save her Anasazi sites. Maybe Dusty had supplied the answer, after all. There was the questionable death of Worthington's Uncle Bill. Was Worthington hiding something? If there was another dimension to the real story of Uncle Bill's demise, she could threaten Worthington with going public with the scandal. He'd not want the publicity. He'd change his mind, back off the *Windjammer*, save his family from the embarrassment, and save his own life in the process.

Anna decided to conduct her own investigation. She looked at her day calendar. Yes, there was enough time before she was due in the Four Corners. But she'd have to be quick. She'd seize this chance to save this man whose power, drive, determination, and devotion to career, to cause, and to family was something to behold.

Chapter Seven

Brenda Turner entered the headquarters building of the D'Camp media empire on M Street, returning the smile offered by the sculptured bust of Henry D'Camp dominating the lobby. She thought about the previous evening's reception for Anna Ardmore and her meeting with Mrs. Henry D'Camp. She had wanted to tell Mrs. D'Camp she probably knew more about her husband's ranch than she did, maybe even more about her husband's lovemaking, but of course she didn't. Instead she had simply satisfied her own curiosity about his wife, who seemed to be a distant spouse lost in her world of charities.

"I'm Brenda Turner, editor and publisher of the *Four Corners Tablet*," she told the security guard.

"Go right on up to the top floor, Ms. Turner." The guard awarded her a salute off the bill of his uniform hat. "Mr. D'Camp is expecting you."

Rising higher and higher in the elevator, Brenda reflected on how she had met media mogul Henry D'Camp. One day, after she had put her weekly newspaper to bed, he dropped by her office in Cortez, Colorado, casually dressed and as casually introduced himself, saying he wanted to chat. Impressed with the powerful man's visit, she self-consciously described to him her own news gathering and reporting experiences. He self-assuredly explained to her about the innovations in printing and circulation and promotion; proudly he described his worldwide news gathering facilities. Later he had bought her dinner at Nero's, offering afterward to show her the sunset from his new ranch house on his spread outside of town. And of course she'd spent the night with him. What woman could turn down such a dashing and powerful man?

The elevator arrived at the top floor. As she waited in the lux-uriously-appointed reception area, she recalled how a few days later Henry D'Camp had called, inviting her to Washington to see the heartbeat of his media empire. She'd accepted, realizing she could also take in Anna Ardmore's presentation. He'd promptly Fed-Exed a round-trip first-class ticket accompanied by a hotel voucher.

The fact that D'Camp himself had shown up at her hotel room around midnight, dressed in jeans, carrying a bottle of twenty-year-old Tawny Port and his latest wire service bulletins, which he insisted on reading aloud to her while she sipped the bitey, complex liquor, didn't really surprise her. He was, after all, a newspaper man. Interested in the news. Foremost and always. But also interested in her.

D'Camp rushed from his office to greet her. He looked quite different in his tailored business suit, no longer the handsome rancher, but instead the handsome executive. Once inside the pri-vacy of his plush office, he grabbed her and kissed her hard on the lips. Drawing back, D'Camp breathed, "I'm going to put a lasso on you and never let you leave me."

"Be careful," Brenda replied, "how you use the reata. Personally, I prefer the hard and fast method, where you tie one end of the braided rope to a saddle horn and then exhibit the skills of your roper's hands."

"Wee-ha!" D'Camp shouted. "Come here, let me show you what I've snared so far. These are my prize cattle—Aberdeen Angus and Hereford. And these gentlemen here," he said, laughing heartily at the down-lighted oil paintings, "are my bulls, ready to service my registered herds."

"As romanticized by the artist on the famed media mogul's Four Corners ranch," Brenda said softly as if she were writing the picture's caption for her weekly newspaper.

"I wish people wouldn't label me as a mogul. My own reporters are told not to, because the description carries a sinister connota-tion. After all, I'm just a plain, ordinary American boy from the streets of Brooklyn who worked hard, and like Horatio Alger, turned his adolescent dreams into reality."

"And the reality is you have a conglomerate of some two dozen daily newspapers, an even greater number of television stations and," Brenda hesitated, "I've lost track of the radio stations and cable television franchises you control from Key West to the Klondike, plus a collection of news magazines."

D'Camp nodded, pointing proudly toward a large map of North America which displayed pins of various colors. "And don't forget my news service. But it's my Colorado cattle ranch that's become my new fascination."

"The Four Corners offers a lot of fascinations."

"As far as the eye can see—fifty thousand acres high atop the McElmo Plateau." D'Camp pointed to a map showing the lay of his land. "To the visitor from back east, my ranch may appear at first blush to be barren, but to me it's beautiful country. My views are superb. Rocking on my ranch house porch, I can see all the way to Shiprock, that magnificent New Mexico monadnock jutting up from the landscape, and to the west in Utah, that lazy, crazy-shaped mountain they call the Sleeping Ute. Why, on a clear day, and most every one of the days I've been there it's been clear as a bell, I can almost see across Arizona to the Grand Canyon of the Colorado."

"Yes, your Bar 8 Ranch is a beautiful spread," Brenda acknowledged. "I'm certain you have many Anasazi ruins on your land. The McElmo Plateau was the Anasazi corn basket for a dozen centuries."

"Ah, no, I didn't know."

"Yes, you see, in addition to farming and cattle, our local economy flourishes only because of archaeology. In fact, the president of our Chamber of Commerce is planning a promotional campaign labeling our town as 'The Archaeological Crossroads of America.'"

"You don't say," D'Camp replied as he tightened his arm around her waist.

"Yes, each year thousands and thousands of people come to see the major Anasazi ruins. Their tourist dollars keep the motels, restaurants, and gas stations flourishing. It's the advertising from these local businesses that support our newspaper; otherwise everything except the local feed store would have closed down and blown away by now."

"I've heard of Mesa Verde."

"Yes, but there are many, many more sites: Hovenweep, Sand Canyon, Aztec, not to mention nearby Chaco Canyon, plus hundreds that have not been excavated. They have names, too, such as Goodman Point, Yellowjacket . . . Dr. Anna Ardmore, our local authority, known and respected internationally, says fewer than one percent of the ancient Anasazi sites have been excavated. I've quoted her in my newspaper as saying, 'There are a lot of mysteries remaining for us to explore, and a lot of answers still to be unearthed.'"

"How do you know these other . . . ah . . . sites, as you call them, actually exist?" D'Camp asked.

"Wolfberry."

"Wolfberry? What do you mean?"

"It's a bush that grows only in rock rubble. You look for a line of wolfberry and, sure enough, they've sprouted up along the crumbled rock of what was once a wall of an Anasazi pueblo. I'm sure I could walk across your ranch and point out scores of sites. In fact, on one of her tours, Dr. Ardmore showed me how to spot these bushes, pot shards, and other traces of this ancient civilization. 'Surveying,' she called our little outing. Unfortunately, many of these sites have been violated, carelessly and illegally dug up by pot hunters looking for the black on white pottery for which the Anasazi are so famous."

"I never knew," D'Camp admitted. "Perhaps you can show me around my own ranch."

"I'd be delighted. You see, for me to write my column about what's going on around town, I have to be up to date on everything happening with Southwest archaeology. Sometimes after an interview with Dr. Ardmore, I feel as if I'm earning my own Ph.D. in the subject."

"Very impressive reporting for your paper, I am sure, Ms. Brenda Turner, editor-in-chief."

"You might like to join one of Dr. Ardmore's excavations, take a week off from your conglomerate, and dig in the dirt. Some people say the artifact they uncover in such an experience is themselves."

"Me? In the hot sun?"

"Why not? Last night I saw your wife at the reception for Dr. Ardmore. She's certainly a strong supporter of archaeology."

"She's on the board of several nonprofits. It's important these days to support causes. In fact, I'm making a very significant contribution to the campaign coffers of one of the congressmen from your Four Corners."

"Orlando DeBaca Roybal?"

D'Camp nodded. "He's running for reelection."

"He's always running for reelection."

"But this time it's doubly important he wins." D'Camp squeezed her. "Now let me show you around our media control center. It's a bit more extensive than your weekly newspaper in Cortez." He moved his hand to the small of her back to guide her.

"We're getting up to date, too," Brenda said proudly as they walked. "At your suggestion I've ordered word processors for our reporters and classified ad takers. We're not into television or cable as you are, but since I've seen you, I've purchased an option to buy the local radio station. I can't decide if I should exercise it, though. None of us are that enamored with country and western music, so we may let the deal drop. On the other hand, we may be missing a good opportunity. I wish I could get some good advice."

"Well, let me tell you," D'Camp said, smiling, "we do things around here to make a profit. If you look at your decision from that point of view, you can't go wrong." He waited a moment before adding, "If you'd like me to, I could have our radio station analyst look at the operating figures."

"Oh, could you? That would be ever so helpful."

"Happy to oblige. Fax the financial data to me personally." D'Camp led her onto a balcony overlooking a busy news room filled with television monitors, cameras, and anchor desks. People scurried about. He pointed to a row of facsimile machines and then to rows of teletypes and desks with banks of red and white telephones. "It's the center of the information world. News stories from around the world come off a satellite somewhere up in the heavens and show up here. We edit them and send them on their way to newspapers, television, and radio stations of our great nation. And to your weekly, as well." He added, "That is, if your paper subscribes to our wire service." D'Camp looked serious. "If we say a story is news, then it's news. "Otherwise," he paused, "the story is ignored by us and consequently by the nation."

"Very impressive."

His arm was around her waist again. "I've come a long way since my first newspaper."

She looked into his eyes, allowing his arm to remain around her waist.

Gently he drew her closer.

"Why did you really invite me here to Washington?" she whispered softly. "To see once again 'your brown-eyed girl?'"

D'Camp chuckled. "That, of course, but, well you see, Brenda, I've decided your weekly newspaper goes with my cattle ranch. When I visit the Four Corners, which I do often, I'll feel right at home."

"You want to buy my newspaper?"

"Of course, I'll keep you on as editor-in-chief, give you a nice office, update your printing presses and your technology with the latest equipment designed for small papers. Why, I'll even buy that radio station for you, if the figures look at all promising, and give you a daily five minute commentary to air at dinner time."

"I've always wanted to be on the radio."

"Good. Then please consider my tender offer. It's . . . well . . . I'm sure you'll find it quite generous." He handed her an envelope.

She opened it. Inside was one page which she read quickly. "Wow, that's a lot of money. You want some sort of . . . ah . . . personal commitment from me, too?"

"No lariats attached, my dear."

Brenda waited only a moment. "Consider it a done deal, then."

"Excellent. I'll instruct our in-house legal staff to draw up the necessary papers. Your local attorney can look the document over, of course." D'Camp beamed. "I'm very happy. And for you, my dear Brenda, so pretty and at such a young age, my acquisition will assure a notable journalism career ahead for you."

She smiled. "Yours is a generous price, I will say that." She kissed his cheek. "Boss man."

"Now I can place two more flags into my wall map, turquoise for your newspaper and orange for the radio station you've optioned, that is, if I buy it. Insert the sharp points of each pin smack dab at the center of my Bar 8 Ranch in the Four Corners."

Chapter Eight

With Emily seatbelted into the front seat, Worthington drove the Volvo down the quiet streets of the exclusive Washington residential neighborhood of Rock Creek to his daughter's private school. The surrounding houses were owned by appointed government officials, career civil servants, lobbyists, and those others who chose not to escape to the Maryland or Virginia suburbs, but who felt instead a kinship with the magnetic power of the District. Here they could feel the pulse of the nation's capital, but not the painful angina of the inner city.

A banner proclaimed, "WELCOME TO ROCK CREEK ACADEMY FATHER-STUDENT NIGHT." Emily pointed up as they entered the school. "My friend Teddy D'Camp helped me paint the banner, Daddy."

"I like your choice of colors," Worthington replied. "Orange letters on a green background."

"Mrs. Carson says we should treasure the color green. She says, 'Green is for the endangered natural world around us.'"

"And orange?"

"'For the destruction we're bringing to it.'"

Worthington started to reply but felt a hand on his shoulder. He turned to see Henry D'Camp with his chubby son Teddy by his side.

The media giant laughed. "You and I choose the most unusual places to meet."

Worthington nodded at Teddy. "We met last time, young man. Your mother was with you." He introduced Emily to Teddy's father. "Mr. D'Camp publishes a lot of newspapers."

"I know that, Daddy." Emily looked at the large hand as it grasped her tiny one in greeting. "But you don't have printer's ink on your fingers, Mr. D'Camp. I do when I help put out our *Weekly Reader*."

Looking down at her, D'Camp chuckled. "I used to, darling, in my early career days, but now, unless I'm on my Colorado ranch, I keep my hands clean."

The long corridors, rapidly filling with fathers and children, displayed student drawings of Eastern songbirds. In Emily's homeroom were cartographical projects: maps of the United States, one showing the vast Louisiana Purchase, another the original thirteen colonies, and yet another the Confederate States of America. It was obvious the maps had been drawn by the students, for their dominate colors were green, and the cities were shown in orange. Worthington was particularly interested in one map dated 1860 labeled "Pre-Civil War Transportation Routes." It showed the serpentine railroad lines and meandering canals of the period.

Emily noticed her father's interest. "I told them all about your bullet train, Daddy. I wanted to draw a straight orange line right across the country, but Mrs. Carson wouldn't let me."

"That's all right, Emily." Worthington put his arm around his daughter. "Your map is a century and half out of date. You need a map of the future to show the route of my train."

"Maps can't be of the future, can they, Daddy?"

"If you label them that way."

"Schools teach the past," D'Camp said. "America loves the past. My press corps likes to delve into a person's past." He looked at Worthington. "But some of us are obliged to plan for the future. Is there some quiet place in this father-child melee where you and I can talk?"

"Right here will have to do," Worthington replied. He looked at Emily. "You and Teddy run along and find your friends, allow me a few minutes with Mr. D'Camp."

"How'd it go with Roybal today?" D'Camp asked.

"I'm optimistic. I gave him my best pitch. But he did surprise me by bringing along his press aide."

"The Indian?"

Worthington nodded. "I know nothing about her."

"You should have called me ahead of time."

"But I wasn't advised . . ."

"Then let me fill you in, Silver Bell in the Night is a role model among Indian women and respected by the men, as well. She has a degree in Native American law. Her grandfather, Cloud on the

Mountain, was a Tiwa language code talker for the Marines during the Italian campaign in World War II. In addition, she speaks Athabaskan and Kersean, important linguistic skills in New Mexico where there are seven different native tongues. Her father's a Taos medicine man, and at thirteen she was qualified as a midwife on their reservation. Her brother is chief of tribal police. Some label her as an agitator for the rights of Native Americans. Our most recent D'Camp-CNN public opinion poll showed her with eighty percent name recognition in her home state. Our poll also showed that Roybal's approval rating rose to seventy percent plus or minus an error factor of three percent after he hired her as his press aide. She's a bright rising star in the Four Corners night sky."

"Jesus! She worried me today, but now I'm really nervous. Say, Henry, don't you own an Indian newspaper in your collection by now?"

"Almost. I'm about to buy the *Four Corners Tablet*. It'll fill a geographic gap in my empire. I think I've got the editor in my . . . ah . . . camp." He chuckled. "But I'm not sure how many Indians read it. They dance to their own chants, you know."

"Actually I don't. That's your job, Henry." Worthington smiled. "And so far you're doing splendidly, molding public opinion across the country in favor of the *Windjammer*. I'm very pleased."

"God, it's noisy in here. Why is it children must scream?"

"Noise feeds on noise," Worthington suggested.

"They're screaming headlines—excited about their lives. They haven't begun making mistakes they'll have to worry about later. Actions that will be subject to scrutiny."

"You're letting all this noise get to you, Henry."

"No, it's that we're coming down to the wire on Congressional approval for the *Windjammer*."

"But why are you worried? The stories you've had your people write and film have been a boon to our cause. You've directed the news coverage with aplomb."

"So far. In their traditional feature stories, our reporters have emphasized family values and pictured yours as the ideal American role model."

Worthington nodded. "Sara really liked the story with the photographs of her feeding the homeless at her charity's shelter in the shadow of the Capitol."

"Yes, but any more, people want to know the dirt about their national celebrities, watch while it all hangs out. Why do you suppose the 'Movers and Shakers' TV talk show commands such high ratings?"

"Maybe you should get me on that show. It would be a chance to speak out on behalf of the *Windjammer* and champion the idea of progress for our country."

The noise in the school was growing louder. Emily returned with two male contemporaries in tow, each looking up in admiration at Worthington. The freckled-face boy proudly held up a small rectangular block of white pine. "Mr. Rhodes, will you autograph my caboose?"

Worthington laughed as he signed his name on the woodblock. "You've quite an imagination, young man."

D'Camp's next words were almost drowned out by the din of the children's excitement. "I think you should stay away from 'Movers and Shakers.'"

"But why?"

"For someone who claims to be so future oriented, your roots are buried in the out-of-date past, my friend. Naive, that's what your children should color you. Let me bring you up to date. It's the questions those talk show hosts ask that worry me. Why, those psyche-mongers will trip you up every chance they get.

"These days there's only so much I can do to manage broadcast and print, even in my own outlets. I can no longer control my own journalists. There are too many public relations firms plying reporters with their hype, too many hidden agendas, too many people with axes to grind who want to place stories, fan distortions, influence the media and the public. News has taken second page to exposés. The good old days of simple, straightforward news gathering are gone—those days before stories labeled 'gate this' and 'gate that.'"

"Gate?"

D'Camp nodded. "Yes, there are too many reporters running around looking for their one big story. If I fired them all there'd be a new batch apply from this year's pool of journalism graduates, and I'd be faced with the same problem of eager young members of the fourth estate searching for that newspaper headline. There are too many prizes for investigative journalism these days. Why, every communication school in the country offers at least one.

"Everyone who fancies himself a reporter is out there snooping, especially in Washington, asking questions about everything. Any subject may be a story and every person of prominence a target, for maybe it's going to be the one little revelation that unravels the plot that wins the Pulitzer. And if that happens, they've made their career mark, their book will be published, and Robert Redford will play them in a movie about their earth-shaking journalistic coup."

Worthington nodded. "I see what you mean."

"The good old days of a reporter verifying facts, confirming sources, assuming an unbiased stance are the rules of yesteryear. Especially now with television. Today a reporter takes the attitude, 'How can I make a name for myself out of this story?' Think of it as fallout from Watergate, the heritage Richard Nixon left us. The days when one man, such as William Randolph Hearst, could control what America reads and thinks are long gone, my friend. Gone on yesterday's train.

"And the writing has become almost mechanical. Why, did you know there are software programs that supply you with libel-free innuendoes, sentences that accuse but don't slander, tried and tested phrases that curdle the reader's imagination, feed their hunger for dirt? All the reporter has to do is caress his or her little mouse—the software supplies the lyrical prose, then insert the name of the person they're after, and bingo, they've got themselves an exposé."

Worthington was silent.

"So, now you know why I'm nervous about getting the final approval on the *Windjammer*. The press is the big unknown. What if they start digging into your background?"

"But there's nothing there to find out," Worthington assured him.

"Let's hope not."

Worthington felt Emily tug on his arm. "Daddy, Mrs. Carson . . ."

Then he heard Mrs. Carson say, "Mr. Rhodes, there's a telephone call for you in my private office. I'm afraid the news is not good."

Chapter Nine

The Beechcraft DX-2 Turboprop from Boston flew low above the jagged coastline of Maine, offering Anna a clear bird's-eye view of this never-never world. Unlike her Four Corners, the sun in this arcadia glittered off a wealth of water: off rivers and inland lakes, off estuaries, and off the ocean itself. Anna began to count the pine-covered islands in the bays and straits, but soon gave up, for often what appeared to be an island turned out to be a promontory jutting out into the sea. But whether mainland or island, each rocky point featured its own unique lighthouse. Out in the vast Atlantic, beyond a far-off island with a cluster of summer camps and another lighthouse, an oil tanker plied its coastal lane.

The plane's cabin ceiling was so low Anna needed to remove the spring straw hat she'd chosen for her journey, a journey that had begun late the previous afternoon. She had found the obituary about Worthington's Uncle Bill on microfiche in the morgue of Henry D'Camp's media headquarters. She read the *Portland Press Herald* notice in the column labeled NOTABLE DEATHS, and then found a later article about Hattie's eightieth birthday celebration at the Chickawaukie Nursing Home in Camden. There was barely time to phone for her plane reservation and catch a few hours sleep before her early morning connecting flight from National Airport to Boston.

"Monhegan." The man across the aisle gestured downward at the large island. "Can you imagine a handful of people shivering the entire winter there? Some say their only social activity is bundling together and waiting for the weekly supply boat, hoping the *Laura B.* survives the twelve miles of open ocean crossing from Port Clyde."

Below her was the Maine described in tourist brochures and travel videos. Even the miniature fishermen she saw might be public relations props. There would be a 1-800 number to call for more information about festivals, restaurants, and accommodations in old ship captain's homes refitted into bed and breakfasts. But what about the real people? Would they bundle together against outsiders? What honesty would Aunt Hattie have for her? Would Worthington's elderly aunt be reserved and shy with strangers?

Anna reflected on how she had overcome her own shyness by wearing hats. Hats enhanced not only her height but also, she discovered, nurtured her self esteem. They offered an efficacious accessory beyond earrings, necklaces, and bracelets. She remembered discovering the charisma of hats while observing Anasazi rock art along the San Juan River in Utah. There, drawing their own images into the desert varnish covering the red canyon walls, the Anasazi had revealed themselves to her across the centuries. She had marveled at how their figures wore elaborately-designed headgear. Yes, hats had worked for these ancient people, and now for her, a woman who studied the past, hats helped her face the world of today. Anna smiled. Hats added a subtle, commanding strength, as effective as stars on a general's uniform.

She responded to the other passenger. "Does springtime unbundle these people, or do they remain uncommunicative with visitors the year-round, Mr. . . . ah . . . ?"

"Pickup. John W. Pickup." He handed her his business card. "Changed my name from Smith so I could say, 'Me and my truck bed are at your service.'" His laugh seemed to Anna as rehearsed and routine as handing her his business card. "But to answer your question, I never try to figure out these people. In my business, I don't want to hear their stories."

She looked at his card. "You repossess lobster boats?"

"Yes, the economy here's in bad shape. The federal government's stepped in and limited the fishing. Each boat gets thirty-five days a year." He shook his head. "It's a joke. Fishermen can't support their families on income from a few paltry days. You see, a few years ago the fishermen used their good credit to buy larger boats and equip them with the latest scanners, onboard computers, and bottom-dragging nets. With these technological advancements, their nets and traps overflowed. The annual lobster catch weighed in at ten million tons. Then one day the lobsters, the haddock, all the coastal bottom fish were fished out. It's sad. Few fishermen can make their payments anymore." Pickup shook his head. "Just the urchin boats are allowed out every day. The Japanese are the only ones who love to eat those cousins of the starfish, and there are still plenty of those spiny pillows down there. Anyway, these Maine lobster boats are powerful and fast, with large capacity for stowing the catch, and my bank's found buyers in Asia."

The pilot illuminated the FASTEN YOUR SEATBELT SIGN. "Don't worry, folks, we'll be landing before we hit that mountain up ahead. For your information, that's our famous Mount Megunticook. Camden, Maine, where the sea meets the mountain—better the sea than us."

Anna and Pickup laughed. "We've got us a real comedian up there," he said. "With this economy we can use a little levity."

Inside the double-wide trailer that served as the terminal building, Anna located the ladies room, and in front of the mirror put on her straw hat. She was ready now to get into the head of Worthington Rhodes by interviewing his Aunt Hattie up here in the wilds of Maine. Lobster boats. Did Worthington remove the radar and radio equipment from Uncle Bill's boat, neglecting to warn his uncle, as Dusty contended? Just exactly what did Worthington do? What was his relationship with his uncle? Was Uncle Bill a surrogate father? Beloved, or hated? Aunt Hattie will have the answers.

Outside, she hailed a taxi with DOWN EAST CAB painted in an arch of white letters on its door. The gray-bearded driver nodded a greeting and opened the back door. "Wheah you goin', lady?"

"The Chickawaukie Nursing home."

"You're not from around heah." It was a statement, not a question. "I'll give you the scenic touah."

As the cab passed the harbor crowded with boats, Anna saw the lobstermen in their yellow slickers sitting on their rope lockers, Winslow Homer foul-weather helmets covering their heads. They were staring out to sea. Their green vinyl-coated-wire lobster traps with their lines attached to their family's distinctively-painted wooden floats were neatly stacked, waiting, begging to be baited and dropped into the ocean, there to lure and capture their soft and hard shell prey.

"No fishing today?"

"Nope," was the driver's one-syllable retort. He pointed. "See over theah? The entrance to the hahbah is blocked by the coast guahd."

Anna had to listen carefully to understand his dialect. "Why are those men just sitting in their boats?" she asked.

"It's all they know to do. They arrive at fouah, five in the morning, sit and wait. Hoping."

"That the Coast Guard cutter will leave?"

"Yup. And the dock inspectahs, too. That is, until the bank takes away theah boat. What else is a man to do? A man pursues his life-long careeah. And then one day the government down theah in Washington decides he's not allowed to work at it any moah. Nope, no work," he added sadly.

"What about another career? Retraining?"

"Staht a gallerah, you mean?" He laughed. "Become one of those hippy artists—paint, take up weaving baskets, or making pots? These are working men, lady, rugged men, not freaky fags up heah for the summah from New Yahk City."

Anna recognized John W. Pickup. He was on the boat dock talking to the driver of a flatbed truck. Pickup pointed to first one, then another fishing boat anchored in the harbor. The sheriff joined them; the three climbed aboard a police boat; and they sped off on their mission to repossess the livelihoods of seafaring men.

At the end of the dock Anna noticed a wooden shack with the letters, DOWN EAST LOBSTERMEN'S COOPERATIVE. It was shuttered, obviously closed for good. What about the families of these fishermen? Their children were probably hungry. Anna's eyes glistened. A lump formed in her throat. The private lives of these men were out in the open for inspection. The boundaries of their public and private lives had merged into a raw drive for economic and emotional survival.

Anna couldn't help but compare these fishermen who had exhausted their ocean resources to her Anasazi who had burnt up their available firewood, depleted their soil by repeated plantings of corn and killed off their game. Would these Mainers, she wondered, imitate her ancient people? Would they abandon their fishing villages as her prehistoric agrarian harvesters had abandoned their settlements, moving to other homelands and building anew? But where would these Maine fishermen go? Along their nautical coastline there were no new harbors, no virgin waters in which to drop their lobster traps.

Someday in a future century, she thought, an archaeologist would excavate this place, by then long abandoned, and determine here was once a thriving fishing village inhabited by men who harvested fish from the ocean. But inexplicably, the natives had left and gone somewhere else. The archaeologist would speculate on the reasons for their departure, trying to draw conclusions from the remains of lobster boats, old ship captain's houses, and rusty, abandoned pickup trucks.

"It's the building over theah." Her taxi driver pointed toward a weathered, three-story shingled structure with a Dutch gambrel roof.

Focusing on her own mission, with her tripod and camera case in hand, Anna paid the driver.

"You in the movies?" he asked, his tone of voice hoping for a tidbit of local news. "Sometimes they come from Hollywood to make movies heah." He paused, looked up and added with sarcasm in his voice, "And theah women always weah them hats."

"No, I'm simply out to record oral history."

He pointed at the sky. "Storm coming. I think it's going to be a bad one. My brother-in-law's put his snow plow back on his jeep. He's uncanny about predicting the weathah—bettah than those forecastahs down theah in Boston."

Anna looked up. A sky full of clouds seemed to have followed her here, for the sun was no longer visible and the sky was dark. During the short taxi ride the temperature must have dropped twenty degrees.

Inside the lobby of the nursing home, Anna looked around. She saw elderly women and a few men, some in wheel chairs, some just staring, some sewing or working with gnarled fingers on their handicraft projects. Sitting at a table were four white-haired wisps of women playing cards. A television set mounted on the wall was channeled to a soap opera, capturing the attention of a few. One woman stroked a cat that sat contentedly on her lap. To the reception nurse, Anna announced herself. "I'm Dr. Ardmore . . . to see Mrs. Hattie Rhodes."

The nurse, whose nametag read MARY MCGUIRE, RN, didn't reply. Her gaze was locked on Anna's hat.

Anna tried a smile and reiterated her request. "Hattie Rhodes."

The attention of the card players turned from their game, their gaze now fixed on Anna. Her head trembling, the woman with the cat looked up. Her glasses were thick. "Something's happened to Hattie." As she spoke the cat jumped from her lap and darted away.

Anna looked quizzically at Nurse McGuire.

Nurse McGuire's voice was weak. "You're too late."

"I knew something would happen to her," the cat woman said. "She was always talking about how magical her Bill was. His magic powers didn't help her last night." The tone of her voice changed, the volume dropped, her speech slowed. "Oh, my dear Hattie . . ." Tears formed in her eyes. With her little crippled fingers she reached out, searching for her departed cat.

Nurse McGuire leaned over the counter toward Anna. "Our dear Mrs. Rhodes is dead."

Anna was stunned. She looked at the nurse in disbelief. "No, she can't be."

"Yes, last evening, in that chair over there next to Mrs. Mittens." Nurse McGuire pointed toward the cat woman.

Shocked, Anna tried to accept the news. She was accustomed to coming upon death by excavating a burial site, albeit centuries later. Now, she was standing inches away from where Hattie, only a few hours before, had left for that afterworld inhabited by wives of lobstermen and perhaps a few lobstermen, too. Where once was life for eight or more decades, now that life had passed on.

Anna gave her condolences to the nurse, and then wondered what she should do. She felt lost. Quentin Ford IV was asking her to sanction the brutal death of Worthington Rhodes. And now, without Hattie's answers, there was no way she could prevent the assassination. Disoriented, frustrated, and afraid to report her failure to Quentin Ford IV, she could barely contemplate the task of picking up her camera equipment. And Anna remained frozen in place, as immobile as a Maine ice pond in midwinter.

She sensed the residents staring at her, wondering who she was, their eyes requiring her to introduce herself. They waited patiently for an explanation as to the purpose of her visit. Why had she suddenly shown up at the Chickawaukie Nursing Home? Even Mrs. Mittens' cat watched, waiting for some signal as to whether to pounce or flee. In her peripheral vision Anna sensed movement. There was someone else. Someone who was not a part of this elderly stage set. She turned toward the door of nurse McGuire's office, and standing there, looking at her, was Worthington Rhodes.

His expression of astonishment developed slowly. "I don't understand why you are here, Dr. Ardmore." His voice rising, he demanded, "Tell me, why are you here?"

"I don't understand either," she replied haltingly. She recovered some degree of her senses, and these words rushed out, "Oh, I'm so terribly sorry about your loss. Please accept my condolences."

"But why are you here?"

Anna said the only thing that came to her mind. "Dusty told me to come."

Worthington's face grew red. "Dusty told you to come?" He bristled. "My father told you to come here to Maine?"

"He told me I should talk to your Aunt Hattie . . . but I had no way of knowing . . ."

"Dusty!" Worthington repeated his father's name. His anger exploded. He couldn't control his rage. "Don't lie to me! You're teaming up with Dusty to destroy me!"

Anna shuddered, the look in Worthington's eyes and the expression on his face were unlike any she had seen before. Anger, perhaps hate, certainly sorrow, each complicated this man's countenance. The only turn of events for which Anna felt thankful was that the nursing home population, along with Nurse McGuire, had shifted their attention from herself to Worthington. But in this sub-culture of the sunset years of quiet serenity, she sensed a communal fear building among them. Ignoring any possibility of harm to herself, she worried what effect Worthington's demonstration of violence might have on the residents.

"Here, now, Mr. Rhodes, you calm down," Mrs. Mittens cried out. "This is a house of mourning. We can't have such behavior." Her cat arched his back in agreement.

Nurse McGuire put her arm around Worthington's shoulder and directed him back into the office. "You and I must speak of the arrangements for Hattie's memorial service which I've scheduled for tomorrow morning in our chapel."

Anna was now free to turn, run, and hide. She opened the front door to meet a rush of cold, icy Maine air.

Chapter Ten

Still mentally frayed from having been set free by a ninety-year-old woman with a cat, Anna fled the nursing home, not having the slightest idea where she was headed, hurrying down the street, almost running, but to where? To what destination? Toward the water! Aunt Hattie, Uncle Bill, and those other fiercely independent souls who had gone down to the sea in ships. Yes, it was the only direction she could think of going. Maine was oriented toward the ocean and so must she be.

The storm came sooner than she expected. A snowflake touched her face. And another. As Anna glanced up the street, she saw the sky was white with spring snow. Cold, wet tingles on her skin brought her to her senses. She asked herself what on earth she was trying to do—playing detective, snooping on Worthington—an act even the best professional sleuths might not be able to carry off. She should leave such matters to those who know what they are doing. She should tell Quentin she was out of her element—an archaeologist trying to dig up dirt about a contemporary man. Quentin Ford IV would have to do it his way, after all.

Anna scoffed at Worthington's accusation that she was teaming up with Dusty. If he only knew her sinister accomplice was none other than Quentin Ford IV, chairman of the Institute and Living Museum of Archaeology in Washington, D.C., and one of the world's richest and most influential men.

But gnawingly, she couldn't dismiss Worthington's intensity, his magnetism, his power. Of course, she realized Worthington's anger was understandable as part of the mourning process. But what about her actions? Or lack of actions? Like a beaten puppy she wanted to roll over and surrender.

Another snow crystal came to rest on her eyebrow. She despaired at not having brought the proper clothing for winter. But April was supposed to be spring. The nation's capital flowered with spring—the Japanese cherry trees were in blossom and it would also be spring in her Four Corners. There were no wildflowers here to tease her with their fragrances. But she could visualize the palette of the Southwest with orange Indian paint brush, purple lupids, and yellow columbine. Spring would be a splendid time to begin her excavation with her group of eager ILMA seminarists. She suddenly realized today was Good Friday. And so far there had been nothing good about it.

Anna wanted to catch a flight out of this place, buy a one-way ticket to Denver, there catch the shuttle to Cortez, and return home to her beloved Anasazi world. But as her pace quickened, she saw the snow accumulating on the street, the roof tops, sticking to the coats of passersby, saw the white stuff on her own flimsy jacket, her tripod and her case. She found herself next to the harbor. The snow was swirling around her and she could barely see the lobster boats anchored there. Everything was white. Even the granite shore and the pine boughs. She must get to the airport. But why? What would she do there? Sit and wait for days in that double-wide trailer-terminal for an airplane that couldn't land?

Be serious, she told herself. The pilot would pass over and continue back to Boston. That's why they had radios. To warn. And that's what Uncle Bill didn't have on board his lobster boat that day he was lost at sea. That fateful day in a fog surely as thick as this snow storm now raging about her. Worthington had removed the radio, or had he? Or had Uncle Bill simply been so headstrong he trusted his own magical abilities to find his way along a coastline he knew like the back of his hand?

Anna saw a bright light out to sea—the harbor lighthouse, its beam so bright the light penetrated the snow. The lighthouse was doing its job—warning ships. In the village she noticed another light, this one shining above a little sign topped with snowflakes, too many to count, enjoying a brief moment on center stage before joining others already covering the ground. Behind the sign, overlooking the harbor, was a weathered shingled house, its pitched roof now white with snow. Approaching the inviting abode, her body growing colder, and although snow was sticking to the sign, Anna made out the lettering, THE MAINE MOOSE B & B.

On the lawn in front of the inn was a kinetic sculpture. Its tapered stainless steel blades, each with a dusting of snow, moved slowly with balance and fluidity atop the Y-shaped polished steel base. The complexity and randomness of its unexpected motion excited Anna; she was sure the artist had witnessed the mutuality between one who acts and one who is acted upon. The work had to be by George Rickey, similar to the sculpture at the gallery in Santa Fe. She now felt a common ground between these remote areas two thousand miles apart.

Opening the door of the inn, Anna was welcomed by a warming fireplace. A plump woman, devoid of makeup, her hair cut short, stood by a picture window and beckoned to Anna. "Come heah and take a look at ouh stohm before I pull the drapes."

"Excuse me?"

The woman turned, raised her arm, smiled and beckoned for Anna to come and join her. "Maybe you'll stay heah tonight? I have one room left."

The draperies were made of fine linen as pure as the snow outside. Above the center of the rod, protruding from the wall, a moose antler supported complementary linen swags which traversed to the sides of the window, fell and gathered into soft folds on the floor.

As the woman closed the draperies, she introduced herself as Hannah. "I'm expecting one othah guest tonight, so if you ahe staying with us, I'll put up the 'no vacancy' sign. Dinnah's at seven."

Anna smiled. "Yes, I'd like very much to accept your hospitality. Maybe I could take a nap before dinner. I seem to be all tuckered out."

"Come on, I'll show you youah quatahs." The woman looked at Anna's tripod and camcorder, then at her hat and asked, "You with the movies?"

"A documentary," Anna said, lifting her still-unexposed film cartridge, hoping her reply would dismiss the matter.

"I like yoah hat," the woman said. "Maine women don't weah them. I mean, you spend all that money on fixing yoah haiah, you don't want to covah it up."

Anna tried to smile, managed a "thank you," and added, "I like your outdoor sculpture."

The woman's smile broadened. "Yup. Mr. Rickey slept heah once back in the 80s when times were good around heah, so I commissioned him. He called it *Maine Wintah*. We're the only inn in town open yeah 'round."

Anna followed the innkeeper upstairs to her room. Gesturing to Anna, Hannah turned down the comforter on the four-poster bed. Anna removed her jacket, her hat, slipped out of her shoes, and fell into bed as the innkeeper brought the soft down coverlet up over her. The last sound Anna heard was the pounding ocean surf of Maine.

Chapter Eleven

There was a soft tap on her door. Anna awoke. She wondered where she was. It was dark inside and outside. She fumbled for a light switch. The knock repeated, and a woman's voice announced, "Dinnah served in half an houah."

"Dinner!" Yes, she was hungry. But first, where was she? Anna found the switch and looked at her watch. 6:30. She opened the draperies. Still barely light outside but sufficient daylight to see snow falling across the harbor. Maine. Yes, that's where she was, and inside it's Moose's Bed-and-Breakfast.

"Our othah guest has arrived and is waiting in the pahlah," the woman advised.

"That's Hannah, the innkeeper," Anna said to herself. But another guest! How could she possibly carry on a dinner conversation with one more of these Down Easterners who practically spoke a foreign language? She hadn't picked up on the tempo yet, so she would have to listen actively to understand their meaning. And she was just too tired.

"I'll be down shortly," Anna managed to call out. She speculated as to who the other guest might be. Just the two of them at dinner. Perhaps he would turn out to be a linguistic scholar on vacation and he would trace this dialect back to old England. Maybe its inflections were Shakespearean. Better still, maybe the other guest would be a perspicacious foreign diplomat, and he would talk to her about customs and people in another far-off land, and she could forget Worthington, his aunt and uncle, forget Maine and certainly put Quentin Ford IV out of her mind.

With anticipation, Anna descended the stairs into the parlor of the small inn. She saw the back of the guest who was peering out the picture window. Surely unbeknownst to himself, he was positioned directly under the moose antler so that the cascading draperies on each side made him look like a desert sheik with antlers.

Suddenly Anna burst into laughter. Uncontrollable, as the days events spilled down upon her in a comedy of absurdities. She shrieked until the tears came, her vision blurred. At last, able to control herself, she retrieved a Kleenex, wiping her eyes. When she opened them, he had turned. And there he was.

Right in front of her.

Worthington Rhodes.

Chapter Twelve

Anna's laugh was infectious. Despite himself, Worthington began to laugh. And then with the two of them laughing and talking at once, Worthington jumbled out an apology for his outburst in the nursing home, and Anna tried to explain her crazy emotions of the moment, their voices harmonizing the cacophony of spoken words. Anna searched for the right words so she could give Worthington assurance she was not laughing at him. But being caught up in the foreign state of Maine, she wasn't sure she could make him understand. She found herself telling him how she'd come upon the B & B and how Hannah's offer of a nap before "dinnah" allowed her an escape from this storm of events. Worthington endeavored to explain to Anna that never before in his life had he lost his temper. He said he'd always known anger could be expressed in a positive way, but he knew this time he'd lost his self control. He tried to tell her how terribly embarrassed he felt, and admitted he'd made a fool of himself.

Hannah entered the parlor and joined their contagious laughter. "My guests usually don't have this much fun."

Brought back to the reality of where she was, Anna's smile vanished. Fun, she thought, this whole experience is not fun for me; I've lost control.

"I've brought you the dinnah menu," Hannah announced. "We're having herb and broccoli soup followed by a citrus ice. Our main course is beef tenderloin with a wild mushroom sauce and glazed carrots and turnips. Then I'll treat you to my wild fiddlehead salad and, of course, coffee and a fresh apple croissant for desseht."

"Sounds delicious," Anna said, trying to be polite. But her voice lacked enthusiasm.

"First, a vintage robust Cotes-du-Rhone—appropriate for a snowy evening by the fire," Worthington proclaimed.

"Right you ahe, sir. I'll go down to the cellah."

Worthington looked at Anna and hoped to bring back her smile. "We should pretend we are two different people tonight, without our histories encumbering us, and enjoy Hannah's wild fiddlehead greens. Maybe I should explain: the fiddlehead is a soft, budding frond of an edible fern that grows along the streams up north in the Aroostook. They say the fiddleheads retain their lusciousness for only an evening."

Responding, Anna's eyes sparkled. "Everything feels different to me here: the language, the ocean, the fiddleheads . . . ."

Worthington was pleased with her change of mood. "For Mainers, fiddleheads are the first taste of spring. Each year in April they strap baskets to their backs, head for the woods, and hone their sleuthing skills . . ." Anna blinked at his reference to sleuthing. ". . . to find these fledgling ostrich brake, or cinnamon ferns—a delicacy adored by those who know where to find them and how to cook them. And fiddleheads, as any enthusiast will tell you, 'need gentling and softening to unveil their quintessence.'"

Hannah enter the room. "Dinnah is served."

Side by side Anna and Worthington followed her into the dining room. Lighted beeswax candles glowed from a brass chandelier above a small round table set with crystal wine goblets, Noritake china, and polished silver.

Worthington held Anna's chair, his head brushing her hair. He whispered, "Ready for 'dinnah?'" accentuating the pronunciation.

"When did you lose your Bowdoin dialect?" Anna asked.

"Wouldn't you rather hear about how we Mainers acquired the dialect?"

"Yes."

"There's a theory advanced by a Japanese linguistic professor who hypothesizes that the English who settled the Down East coast of Maine came from the Stratford-upon-Avon area and brought with them a true Shakespearean language."

"I must have read the same account because the thought crossed my mind earlier this evening."

"Maybe our interests are not that far apart."

The innkeeper showed Worthington the wine bottle, and poured a taste into his glass. He sniffed, sipped, nodded his approval, and when their glasses were full, he proposed a toast. "No matter what language we speak this evening, may we communicate openly with each other."

"*Pour plaisander, par plaisanterie.*"

"Of course, 'for the pleasure of it,'" he translated.

Overhearing as she returned, tureen in hand, Hannah said, "And now for yoah dining pleasuah, heah is the *soupe du jouah.*"

Worthington looked at Anna, and together they broke out in laughter.

"You know," he said, "laughter is the universal language."

"And so is art."

"You saw the Rickey sculpture outside responding to the snow flakes."

"Yes," Anna replied. "I was enraptured by it."

"For me, this artist captures the maxim that nothing remains static, that we humans are powerless to forestall change and its affect on our lives, anymore than we can deny the ocean its tides, or the wind its currents."

"But can we survive the storms?"

"Tonight you and I are sheltered from the elements."

When they finished their dinner, having eaten in silence, Worthington said, "The snow has covered up our words."

"But not our thoughts."

"Would you share your thoughts with me?"

"Earlier I thought our sculptor, in his work, expressed the notion of one who acts and one who is acted upon. But your interpretation that we are powerless against the argument for change reflects the mood I am in tonight. I feel you are the one who acts and, for the first time in my life, I want to follow someone else's lead. I'm rather enjoying this juxtaposition."

"For a change?"

"Just for tonight."

"I'm going to make love to you, Anna."

Chapter Thirteen

Anna called Quentin Ford IV from the telephone on the Boeing 767 after the jet was airborne on its Saturday afternoon nonstop flight from Boston to Denver. With the Maine airports still closed from the storm, the bus had been the only way out for her—a long, grueling ride from Camden down the twisting US Highway 1, its potholes and frost heaves not yet repaired from the severe winter. Arriving in Boston, she debated whether or not to go back to Washington to see Quentin in person. But she rationalized the bus trip had been too exhausting, so she elected to fly out of Logan Airport and communicate with him via the plane's telephone.

As she had during her motor coach journey, and as she did in the air terminal, and then during the plane's taxiing and takeoff, Anna labored with the message she knew she must convey to Quentin. Not only did she agonize about her Anasazi and the importance of the preservation of their sites, she anguished about the fate of Worthington Rhodes. The fallout from the emotional storm of the previous evening, while marooned together in Maine, made the situation even more difficult for her. Finally, high above the Appalachian Mountains of Pennsylvania, she placed her call.

"Quentin," she began, trying not to be overheard by the man in the seat beside her, hoping he was indeed asleep, "I've come up with nothing in the time you've allotted me. From here on, I'm sticking to Southwest archaeology, an academic field I know something about. That's where I'm headed now—to lay out our excavation plan, so I'll be ready for my seminarists when they arrive Monday."

"My dear, if you weren't so headstrong, I could have saved you a lot of trouble. Stuart and I will take care of matters with a professional . . ."

"Yes," Anna said, "the archaeological record tells us that sometimes, some people were sacrificed for the benefit of all of society. So, do what you must."

Chapter Fourteen

Stuart Wales sat on a bench overlooking the Georgetown lock of the restored Chesapeake and Ohio Canal, waiting for Quentin Ford IV. Growing impatient, he looked at his watch, stood, and paced back and forth on the towpath, that same towpath Supreme Court Justice William O. Douglas hiked and where he probably got the idea to spearhead the campaign to preserve this early-nineteenth-century transportation relic.

Stuart stopped to read again the message on the canal's commemorative plaque that he himself had composed for ILMA years ago. If he were to rewrite that inscription today, given Worthington Rhodes' *Windjammer*, he'd take a different tack. Instead of simply glorifying a mighty canal network that stretched out through the Appalachian Mountains to open up the American Midwest back before the onslaught of the industrial revolution, he'd issue a wake-up call for America to address the transportation demands of an exploding population in a rapidly-expanding commercial environment. While he could never let his boss know what he thought, Stuart surmised that Ford's adversary just might be on the right track.

Stuart looked at his watch again. He glanced up the brick sidewalk that led to M Street, expecting at any moment to see his chairman's limousine arrive. He was puzzled why Ford wanted to meet by the C&O Canal. Ford wasn't into exercise, so they weren't going to go for a run along the towpath, although Stuart craved to do so, for he needed one more training run to be prepared for tomorrow morning's Cherry Blossom Ten-Mile Race. Usually, when he and Ford did talk, other than at ILMA board meetings, the location would be at Ford's private club overlooking the Potomac or in his limousine as his chauffeur drove along the back roads of the Virginia countryside. Ford liked to visit Mt. Vernon and then afterward drive past eighteenth-century farmhouses, admiring especially those structures that dated back to the Revolutionary War. Pointing to the royal-chartered manor houses, their stone fences, and an occasional remaining slave quarters behind, Ford would say, "My boy, before you is America, its people and its heritage, a heritage that has molded this country into the greatest nation in the world." He had a favorite way of concluding the ride, saying, "Our responsibility—yours as executive director and mine as chairman of ILMA—is to preserve our nation's past at all costs."

Stuart wondered how long he should pace. Another half hour, certainly. An hour, maybe. Two hours, well, if Ford hadn't shown up by then perhaps he'd be free to leave, but one didn't stand up Quentin Ford IV without a damn good excuse and expect to keep either their job or their head around this town.

As he completed another back-and-forth, Stuart looked up, this time to see Quentin Ford IV hurrying toward him, mopping the perspiration from his forehead. As usual the chairman was dressed in a tailored suit of American fabric and design, not Italian, for Ford insisted on buying only American products. Stuart reflected that, perhaps in addition to the silver spoon Ford was born with, he had come into this world impeccably attired, his shoes shined. Being able to look rich was a genetic trait of wealth, but the acquired mannerisms, attitude and mind-set were the result of the environmental influences of money. Quentin Ford IV was blessed with both as he carried on his legacy of status. Stuart wondered if the Ford dynasty would endure for centuries. Would there be a Quentin Ford IX, even XXVI?

"Good afternoon, my boy."

"Afternoon, Mr. Ford."

"I took the Metro to Foggy Bottom—closest station—a ways to walk, but I don't want anyone to see us meeting. My automobile does attract attention. There's always some reporter nosing around for a story, asking if I'm a government official using the vehicle on private business."

Stuart fell into step with Ford as they walked along the towpath. Stuart nodded at a passing runner. He and his chairman split apart, allowing a bicyclist to pass between them. Back together, side by side, Ford began. "Here, we're like two friends out for a walk. No one will suspect we're discussing how to put an end to Worthington Rhodes. What I am going to tell you is confidential—

most confidential. It requires . . ." A jet plane taking off from National Airport across the Potomac flew low overhead, drowning out Ford's voice.

Stuart had to ask his chairman to repeat himself.

Annoyed, Ford verbally retraced. "My plan takes for granted your dedication to a higher cause."

"Of course."

Ford continued. "The canal we are walking along was once thought to be the ultimate in our nation's transportation needs. But in hindsight, canals were short-lived."

"Thirty years at the most, before the railroads arrived on the scene."

Ford nodded slightly as if concurrence was redundant. "People were eager for progress in those days. Many interpreted a Bible passage to mandate progress."

"The one in which God says to Adam He would give him dominion over the world and everything in it?"

"That's the one. And man was off and running, killing off the animals, plowing up the flowers, devastating the natural countryside." Ford paused. "Let's sit for a minute. I'm not accustomed to so much walking." The two men found a bench in the recently-dedicated park memorializing Francis Scott Key. "You see, Stuart, I've come to a conclusion. If we lose both our prehistoric and historic national sites, we'll lose the fabric that is the greatness of the American experiment, an experiment the results of which have miraculously endured for more than two centuries."

Another jet plane flew low, its noise pervading the area. This time Ford waited for quiet before resuming. "My family has so much money that in my life I accept wealth as a given. No matter how much I spend or donate, there's always more."

As he watched his chairman, Stuart realized Ford was such a believer in his cause of preservation that he could rattle off his arguments without notes and probably, Stuart concluded, did so in his sleep.

"What I'm trying to say is that I've worked all my life for the cause of heritage preservation, and now I have come to a decision, having debated with my conscience. What I am about to instruct you to do is the only course of action open to us. Because to pursue the more conventional avenues of contributing money and lobbying Congress—the customary Washington methods—well, they just aren't working this time. We're being outgunned by Henry D' Camp and his media empire, by the giant construction companies, by the socialist labor unions, and by landowners who hope their properties may be designated for one of those new cities. Stuart, my boy, there is only one way we can change the course of events. And you must carry out the act."

"What exactly are you talking about?" Stuart's mouth was dry.

"Let me be specific." Ford put his hand on Stuart's shoulder. His tone of voice was firm. Ford hesitated for only a moment. "We at ILMA find ourselves playing in the big leagues. We're no longer tossing easy pitches in a sand lot of little league players. And the stakes are more, much more, than this year's league championship. The stakes are our country, our culture, our environment. We're champion players in the real world series. And in this real world we are far removed from simply frolicking like children in an amorphous cloud-like dream world of sweetness, fair play, and light."

"But surely . . ." Stuart started to protest.

"Wake up to reality, my boy. We're playing hard ball in a game in which the rules, if there are any, decree that the loser really loses, and I mean loses big."

Trying to follow Ford's baseball metaphors, Stuart was reminded of those Mesoamerican ball courts and the deadly games played therein. His hand flew protectively to cover his heart as he thought about how those ancient people, after their games were over, conducted the bloody sacrifice of the losers in reverence to their gods. Sitting beside the C&O Canal in the growing dusk, and in the brief interlude of silence between arriving and departing jet airplanes, Stuart Wales thought about the party line of all recruiters: death in the name of God and country.

"Stuart, pay attention. I have some very grave instructions to convey to you . . . inside this envelope." He handed Stuart two envelopes, not ones embossed with the prestigious return address of Quentin Ford IV but rather the inexpensive kind found in the small box of twenty purchased in the supermarket stationery section. They were sealed with ordinary scotch tape. "There's an awful lot of money in the thick one." Ford's laugh was shallow and quickly done with.

Stuart accepted the envelopes.

Ford looked around and then at his executive director. "For Christ sake, man, put them away before someone sees."

Quickly Stuart stuffed the envelopes into his jacket.

"You're planning to compete in the Cherry Tree race, aren't you?"

"Yes, sir." Stuart didn't correct his chairman with the proper name for Washington's annual spring athletic event.

"You are a fanatic, my boy. But this time your eccentricities will serve our country well."

"Excuse me?"

"There will be thousands of your jogger friends, each bent on winning, so no one will notice your covert mission." Ford tapped Stuart's jacket. "Just follow my instructions to the letter."

Chapter Fifteen

Worthington knew there was no predictability in a Maine springtime. One minute snow covered its world and then, almost as quickly, melted away. Disappeared. Gone. Anxious to leave, too, he somehow managed to get through the emotionally charged memorial service in the chapel, the funeral in a snow-covered cemetery, bid good-bye to Aunt Hattie's friends and Nurse McGuire, and return to Washington in his chartered jet Saturday evening.

With the events of the past two days framed in his mind, Worthington drove the Volvo slowly through the sparse traffic from National Airport, crossing the Potomac on the Memorial Bridge. Being back in the District brought benchmarks of stability, but nevertheless he remained mentally frayed.

As he passed the illuminated Capitol, he forced himself to think about Congressman Roybal and the meetings of the Appropriations Committee of the House of Representatives that would soon be held in their crowded committee room off the massive chamber of the House. Waiting for a traffic light to change on Pennsylvania Avenue, he tried to rehearse the testimony he would give to those men sitting in their giant leather chairs in their semicircle of power, microphones in front, staff aides to their rear, all looking down on him as if he were under a microscope in some legislative laboratory, and they, the scientists of politics. He would be pleading with them—no, he told himself, he would be advocating his cause, reminding them that they, too, would be the real winners in the eyes of their constituents by supporting construction of the *Windjammer*.

But Worthington's mental attention darted off, returning to Maine. To a little inn by the harbor in a snowstorm. To a dinner by candlelight, all the while the face, the body, the presence of the woman with whom he had spent the night—a sleepless, athletic night—reappeared before him. How could he have accused her of wanting to destroy him? She gave him life.

The traffic light changed to green, but he sat there immobilized until a horn from the car behind urged him forward. At the White House he stopped the Volvo and sat for a while admiring the lighted mansion, its radiance highlighting the budding trees displaying their spring vitality. What mysterious process, what sensual stimulus caused them to bud? He was budding, too. An outgrowth shocked by a distant liaison in the passionate never-never world of his previous evening.

There he'd been singularly in charge as if in his most erotic dream he could have done anything, and she'd have gone along with his every desire, following his lead, willfully. God, how she had responded! He visualized her again, felt her body next to his, her soft skin, her cerulean eyes watching him. He was thrilled with her expressions, certainly her series of orgasms. And then she was expectant again, ready, anticipating, waiting. Not for a replay, but rather his inventiveness. Her eagerness for his new ideas told him they spoke the same language.

Yes, sex was supposed to be a regenerating act, drawing upon the imagination, it's climax suggesting the ultimate liberation, but for him, sex seldom turned out to be such a dramatic declaration. Not with kids having to be first bedded down, doors in the house locked, the alarm system coded for the night, servants politely bid good evening, teeth brushed, lights turned out . . . . Having complied with all that routine, the spontaneity of sex had tiptoed away.

His encounter with Anna had been ever so more impetuous. He asked out loud, "Again?" Would he and Anna meet again to rise to even greater heights? If so, where? And when? How and where would he, could he, arrange it? Last night was indeed extemporaneous—not one of those scheduled events entered in his daily calendar weeks ahead like his forthcoming cross-country tour, the details having been arranged by his staff: city to city, hour by hour, person after person, each to be sold on the idea of a magnetic train, each to be convinced of its merits, each to be won over, each like a tart of the night to be promised some favor for their support.

Driving along his favorite back streets of Georgetown toward his Rock Creek home, Worthington contemplated what still lay ahead for him this evening. Was he the returning traveler reluctant to face Sara? Or was he the father happy to be home in time for tomorrow's Easter egg hunt with Emily and Danny? Elizabeth was, of course, too old now to participate; she was interested in bonnets and bunnies, the chocolate kind.

Yes, he was nervous about seeing Sara, about the look of betrayal she might see in his eyes. It had only been two days since he had left for Aunt Hattie's funeral, but so much had happened, or had it really? Was the tryst another of his dreams?

No, the affair had actually taken place, and in his real life. The events of the previous evening had not been a dream. For certain, he mustn't tell Sara, even hint, although she might suspect. Worthington admitted he wasn't good at deception, only advocacy for a cause. And what does a man advocate to his wife of fifteen years? A fresh color for their children's Easter eggs?

He congratulated himself for remembering to buy a carry-on prepackaged pair of lobsters at the Boston airport for their Easter dinner. But such a gift is no present, for she'll have to cook them. No, this time he'd take the lead, cook the dinner himself. Yes, he'd tell her to sip her wine while he donned his apron proclaiming him "chef" and do the cooking. That would be Sara's treat. He knew how to handle lobsters. And how to prepare the broth in which they were cooked. Aunt Hattie had shown him the technique years ago. Dear Aunt Hattie.

From inside the Volvo Worthington triggered the automatic garage door opener. Sara must have heard the rolling, vibrating sound, for she was standing there by the kitchen door, immaculately dressed, her sweet self, her long blonde hair done into twin pony tails with bows of pink, waiting, smiling, welcoming. God damn it! What had he done? To himself? To her? He saw Anna's beautiful face again. Jesus! He'd rather be naked and tongue-tied before a Congressional committee than get out of the Volvo, prepackaged lobsters in hand, moving ever closer to Sara's embrace. God! At times like this why can't we each be two separate people, clones diverging, each pursuing two separate lives? But even if it would have been possible last night for him to have been a clone of himself, his other person going down a second track, tonight both of his life's rights-of-way were now merging together again, converging into Sara's arms, feeling her kiss and returning it.

Sara whispered, "The children are in bed . . . I put them down early . . . they are so excited about tomorrow's hunt." She drew back, looked at his face, and said, "Oh, you poor dear, the funeral service for Aunt Hattie, and I saw on TV the storm was bad, too. You've had an awful trip." Then she saw his package. Sara laughed, her soft laugh, the laugh of anticipation he knew so well. "You've brought live lobsters."

"Yes, I'll cook them tomorrow just like I used to for the two of us."

Sara smiled. "Yes, I'd like that. Too bad we can't go back to the way we were." She turned toward the kitchen and called out, "Françoise, Mr. Rhodes is home."

The *au pair* looked up from coloring eggs and nodded a greeting. Worthington smiled at her.

"Why don't you go on to bed," Sara said to the nanny, "we'll finish up here. Remember, six A.M."

The *au pair* smiled, placing another egg in the brimming basket of colors. "Do you want me to carry Mr. Rhodes' cleaning upstairs?" she asked.

"No, Françoise, I'll take care of that, and his shirts are still out in my car, I haven't had time to bring them in."

Sara turned to Worthington. "I have your clothes ready for your cross-country tour. Unless you're taking this Italian one." She pointed at the suit he was wearing. "I'll need to have it pressed, too."

"Ah, no, this one's for inside the Beltway. I didn't have time to change before I flew off to Maine on Friday. Charlene has advised me not to be overdressed out West."

Sara nodded. "Tomorrow with the children will be fun . . . allow you to regroup from the cold events of Maine before you travel on."

"I wish you were coming with me."

"Be serious. I've too much to do with the children, their school, and my charity work for the homeless. They're all depending on me, and I can't let them down."

"I'm afraid I've let you down."

Sara looked puzzled.

"I mean, you have all the responsibility for the kids, the house, keeping things in line around here, all the activities . . . while I just go off . . ."

"Nonsense. You are very much a part of this family. For better or for worse."

Chapter Sixteen

If the spring morning sky had been clear, the Washington Monument would have cast a long, thin shadow across the staging area of the Cherry Blossom Ten-Mile Run toward the Lincoln Memorial. Instead, prior to the eight o'clock start on this early Sunday, dark clouds, threatening an April thunderstorm, faded the bright pink of the Japanese cherry blossoms embracing the rim of the Tidal Basin. Also up in the sky, several TV helicopters whirled, underlining the newsworthiness of the event and heightening the excitement of the remaining pre-race minutes.

Stuart Wales was eager to race. Magical, he thought, how ten thousand runners come together, bringing with them their months of rigorous, disciplined training. Now assembled, the combined energy of their anticipations electrified the atmosphere around the starting banner draped across Independence Avenue.

Looking into their faces, listening to fragments of their conversations, Stuart searched for the man who would signal the start of his covert mission. His attention, however, was diverted by several benefactors of ILMA, who greeted him with boastful predictions of their times in today's race. His search was also detoured by a group of Native Americans who were demonstrating. They were being organized by a young woman in a long dress, its fringed hemline sweeping across the grass. He recognized her—she was the new press aide for Congressman Roybal. Their placards shouted the messages: STOP THE *WINDJAMMER* and DON'T DESTROY OUR SACRED SITES. Stuart said to himself, "Silly woman, she'll lose her job. In Washington, you don't defy superiors."

Stuart elected to stand by himself, away from the others, waiting, but still no one took an interest in him. As he stretched his Achilles tendon, Stuart became edged with Quentin Ford IV for not having provided a description of the person to whom he was to hand the money. Ford's instructions had read, "Hand the thick envelope to the runner who says, 'Did you bring my trophy?'" Stuart hoped the drop would occur before the race so he wouldn't have to run with the money taped to his belly. Not only did the envelope give him a spare tire, it also weighted him down. He had even gone so far as to pin a dollar bill to a corner of the race number affixed to his T-shirt. Some people did eye the greenback, a few smiled, but no one stopped him.

"Three minutes to start," the race director announced into his hand held bullhorn. "Runners, please line up according to your expected completion times so we don't have anybody trampled to death."

Stuart joined those who would strive to run at a seven-minute-mile pace. Positioned at the starting line were the invited world-class runners who, at the crack of the gun, would burst forth, accelerating with the grace of African gazelles, and speed through the course, racing the entire distance at a sub-five-minute-mile pace.

Watching the overhead digital clock, its large white numerals clicking off the seconds, ten thousand runners counted down in unison, their vocal crescendo rising to drown out the firing of the starting gun. Soon the long parade of athletes crossed the Potomac River on the Memorial Bridge, followed counterclockwise around the Virginia-side traffic circle, then recrossed the bridge, returning to the District.

Stuart concentrated on maintaining a steady, even pace. He thought about his form: arms low, fanny tucked in, head high. Looking to his left he noticed a woman running smoothly by his side, matching his pace. She looked over at him and laughed. "They didn't collect the RT bridge toll."

Stuart smiled. "The Department of Transportation passed up a sure source of revenue this morning."

"A dollar per runner," she replied, "would add up to a sizable sum for a Sunday morning offering."

Side by side they ran on as the course made a U-turn at the Kennedy Center. Passing the Mile Four marker, she picked up her speed and called out over her shoulder, "Do you have enough of those greenbacks on you to pay for all ten thousand of us?"

Stuart wondered how she knew what he was carrying. Was she his contact? Surely Ford wouldn't have arranged for a woman assassin. Anyway, she now disappeared, lost up ahead in the crowd of runners. Stuart's attention focused on his own physical endeavor. Passing the Jefferson Memorial, Stuart heard a runner behind him exclaim, "Here come the leaders." From the opposite direction came the Kenyan juggernaut, loping along, seemingly with ease as if they were out for a casual Sunday running jaunt. Stuart said to the older man now running by his side, "I wish I could run at their world-record pace."

"Maybe you could if you weren't carrying so much extra weight," the man said.

Nervously Stuart pointed to his belly, hoping the man was his contact. "I'll never get a trophy being ten pounds overweight."

"Think of the extra weight as ten one-pound packages of butter strapped to your midriff," the man analogized. "Take my advice and reduce your calorie and fat intake. You'll soon lose that excess baggage." To make his point, the man sprinted ahead.

The temperature was dropping. The sky was darkening. By the time Stuart and those around him made the turn at Hains Point to run along the Potomac back toward the finish line, the wind was picking up. He looked over at the river and saw white caps. Lightning cracked overhead. Thunder roared. Rain began to fall and the temperature dropped even lower. As they raced the final leg of the course back along the Tidal Basin, the rain pelted them. The wind blew off the Potomac with gale force. Cherry blossoms, freed by the squall from their delicate branch moorings, filled the air with trillions of flowery flakes for the spring storm. The wet asphalt was quickly covered with pink petals as were the runners. The treads on their shoes were not designed to track on a surface of wet cherry blossoms. Some runners around him began to slip. Suddenly Stuart felt his feet flying out from under him, his balance lost. His hands reached out, trying somehow to prevent his fall. The next thing he felt was pain, his breath forced from his lungs. Wet cherry blossoms were his only view, his nose and face flat on the now-pink asphalt pavement.

To his surprise it was the woman runner who had paced him early in the race who was helping him up, steadying him, asking with concern if he was hurt. Stuart looked down at his body, felt his legs, his arms, his ribs, and announced he was okay, apart from blood here and there, and he thanked her for her concern.

"Take it easy, Mr. Wales," she said. "The finish is just up ahead."

Surprised once more, Stuart asked, "How'd you know my name? And what's yours?"

She smiled the smile of one runner to another. "I'm Angela. After you finish the race, climb the stairs and wait at the foot of Abraham Lincoln. My associate will meet you and expect you to hand him your little package."

"But how will I know him? And what's his name?" Stuart managed to ask as he resumed his running.

"His code name is 'Booth.'" Angela darted ahead and was lost in the swirling cherry blossoms and the crowd of slipping, sliding runners.

Stuart crossed the finish line, taking notice of the digital clock's one hour and fifteen minute reading. He grabbed a banana and a bottle of water offered by a race volunteer and collected his commemorative T-shirt. As he continued on at a slow jog toward the Lincoln Memorial, he looked at the race shirt and saw, silk screened on its back, a bullet train. The *Windjammer* was the sponsor of the Cherry Blossom Ten-Mile Run. Yes, he certainly had to hand it to Worthington Rhodes. He was a far-sighted man with imagination. Pity.

Ascending the steps toward the munificent Abraham Lincoln, dodging tourists with umbrellas and other race finishers seeking cover behind the fluted Greek columns, Stuart dreaded his rendezvous with a man called Booth.

"Did you bring my trophy?" a voice asked.

"A trophy?" Stuart replied, puzzled at first. "Oh, you mean this?" He reached under his sweat-soaked shirt and ripped the tape from his skin, grimacing. He handed Booth the thick, sealed envelope.

"It's too bad," Booth said, tucking the bulky envelope under his shirt.

"Why?"

"Well, in this case by performing my job properly—which I plan to do, of course—I'll be disappointed."

"Why is that?"

"I was looking forward to riding the new bullet train to Los Angeles. I like trains. I'm deathly afraid of flying."

"How do you get to your destinations so you can perform your . . . ah . . . assignments?"

"Oh, I've this red Mustang convertible." Booth beamed proudly. "My prize for winning a marathon. I use it to commute to work. You see, I savor the privacy a car affords me during the gap-time between home and my job."

"You regard your work as a job?"

"Yes, and I'm very good at it. Angela and I will tackle this assignment right away. Meanwhile, I'm going to run the Boston Marathon a week from tomorrow. I hope to finish in the top ten. I believe in staying fit. Besides, running is a right brain activity. It stimulates my creativity, you see, and makes my mind work. So, while exercising—usually after about five miles—I'm able to devise new and clever ways of executing my assignment."

"But there's only one way to pull a trigger."

"Perhaps," Booth said. "But the journalistic volleys I deliver are faster than a speeding bullet and more powerful than a locomotive."

"What do you mean?" Stuart asked, surprised. "You are an assassin, aren't you?"

"Yes indeed, and a very thorough one, too, the best of the professional character assassins inside the Beltway."

Dumbfounded, Stuart repeated, "Character assassin?"

Booth nodded. "A fate worst than death if administered correctly. I advise my wealthy clients it's the best way to exert power today—supersedes the old methods of massive campaign donations, bothersome lobbying, and political horse trading. No Federal Elections Commission watching over, no bureaucratic reports to fill out and file, no registrations, no diaries to keep."

Stuart's mouth dropped as he watched Booth, quite the richer, dart away. The assassin was quickly lost among the arriving hordes of visitors who were now exiting tour buses from Maine and Illinois, intent on photographing a chapter of American history.

Chapter Seventeen

Four Corners—a splendor of Anasazi architecture: Chaco Canyon, a cultural center dating from A.D. 1000, its Pueblo Bonito with multiple tiers of coursed rock rising into the New Mexico azure sky; Canyon de Chelly, its chalky White House tucked into a protective alcove of a prodigious Arizona cliff; Chimney Rock, commanding a mesa top, its astronomical turrets surveying the mysteries of the Colorado night sky; cavernous Hovenweep, a captivating sense of place within a Utah canyon, its Square Tower watchful in the early morning shadow of the Sleeping Ute. Anna Ardmore's Anasazi welcomed her home.

Returning to her familiar Southwest environment, she found her affinity with the area hadn't changed, but, she wondered, had she changed? She felt her pathways of the past two days were as enigmatic as the yet unexplained prehistoric roads. Had her ideas about sex being only for recreation changed? She acknowledged that Worthington Rhodes was the first man to ever penetrate her very soul.

To clear her mind, she must hike in and scout the dig site. She must take her computer, her maps, aerial photos, carry plenty of water, and pack a lunch. In this high-altitude refuge there would be no dinner served by candlelight. If she could deny the existence of Worthington Rhodes, she could annul that sea level consummation, and she would be on firm ground again.

Ten years ago, with the guidance of Spider Woman, Anna had chosen the site on which to build her home, a home she fashioned after an Anasazi houseblock. To Anna, the Pueblo Revival style of architecture was simple, straightforward, and of the earth itself:

three foot adobe walls supported viga roof beams that supported the flat roof. These thick walls kept the interiors cool in the summer and warm in winter. Anna's bookshelves lined these massive walls. Seeing her own familiar library, her personal photographs, her working papers partly organized, partly scattered, her wardrobe of Santa Fe style clothes, her shoes, belts, scarves, and hats, and especially the striking wrought iron well-head sculpture she had placed in the middle of her living room, Anna knew she was home.

Her attention was caught by the red light blinking on her answering machine. The message from Alexander Parish advised her he was arriving a day ahead of the other participants. "Gosh, Dr. Ardmore, I'm eager to begin our dig, and I'm anxious to see how your computer plotting program works, so may I please, please accompany you on your survey of the ruins?" Anna listened to his persuasive voice. "If so, and hopefully so, I'll be waiting for you at the trailhead at seven sharp Sunday morning."

As Anna drove her Jeep to the trailhead, a thousand years of prehistory jumped out in front of her as nimble as a jackrabbit crossing the road. It wasn't so with the East Coast. Here, in her Four Corners, much was unspoiled, undiluted, and untampered with. Barely a hundred years had passed since man began to explore its mysteries. Of course, there had been conquistadores, missionaries, mountain men, and prospectors, but their impact had been limited to military conquest, religious intervention, animal depletion, and mineral removal. Impact enough, certainly, but not the same as building cities and railroads everywhere. Pedro de Peralta laid out the Spanish capital city of Santa Fe in 1608, the same time as Captain George Weymouth and the earliest of the English settlers were struggling to build a community on the coast of Maine, and a dozen years before the Pilgrims landed at Plymouth Rock. She thought how, throughout the next three hundred and seventy-five years, immigrating Europeans had reshaped the eastern landscape, crowding its streams with mills and factories and overlaying its countryside with sprawling cities.

Wanting only to study the past, to become lost in its billowing skirts of time, to hide in the recesses of its caves and wander in the labyrinths of its architectural ruins, she renewed her vows to harmonize with her prehistory people. Here she could forget the present and ignore the future. In the context of studying her world of antiquity, weren't they both simply irrelevant? She would be removed from the issues of the day, excused from participating in the national debates. And she'd not be alone, for there were research chemists, historians, artists, and professors, many of whom had chosen their own grand escapes. Let modern times advance with each invented technology. Let modern times always be modern times, not held back by tenets of the past or restrained by those who fear change. Let there be jobs for those out of work, such as those seafaring lobstermen. Yes, let the entire national economy bubble up into prosperity for all. And let Worthington Rhodes—if Quentin's dreadful scheme failed—build his train and his new cities. Or let him be gunned down in cold blood at some shopping mall or while speaking to his faithful from some platform. So be it.

A grinning Alexander Parish greeted her at the trailhead, and they set off in search of ILMA's excavation site, she leading him.

"Will we be digging in a kiva, a plaza, or a trash heap?" Alexander asked as they hiked.

"That's the beauty of my software program." Anna gestured to her backpack. "Archaeologists have their individual biases about where to dig, so by the computer randomly selecting one-meter squares, we will adhere to a scientifically correct sampling. Tomorrow, we'll each insert our trowels and our curiosities into our assigned squares."

"And not dig up the entire town?"

Anna nodded. "Just sample it. Leave the rest for future archaeologists who undoubtedly will devise new and improved techniques."

"At last, I'm actually going on an archaeological dig. For me this trip is as exciting as a World Series."

"I hope all our seminarists share your enthusiasm."

"You turned me on, Anna, with your presentation the other night in Washington."

"Tell me about yourself, Alex. How'd you get into this baseball career of yours?"

He laughed. "Well, I was born with a bat in my hand. I played Little League and then Babe Ruth, high school ball and then college at Arizona State. I was drafted my junior year by the Yankees."

"The New York Yankees?"

"Yes, their scouts travel all over the country, even to Arizona."

"So you played in Yankee Stadium?"

"Not right away. I was in the minor leagues for a year with their farm team in upstate New York. Oneonta is a beautiful little town, and its ball park . . ." He laughed.

"What's so funny about it?"

"The outfield fence is painted with advertisements promoting local businesses. That summer, each time up to bat, I tried to park the ball over a different logo to win each merchant's home run prize. Pull the hit as they say."

"And did you collect all the prizes?"

"Yes, except for the Catskill Funeral Parlor."

Anna choked, and Alex offered her his water bottle. "Thank you, Alex. It's thoughtful of you to remind me how quickly we forget to drink enough water out here in this dry, sauna-like heat. I must warn our people tomorrow when we gather at the Cross Cultural Trading Post. We don't want anyone suffering dehydration."

The trail climbed out of a sandy arroyo and wound upward through a copse of bright green aspen. Alex's long legs and faster pace carried him ahead. A lesser gait seemed uncomfortable for him. Anna walked more slowly now, stopping to search the rocky soil for shards and projectile points. Occasionally she would find one, pick it up, and examine it.

Observing her, Alex called back, "These hills are alive with broken pottery." He stopped and waited for her to catch up. "George and Martha said there are federal laws protecting these ruins."

"Yes, but people have to uphold the laws."

"You should become a full-time agent for the Anasazi, Anna. Protect their interests and maybe even negotiate an attractive bonus for them."

"You may have something there."

After a while, Anna circled her hand and announced, "We're here, Alex. We've arrived at our excavation site. See, over there is a crumbled rock wall of a tiny farming tract. And there's the remains of a stone signal tower. And over there," she said, turning to her right, "are walls of houses, a whole row of them, and behind them, still more. Alex, we're surrounded by an Anasazi pueblo. You and I are standing in the plaza of an eight-hundred-year-old city. And in front of us . . ." Anna pointed. ". . . see that round, sunken area?"

"A swimming hole?"

"No." Anna laughed. "It's their grand kiva, the village's main ceremonial room. The roof has long since collapsed, and down through the centuries soil has blown over, concealing its secrets from us."

"Too bad, I would have loved to have gone skinny dipping with you." He looked around at the ruins. "But this is a ghost town. The stands are empty."

"Even so, Alex, I almost expect someone to peer out through that window in the tower, or to climb up out of the kiva on a pole ladder to greet us."

"Or sing the national anthem and tell us to 'play ball.'"

"You're right, Alex. We must get to work."

"We could set up a concession stand and sell peanuts and crackerjack 'cause I don't care if I ever get back."

Anna laughed again and set her pack down at the edge of the kiva. "I'll get out our maps and computer. Here, you can help."

"And now, fans, batting cleanup with the bases loaded is our beautiful Anna Ardmore," he announced as he spread the maps on the ground, anchoring them with rubble from a nearby wall. Alex feigned whistles and cheers from the Anasazi spectators.

Anna looked up from her keyboard and tried to keep from laughing. "Here, you take the measuring tape over to that far corner of the settlement beyond the tower and call back the distance in meters."

"I'll beat out the bunt," he called over his shoulder as he raced off. He shouted back, "Forty meters to first base."

"Good, now do the same on the other corners. I'll enter the figures and put the computer to work."

"This is great! It's like chalking out the infield diamond before a game." He bounded off again, tape in hand.

Anna watched his boyish antics. He had taken off his shirt, revealing muscles toned to perfection. Was Alex flaunting his masculine body? No, he was simply an athlete proclaiming no bounds. This baseball player was good medicine for her.

Returning her attention to her screen which now displayed the parameters of the site, Anna watched as it sectioned the entire area of the ruins into a checkerboard pattern and then selected, at random, a dozen squares. She called to Alex to come and see her lottery results.

Their heads together, he whispered, "There's one thing your computer doesn't tell us."

Anna looked at him curiously.

"Where are the bedrooms? That's what I want to explore."

She handed Alex a roll of twine. "Behave yourself and follow me. I want you to tie this string around the marker stakes which we'll drive into the ground at each corner of our special squares. We'll begin out there in the farming tract and work our way back to the plaza." When they had completed their rounds, Anna announced, "We're done, Alex."

"Can we explore that bedroom now?" Alex pointed toward a vertical fifteen-foot ascent up hand and toeholds carved into the sandstone cliff leading to the opening of a natural cave. He took her hand and she climbed up with him. Once through the small entrance, the cave opened into a vault ten or so feet in diameter. The room was almost as high in the center where, down through the eons of time, its crescent roof had been sculpted by the rushing waters of flash floods. The centuries had collected an ocean's worth of sand to carpet the floor. On the back wall, the last Anasazi resident had painted a figure of Kokopelli playing a flute while displaying a thirteen-point-three-four centimeter erection.

"Look at that stud!" Alex exclaimed as he took off his pants. He put his arms around her. "And what is your favorite Anasazi position?"

"We'll have to observe the animals," she replied. She turned toward the bedroom wall, whispering over her shoulder, "Before the missionaries came, the animals wrote the prehistory sex manual."

A little canyon wren, its brown tail bobbing, flitted into the cave, chirping at them ceaselessly. "We've finally got a spectator," Alex managed to say. The wren darted behind Anna's pack, leaving its tiny prints in the sand. Back and forth, in and out, the bird paced.

Anna responded to Alex's orgasm, but she found no release from the complexity of her thoughts. Continuing to watch the bird, she whispered, "The wren's upset. This is her home and we've intruded."

They heard chirping overhead. "Up there," Alex said, nodding his head toward the cave ceiling.

"Inside that little recess." Anna pointed toward a ceiling coffer. "She has a nest up there."

The canyon wren boldly flew past them and disappeared into the niche. Her chicks greeted her with a medley of joyous cries.

"Let's all celebrate." Alex reached into his pack, pulled out a bottle of New York wine, stuck a candle into the sand and lit it.

Anna stared at the lighted candle. Memories stormed across her mind. As Alex unfolded his Swiss Army knife and popped the cork from the wine bottle, she threw up her hands. "Enough!" she exclaimed. "I've had enough of these candlelight ceremonies!" Leaving Alexander Parish stunned, she fled the cave. With alacrity, Anna descended the hand and toeholds down the face of the cliff.

Chapter Eighteen

Clarence Short lived in an old boxcar with his dog named Willie. Surveying the ten acre parcel for his freight car home had been a labor of love. Even transporting the weathering car from the siding of the abandoned narrow-gauge line outside Farmington had proven to be an enjoyable engineering challenge for him, as had plumbing and electrifying its interior. He had cut an entry door into one side as well as four round windows, one of which eliminated the RR of the still visible but fading black letters, DENVER AND RIO GRANDE RR. He had yet to build the entry steps, but he hadn't planned on inviting guests and he enjoyed climbing the rungs of the freight car's rusty metal ladder. Besides, it was fun to watch Willie make the leap.

Clarence wasn't short of money. His British-made four-wheel-drive vehicle parked on the gravel pad outside his boxcar attested to that fact. Nor was Clarence lacking in personal prestige. For since moving to the Four Corners only a few years earlier, he'd made quite an impression in political and construction circles. His notoriety of wealth and political power sent shivers through those who must either work for him, get along with him, or both.

According to rumors now circulating, Clarence's assets were extensive. In reality, all he had done was buy, back in 1962, a small Palo Alto tract house which, luckily for him, benefited from California's wild real estate inflation. Decades later, he had simply sold that very same house for exactly sixty-seven-point-two times what he had paid for it.

True, he said to himself, he had to deduct from his profit one repainting and a kitchen remodel, both insisted upon by his wife, and a driveway resurfacing caused by movement of the underlying unstable soil. And, compelled to do so by her nagging, he had installed an automatic garage door opener so she wouldn't have to get out of her American Motors Rambler during winter rains. He was responsive to her wishes, he had explained to his buddies at the Legion Hall because, after all, women are smaller and weaker and that old door's exterior plywood sheets framed into one heavy section was pretty weighty for her to handle. They had laughed, guffawed the way men do when they understand the other, saving the effort of unneeded conversation. Why, one properly intoned guffaw replaced at least three minutes of composing one's thoughts into an intelligent statement of sentences and paragraphs.

When the little woman died, it rather broke him up. Life alone in that house became difficult for him to cope with. He needed a change, a new home, fresh scenery, and a dog, as well. So he took early retirement from his state job. Trying to free himself of all his memories, he advertised an absolutely-everything-must-go garage sale. And he left, hoping to find a new point of beginning.

He decided to emulate the behavior of those who were influential. He would throw money around, give and get favors, drive an expensive vehicle, join a country club, wear a ten-gallon hat, and own a Rolex. Yet, he vowed he would always remain a red-blooded working American engineer and surveyor.

Clarence learned the *Windjammer* was to angle across the Four Corners and that New Mexico had a job opening in charge of surveying its wide right-of-way. The state was also in the midst of a gubernatorial election. Clarence put on his best western suit, donned a silver bolo, and met one of the governor-to-be hopefuls at a campaign rally. He shook her hand, behaved his best, sounded his smartest, and talked about the *Windjammer* with a mixture of admiration and "American can-do."

Cornering one of her aides and acting wealthy and wise, mature and nonsexist, he said, "Honey, my name is Clarence Short. I'm interested in your filly's race. She's doggone good looking and I think she'll make a mighty fine governor. I'm also prepared to make a sizable campaign contribution and, by the way, I'm sure interested in that new job in charge of surveying our state's section of the *Windjammer*. I don't mean to tie one to the other, but you know how it is today—everybody's real busy and it's easy to get things confused, especially for women, you know what I mean? So I'd really like to go to work on this here *Windjammer* project, and I'd also like to help move your little woman out of the State House and into the Governor's Mansion." He tried a guffaw, but it didn't score big with the campaign aide. Women are different, don't share male understandings, he concluded.

The little lass watched him drive off from the garden party by the swimming pool at the country club outside Gallup, noting his top-of-the-line four wheeler with its four antennae. Sufficiently impressed and remembering him from his construction-like talk, as well as his lavish description of the private railroad car in which he lived, she relayed both his job request and his offer of financial support. Anyone with four telephone lines on their vehicle had to be pretty important, she advised in her verbal summary. For clearly one line was for incoming fax, another for a modem, the third for everyday cellular communication, and the fourth an answering machine for when the other three were busy. Besides, his dog was cute. Her candidate prevailed, and Clarence received the appointment.

This midday, standing by his all-terrain vehicle at the end of a disused jeep road, Willie by his side, Clarence looked through powerful Japanese binoculars out over the arroyo below. His solicitous assistant, Dillon, stationed at a portable computer placed on the vehicle's hood, inputted data as Clarence dictated.

"Dillon, our route will cut across the Continental Divide and span that broad arroyo way down there at the foot of this mesa."

"Crossing the 37th parallel at . . ." Dillon calculated. ". . . 6,828 feet. I can see where the right-of-way will run . . ." He looked up and pointed. ". . . off there toward the horizon." Dillon's fingers flew across the keyboard advancing the right-of-way westward. "And once across the Four Corners our train will head bullet-like for the Southern California beaches."

"Yes, smack across the Four Corners itself, roll right over the precise spot where the Page-Lentz surveyor's monument was set in 1899, back before Arizona and New Mexico became states." Clarence took a drag on his cigar. "And re-monumented in 1931. I remember that question from my California license exam years ago. Re-monumented in 1962 and again in 1992, the last time by Wilson and Eaves." He turned to Dillon. "Had to know that in order to pass my New Mexico exam."

Dillon nodded, showing his admiration. He unfurled a large map. "Our Native American Reservation Map shows that the exact point where the four states meet lies within the Navajo Nation. In fact, there are lots of Indian lands around here."

"Damn Injuns getting in the way of progress again." Clarence shook his head.

Dillon nodded. "So, where will they locate the huge new Four Corners city?"

Clarence took a deep draw on his cigar, exhaling slowly into the warm spring breeze. A cloud of smoke floated over his dog and Dillon. Willie sneezed. "I'll let you in on my little secret, Dillon, if you keep it to yourself."

"Yes, sir, I will."

"My favorite congressman, Orlando DeBaca Roybal . . ."

"Was that your cellular phone call from Washington early this morning?"

"Yes, Dillon, you'll find it pays to make the right campaign contributions. That's what money's for, I've learned. I always advise younger men such as yourself to court influence."

Dillon's respect was apparent. "What did he say?"

"Congressman Roybal is going to make good on his campaign promise to a big contributor," Clarence told him. "Favor for favor, you see. So, it's a sure thing the new city will be built on the Bar 8 cattle ranch."

"Belongs to some big eastern dude in newspapers and television, so I've heard."

Clarence smiled. "Right again." His cigar having gone out, he chewed on the stub and puffed out his chest. "Remember, Dillon, this nation was built by surveyors like George Washington and Daniel Boone, and now Congressman Roybal has asked me to survey his new city. He's already coloring in the plans, but he confessed he needs the help of a real mapmaker."

"Fits you to a tee," Dillon fawned. "Say, won't you need a good assistant with a job as big as that?" Eagerly observing his boss, he waited for a reply.

Instead, Clarence was glued to the binoculars, his attention elsewhere, a smile forming. "Over there, Dillon, that cave. Something's moving." He handed the glasses to his assistant.

Dillon looked and returned the binoculars to his boss. "I don't see anything. Probably a deer. But I do see some Indian ruins way down there below the cave."

"They're of no consequence," the surveyor muttered. "Remember, Dillon, our *Windjammer* has police powers—the right of eminent domain. The roadbed will plow right through that cliffside, wiping out everything in its path." Clarence managed one of those guttural laughs heard only in blue collar bars, a communication between males who know and understand the workings of the world, whether the subject be geopolitics or sex.

Peering into the binoculars again, Clarence exclaimed, "Look there, Dillon, there is something moving. It's a woman, and she's coming out of that cave. By God, she's naked as a jay bird . . ." Clarence's mouth was open.

Hoping to be offered a look, Dillon's hand rose, his fingers outstretched, waiting to grasp the binoculars. But Clarence held on, glued to the glasses. He watched as the woman adroitly descended the cliff. He rotated his focusing knob back and forth. With the scene now crystal clear, he saw the hand and toeholds on the face of the cliffside. "Wow, Dillon!" Clarence's voice rose in excitement. "Has she got a pair of hooters!"

Chapter Nineteen

Breakfast at the Cross Cultural Trading Post with Dillon was the only social activity Clarence penciled onto his calendar during his surveying assignment in this remote country. With Willie begging for table scraps and drawing public attention, he could meet the most interesting people.

The Cross Cultural Trading Post was established in the mid 1800s as a place to conduct barter between the nearby Navajo and Ute Indians and the mountain men of the Rockies. Fortunate in having the state highway built past its entrance in the late 1920s, the log cabin adapted to progress with the addition of a breakfast cantina. Today, with its reputation known across the country, the trading post catered to collectors of baskets and pottery, turquoise and silver jewelry, woven rugs and blankets, fetishes and kachinas, as well as enticing tourists with a menu of huevos rancheros, blue corn tortillas, and chorizo sausage.

Along the exterior foundation, next to the massive wooden entry door, a row of hollyhocks, climbing their strings, escaped the gravel parking lot. The trading post's interior log walls, having accumulated more than a century of dust, offered the perfect display for antique snowshoes and wooden skis. In addition, elk, deer, and pronghorn antelope trophy heads, cobwebs spanning their antlers, looked down on those below with animal curiosity. Hanging from overhead beams were leather saddles and chaps, spurs and hats of all sorts. Packages of beef jerky and bags of potato chips decorated the old wooden counter, behind which were countless cubbyholes loaded with vital supplies awaiting modern-day cowboys, outback hikers and backpackers. With its Wild West decor, the trading post delighted all those who drove the long distance to its remote location to taste and smell the frontier spirit.

Clarence Short gestured toward the big round table in the no-smoking section. "Look there, Dillon, it's the woman I saw climbing down out of that cave yesterday."

Dillon gave a low whistle. "Like you said, Boss, she's got all the right equipment."

"And do you known who that man is next to her?"

Dillon looked puzzled. "The old guy with the beard and leather hat?"

"No, no, I mean the handsome, clean-shaven fellow with the baseball cap."

Dillon's look remained blank.

Clarence showed irritation with his assistant's ignorance. "It's Alex Parish, the Washington Slugger's third baseman. He batted over three hundred last season. Thirty-four home runs—one for each year of his life—and then he retired. Prematurely, I told everyone at the country club."

"And who's the dude with the Australian outback hat?"

"They sell 'em right over there at that counter." Clarence nodded his head toward the outdoor clothing section. "He looks well-heeled like the rest of the group. I'll bet they're out here looking for adventure, and our cave lady's providing it."

"She and those other three young fillies," Dillon stated. "I'll take the blonde with the short shorts."

"You'll have to get around those chaperones from Texas."

"How do you know where they're from?" Dillon asked.

"She's got one of those Texas hairdos and see all her Mary Kaye makeup. And his bolo is a silver oil well."

Dillon nodded and leaned forward trying to hear the conversation at the large round table. But all he heard was the sound of tires grinding to a stop on the loose gravel in the parking lot. A truck door slammed, followed by the sounds of bolts sliding across metal and hinges squeaking. Willie's ears went up.

Suddenly the heavy trading post door was pushed open. A tall, bewhiskered and lanky man wearing old bluejeans, a dirty western shirt, and a large black hat entered. He wore a Navajo beaded nametag that introduced him as TONY, YOUR LLAMA MAN. Tony shouted across the trading post, "Who's got the dog in here?" Without waiting for an answer he yelled, "My llamas know there's a dog in here somewhere. I can't unload my prized possessions from my transporter until the dog's gone."

Leon, the owner of the trading post, appeared from out of the blanket section. "What's all the ruckus about, Tony?"

"There's a dog in here somewhere."

"Oh, that's Mr. Short's dog. He won't bite."

"My llamas don't know that. They can smell a dog a mile away. Get that bitch outa here." Tony saw Anna and stated emphatically, "Dr. Ardmore, you're not planning to bring a dog on this trip, I hope."

"Mr. Short's one of my valued customers," Leon protested. "I can't . . ."

"So am I," Tony shouted, his face growing as red as the bandanna around his neck.

"It's okay, Leon," Clarence said. "We've got to get to work anyway. Come on, Willie." He snapped a braided leather leash to the dog's bright red collar, tossed a twenty on the table, politely tipped his Stetson toward Anna, and with Dillon and the dog in tow, exited through the back door.

Anna addressed her eight acolytes at the round table. "As you heard, Tony's llamas will be carrying our gear. He's waiting outside to introduce us to them. They answer to their own names."

Dusty started to say, "You can call me Dusty," but the scraping of chairs as the group pushed away from the table and the last clinking of coffee cups drowned out his voice for all but those close to him. A telephone rang somewhere among them. Immediately the group quieted, looking around in puzzlement. To his surprise, Dusty realized the ringing was coming from inside his jacket. Embarrassed, he extracted the hand-held instrument, unfolded the mouthpiece, and pulled up the antenna. Hoping no one would notice, he said softly, "Hello?" Unable to dismiss the curious looks from the others, Dusty held his hand over the mouthpiece and explained, "My granddaughter wanted me to carry one of these— told me I should 'get with it.'" He added with a sheepish chuckle, "In case we needed to order pizza from the dig site."

With everyone listening, Dusty spoke into the instrument, "Yes, Emily, this cellular phone really does work." He laughed. "Why, I'll bet I can even call my archaeology friend at his excavation way over there in Greece. How about that, Emily, ruins in the New World talking to ruins in the Old World." A pause. "Yes, precious, I promise I'll call you from the kiva as soon as I unearth Ixtill Eight's wheel."

A hint of a smile appeared on Anna's face. "All right, my friends, let's hike out to our Anasazi settlement and see if we can dig up this legendary wheel."

Outside, a calmer Tony, looking as though he deserved credit for having genetically engineered a new breed of pack animal, was ready to help everyone load their possessions.

Anna heard Paul, who was an eminent economist with Merrill Lynch in New York, ask Tony, "How will I ever equal the load on each side of this llama's woolly back?" He adjusted his Australian hat. "It's going to be as difficult as balancing the nation's budget."

Tony produced what he referred to as his Lady Justice scale with two empty trays. "Okay, listen up, everyone. Fill your two panniers with gear, and then we'll weigh the wicker baskets." He hung the scale on a metal rod which he extended from the back of his transporter. "Whatever you put in one must balance with the other, and no more than twenty pounds in each."

Paul laughed. "Tony, the nation should hire you to correct the deficit in our foreign trade balance."

The blonde in the short shorts, Daisy, weighed in and then reluctantly threw out her hair drier. Anna watched as she discarded even more possessions on the ground. Her friend Greta, the school teacher, passed the weight test.

The third woman, Margaret, having announced she was a banker from Chicago—a loan officer specializing in emerging businesses—had far less equipment filling her baskets. She said sarcastically, "I hope this isn't another one of those experiments in the arid West that goes dry. I'm reminded of Edward Beale's expedition back in 1857."

"You mean the twenty-five camels brought over from Morocco?" Tony asked.

"Yes. Another harebrained scheme that didn't work."

"What would the world be without someone trying new ideas?" George asked as he loaded his and Martha's panniers.

Margaret frowned. "There'd be a lot fewer losses of depositors' money on bad loans, let me tell you."

Alex helped Daisy lift her sleeping bag. "My coach used to say, 'If you don't swing at the ball, you'll never get a hit.'"

"You're right, Alex," George agreed. "If you never drill a wildcat well, you'll never get a gusher."

"Oh, you'll all lose your money," Margaret said and walked away.

Tony began checking the straps on his animals, making sure they were neither too tight nor too loose.

"No more weight," he admonished Daisy, "or my friend Paco here will become out of sorts and spit."

"Ooh," Daisy cooed. She looked at Greta. "You never me told me about that."

"You never asked. Personally I wouldn't spit at an adversary. I'd practice the Japanese discipline of *aikido*."

Dusty looked at Greta questioningly.

"It's a beautiful philosophy," she explained, "a harmony of oneness with the Earth. It's a nonviolent technique of self-defense, especially good for women because it requires little upper body strength. I'm a devoted disciple and I teach it to my students."

"She'll demonstrate for all of us, won't you, Greta?" Daisy said to her.

Greta eyed Dusty. "I hope I don't have to use it, but I'll be happy to show the group the various movements."

Tony announced in a loud voice, "Okay, folks, now all you have to do is lead your llama with the rope. Don't tug, they'll follow quite willingly. They're gentler than horses, they don't tear up the trails, they eat a lot less, and they're happy to be accompanying you."

Tony waited for Anna's signal that their excursion was ready to depart. Receiving her nod, he waved his hand, smiled at each of his animals and urged them by name, "On Paco, on Herbert, on Henrietta, on Dolly . . . ."

Chapter Twenty

Arriving at the Lackawanna Station Hotel in Scranton, Pennsylvania, Worthington Rhodes barely noticed how splendidly the old French Renaissance depot had been made over into a modern four-star hotel. The bronze plaque dating the Erie and Lackawanna Railroad Station to 1907 and stating it was listed on the National Register of Historic Places escaped his attention. As he walked across the Italian marble floor, he failed to look up to see the ceiling's magnificent stained glass dome. Nor did he pause to admire the model railroad trains in glass cases with their tiny engines and miniature coaches displaying the logos of the early eastern passenger lines. Instead, his mind and heart occupied another place, another time.

Absentmindedly he walked toward the hotel's banquet room where the first public presentation in his cross-country tour was scheduled to take place later that evening. He was early, but he had been anxious to get out of Washington.

While he and his staff had thoroughly reviewed the *Windjammer* promotional tour, Worthington now only vaguely recalled the itinerary. Scranton tonight on his own, then Cincinnati where someone—he couldn't remember which staff person—would join him, then on to Indianapolis, or was it Louisville? His public appearances had been planned for cities that took community pride in their recently restored grand central stations—architectural wonders of the American railroad heyday.

In addition to his public presentations he was scheduled for private audiences with state governors and members of Congress. He was also booked for formal speeches to environmental groups,

Rotary clubs, colleges, chambers of commerce, and even cameo appearances at grade schools, not to mention the press conferences and the local radio and television talk shows. Worthington empathized with political candidates locked into their grueling campaigns.

Walking down the hotel corridor, he tried to concentrate on the list provided by Charlene of this evening's invited guests. The local mayor, city councilmen, and planning commissioners plus a host of state dignitaries were expected, along with Henry D'Camp's press corps and a few others who were not under Henry's thumb. Among them all, he couldn't remember a single name.

Seeing the lectern in the banquet room, he knew he should rehearse his script. Instead, he found his thoughts continuing to wander back to a little inn on the coast of Maine. He had to see her again. Where was she now? She was a million miles away from him. And what was she doing? Oh my God, Dusty was there. How could he bring himself to concentrate on tonight's agenda?

Sara, his Sara, always on top of the situation—hadn't she arranged for little Emily to give Dusty a going away present? That present could be his opportunity to communicate with Anna. He had to talk to her. But how could he place the call, knowing Dusty would answer the cellular phone?

Suddenly he realized he was far from being on top of his own situation. He had forgotten to bring his audiovisual equipment. He would have to call Charlene and tell her to drive down here right away. He looked at his watch. Barely time for her to make the long drive on the interstate.

He found a pay phone, and then couldn't remember his office number. Frustrated with himself, he finally retrieved his own business card to find the number, and then he realized he'd forgotten his credit card pin number, and so he was reduced to calling his own office collect. And, of course, at first they didn't believe it was him, so there was an additional delay while he established his own identity by eventually remembering and telling an office joke unknown to any outsider. Why, he asked himself, was he having this mental block about placing telephone calls?

Finally Charlene came on the line and he explained his predicament. "I'll be right there, Mr. Rhodes, don't worry. Now you concentrate on memorizing all those names I gave you before you left and leave the rest to me."

With relief, he thanked her, went to his room and started the Jacuzzi. With the water jets bubbling around him, Worthington studied page after page of names. He employed all the memorizing techniques he had learned at Bowdoin as he crammed for his evening's exam. Later he fell asleep. Sprawled on the king-size bed, he dreamed of names and faces floating in front of his eyes, voiceless spirits in a snow storm on the coast of Maine.

He heard the phone ring. Charlene was calling from the lobby, expressing her concern. "Mr. Rhodes, are you all right? I've been ringing your room for the last five minutes. I looked for you in the banquet room . . ."

"I'm fine, Charlene. What time is it?"

"We've only a few minutes. I'll set up the AV equipment. You should get down here right away. Sounds like you were sleeping. I barely made it. The highways were jammed. I opened my Porsche up on the clear sections. Got a ticket for speeding. Had to slow down in the gridlock around Baltimore and Harrisburg. I should have gone by way of the Philadelphia perimeter."

"Probably worse this time of day. Someday soon we'll all be able to ride a high-speed train."

Charlene voiced a perfunctory, "Yes," then added, "meet you in a few minutes. Oh, before I forget, sir, I must give you the latest news. We've moved way up in the CNN-D'Camp public opinion poll. Nationwide, more than two-thirds recognize your name and also believe the *Windjammer* will be good for the country. Twenty per cent don't know, and the rest—and there's always a negative lot—are opposed, but their numbers are small, less than ten percent."

"That's great."

"Yes, Mr. Rhodes, even President Bush after Desert Storm didn't score that high."

"But I'm not a politician."

"Everyone's a politician these days."

A relaxed and smiling Worthington stationed himself at the entrance to the banquet room where he greeted the crowd of faces as they arrived. He was, indeed, able to put names to each of them, his memory cells functioning at their best. His presentation was a monumental success, judging from the spirited applause and the thumbs-up he received from Charlene from the back of the room. Once again he felt in command of the situation.

Responding to the questions from the audience, Worthington waved the red, white, and blue colors of the magnetic train, clocked its three-hundred-mile-per-hour speed, and favorably compared the price of a ticket with driving a Porsche across the country. Henry D'Camp's reporters cooperated with more innocuous queries that allowed Worthington to elaborate on the role the

Windjammer would play in bringing the nation together. He thought the question and answer session was over, as a number of people rose to leave or head for the bar, which he had announced would reopen.

But then an attractive woman in the front row stood up. "I'm Barbara Waters with World News Syndicate." Worthington didn't recognize the name of her press service, but he suspected it wasn't D'Camp's. "My question is, can you explain for my readers the circumstances surrounding the unexplained and mysterious death of one William Merlin Rhodes?"

Those who had started to leave turned back as the audience murmured. Others returned to their seats. The bartender paused in the act of setting up his beer and wine bottles. Charlene stood, a look of dismay on her face. By emphatically drawing her finger across her throat, she signaled for him to cut the meeting off—end it right now. As part of their preparation, trying to anticipate every eventuality, including hecklers, he and his staff had brainstormed every conceivable question, formulating positive answers. But no matter how much rehearsing, none of them had forecast such a question. This one came from out of the blue.

Worthington recognized Charlene's signal, but he was perplexed by the newspaper woman's delving into his family history. He struggled to formulate a terse answer that would unequivocally dismiss her. But the question was such a surprise he couldn't think of what to say. For a moment he speculated his father had put this Barbara Waters up to her question, hoping to discredit him. The unpleasant ordeal with Dusty threatening to prejudice the Bowdoin College admission officer came to his mind. But as to his father being the architect of this scenario, he quickly dismissed Dusty as a benighted academic.

A television cameraman moved closer, ready to film his every frown, scowl, and bead of perspiration. The press corps waited, ready to quote his answer verbatim. The eyes and ears of the media were focused upon him. He couldn't walk away, leaving the question unanswered. It wasn't that simple. He would have to explain later to Charlene. Finally Worthington managed to say, "The tragic accident you are referring to happened a long time ago. My family felt a deep loss."

The woman followed up. "But weren't you the one who deliberately removed the radar equipment and radio from his lobster boat?"

"No!" Worthington exclaimed. "That's not true. How could you possibly say such a thing, accusing me . . . ?"

"You deny any culpability?" the woman asked.

"Yes, of course," Worthington said bitterly.

Worthington detected a wry smile on the woman's face as she continued to confront him. "Probate records filed in Waldo County, Maine, show you stood to receive his entire estate. Isn't that right, Mr. Rhodes?"

"Well, yes, but . . ."

"And you insist you had nothing to do with his tragic death?"

"Absolutely not!" Worthington added emphatically, "And that's the end of tonight's session!"

Afterward, he shook more hands and expressed his thanks to the political dignitaries for coming. To his relief, Ms. Waters left with the other media people, and no one else seemed interested in the subject of Uncle Bill. He dismissed the whole episode as a fluke.

Worthington found the hotel lobby bar and sat there, sipping a beer, and then another, along with Charlene as they reviewed the evening. She touched his hand and cautioned, "Better call it a night, Mr. Rhodes. You're tired from the tensions of your first presentation—so many handshakes."

After the bar closed, Worthington went to his room and tried to sleep but couldn't. He thought about calling Charlene, but realized any further contact with his assistant at this hour of the night could be misconstrued. And Sara would be asleep, so he didn't call her. Taking a walk around downtown Scranton appealed to him, but that wouldn't be smart at two in the morning, so he dismissed the idea. He finally admitted to himself, after having suppressed the desire all day, that what he really wanted to do was to make love to Anna. With the comfort that is derived from honesty, Worthington fell asleep.

Chapter Twenty-one

As daylight filtered into Worthington's hotel room, the phone rang. "Mr. Rhodes, you better have a look at the morning papers. I'm afraid your cross-country tour may get a little bumpy," Charlene warned.

"What do you mean?"

"Another media person has phoned already this morning. I took the call and tried my best to fend him off, but he's not buying my 'no comment.'"

"Bring me the papers and we'll sort this out."

Charlene arrived a few minutes later with an armful of newspapers. She pointed to an article at the bottom of page one of the *Scranton Times*. "It's a dispatch from the World News Syndicate with Barbara Waters' byline."

"Would you mind calling room service and getting us some coffee?" Worthington asked.

Charlene picked up the phone and ordered two continental breakfasts with a full pot of coffee.

"So, what does the World News Syndicate have to say?"

Charlene handed him the paper. "Her lead paragraph reports your vigorous denial of any fault on your part in the death of your . . . ah . . ."

"Bill was my uncle. I denied removing the radar and radio from his boat, she's reported my denial, so what's the problem?"

"It's the third paragraph about the nonprofit association you and your Uncle Bill were involved with up in Maine years ago."

Worthington looked puzzled, searching his memory. After a moment, he expressed disbelief. "Is she talking about the Fisheries Improvement and Save the Harbors Association?"

"Yes," Charlene replied. "FISH." She looked up at him, a smile forming. "Are you the one who devised that acronym?"

Worthington smiled back. "Yes, I was still in college, and a bunch of us were into acronyms—at the time we were studying the New Deal. You know, NRA, WPA . . ."

"Before my time, Mr. Rhodes."

"Well, mine too, but it is part of our history. So what do they say about my FISH?"

"That you absconded with all its funds."

"What!"

"They don't come right out and say that in so many words, of course. But the article quotes a source in the state capital, a nameless source in the corporation commissioner's office, who says official state records show the association failed to file annual reports after the year 1975, including required state income tax returns, and that repeated notices of default sent to the officers received no replies. The source states you were listed as an officer. That means you have responsibility. The story also goes on to say that credit bureau records indicate FISH has a long list of bills from suppliers and others that, to this day, remain unpaid."

"Anything else?"

"Yes, one more item. The article says there was a federal government grant to FISH for building an experimental docking facility in a little harbor. The reporter quotes a source as saying the work was never completed, and that final reports were apparently never filed with the appropriate federal agency in Washington. The reporter asks if this isn't misappropriation of federal funds."

"That's ridiculous."

"That particular federal agency has been merged into another, and a government official there now promises an investigation into the mystery."

"That's it?"

"Yes."

"Well, it's all easily explained."

Charlene waited.

"After Uncle Bill died his attorneys were supposed to wrap up FISH and bury it."

"In an old newspaper?"

Worthington smiled. "Exactly."

"It seems they left FISH out, and now it's beginning to smell."

"That's not funny, Charlene."

"I didn't say it was, Mr. Rhodes."

"You suggested . . ." Worthington stopped and looked at his assistant. "I'm sorry. I guess these wild implications of impropriety have made me a bit testy this morning."

"That's all right, Mr. Rhodes, I understand. But what we should do now is formulate believable replies, because you'll get hit with more questions as you cross the country."

"Where's my next public appearance?"

"Indianapolis at the shopping mall in their restored Union Station." Charlene consulted her leather-bound notepad. "Meanwhile you're scheduled for a number of private sessions plus a press conference in Pittsburgh."

The waiter arrived with their breakfast trolley.

Following the interruption, Worthington asked, "Should we cancel the press conference?"

"I don't think that would be wise. Let's go over your explanations."

"Like I said, his attorneys were supposed to . . ."

"But apparently they didn't."

"Maybe not. I was in college at the time. I mean, how should I know what happened or didn't happen. Kids in college are not in touch with the real world. You know that."

"But you were an officer of FISH."

"So were a lot of people. They needed Mainer names for their letterhead. FISH was a nonprofit foundation."

"Answers, Mr. Rhodes, plausible, satisfying answers. That's what we must have. In all due respect, sir, you're arguing your case. The media will want simple, close-out types of answers."

"Such as?"

"Well, the boat with the all the records sank in a storm . . ."

"Like Uncle Bill?"

"Yes, or there was a fire and all FISH's records were lost. Or . . ."

"Or, this whole story is a put-up job."

"Yes, and if that's the case, then you've got to lay blame on somebody or on some organization. And who would that possibly be?"

"I don't know."

"You've haven't a vindictive ex-wife or a mistress . . ."

Worthington's face grew red. "Of course I don't."

"So then we must script some quick, easy answers these investigative reporters will buy. That way, they'll quickly lose interest and go back to their regular routine of real scandals and real murders."

"Yes, that's a good idea. I'll memorize your answers as I did your list of names last night."

"Let's put some humor into our script. You're good with acronyms. So think up new words for F-I-S-H that would disarm the reporters and get them off their serious pursuit."

Worthington thought for a moment. "How about 'Futile Investigation Suggesting Horseshit?'"

Charlene laughed. "Yes, that's good. Now to their questions."

Worthington started to sing, "'F' is for the many facts dis-tor-ted; 'I' is for the irony of it all; 'S' is for the snooping of re-por-ters; 'H' is for the hack writers we abhor. Put them all together they spell 'F-I-S-H-Y,' a word that means the death of me."

"You've got to be serious, Mr. Rhodes."

Worthington looked at her intently. "Charlene, there's nothing to be serious about. There's no substance to these accusations. Believe me. Moreover, this entire arena is a family matter—private, and certainly no one else's business."

Chapter Twenty-two

Worthington was in a good mood. "Did you see our TV spots on the local Pittsburgh station last night?"

"Yes, doesn't D'Camp's Hollywood production company do a good job? Here's the media blitz schedule they faxed to us." Charlene held up a curled sheet of thermal paper. "The commercials are running on cable, too, timed to coincide with your press conferences and public appearances."

"The old steam train chugging across that high wooden trestle was quite picturesque."

"And the handsome actor comparing the *Windjammer*'s comfort and speed to that of those early transcontinental trains should help our image with the press this afternoon." Charlene looked inquisitively at him. "It's time, Mr. Rhodes. Are you ready to take them on?"

Worthington nodded. "Even the World News Syndicate."

The hotel meeting room, windowless and austere, offered no friendly embrace, only an enclosure poised to entrap. The press corps, seated in rows of cushionless metal chairs, appeared eager to fire their questions. Cameramen aimed their lenses. Worthington positioned himself in the center of their bull's-eye behind a picket fence of microphones, his hands grasping the edges of the wooden podium, knuckles white.

He and Charlene had decided to present an opening summary before inviting questions. He did so as the lights dimmed, his deep baritone voice resonating from the speakers. Charlene worked the audiovisual equipment. The *Windjammer*'s transcontinental route and pictures of its magnetic engine and coaches were displayed while rousing background music filled the room. With his pointer Worthington explained the slides showing the magnetic train's guideway and workings. He concluded on a patriotic note, assuring the press that America could now look forward to implementing the most advanced rail system possible, once again enjoying a position at the fountainhead of world transportation technology.

The chandelier overhead brightened for the questions which dealt with the *Windjammer* and fell into anticipated categories. Yes, the train was fast, three hundred miles an hour. Yes, the price of a ticket to ride in one of those comfortable coaches would be inexpensive, all costs considered. Yes, the use of magnetic power meant no toxic emissions, not even noise pollution. Yes, the system would pay for itself and not threaten the nation's finances.

Worthington individually addressed each member of the press who spoke, smiling at them as he endeavored to humanize the spirit of the moment. Although the television lights made looking past the first few rows difficult, he searched the room for Barbara Waters. Not seeing her, he was relieved.

A man's voice spoke up from the rear. "Mr. Rhodes, I'm Johnny Redgrave from World News Syndicate. This morning there's a wire service story out of Maine quoting a state government source to the effect a certain charity—FISH, I believe it is called . . ." There was some laughter. ". . . of which you were an officer, has not filed annual reports, and further, that monies contributed to it by individuals and also federal monies it received have not been properly accounted for. Can you, sir, clarify the situation for us? And also, while you're at it, address another story to the effect that the year after FISH filed its last report, state records show you acquired, apparently for cash, a new Cadillac automobile, and in addition, according to town records, also bought for cash a new home on the coast of Maine at Orrs Island south of Brunswick."

"That's more than one question."

"May we have your comment, sir?"

"Well, as you know, I went to Bowdoin College there in Brunswick. And, while I think these are family matters and have no bearing on our subject here this afternoon, I will nevertheless answer your questions. Everyone needs a place to live, even students, so my aunt and I bought a little log cabin with a loft where I could sleep and study . . ."

The reporter interjected, "That ocean front cabin is worth today, according to the town assessor, more than half a million dollars."

"But that's not what we paid for it back in 1975."

"But that's not the point. Where'd you get the money?"

"Well, part of it came from the proceeds of my uncle's life insurance, and the rest, as I recall, came from my share in his estate."

"Probate records show you inherited everything."

"What I meant was, I felt it was my responsibility to care for my widowed aunt."

A senior member of the press corps whom Worthington recognized as one of D'Camp's correspondents stood up. "Ladies and gentlemen, the time allotted for our question period has expired. We'll have to continue this in Indianapolis at the next scheduled public forum."

Turning to leave, Worthington heard the reporter in the back shout, "Mr. Rhodes, have the annual reports of FISH been audited by an independent accountant?" Worthington walked briskly toward the side door, but he heard the reporter's voice shout even louder, "Mr. Rhodes, will you make your personal income tax returns for those years available to us?"

Worthington stopped. He stood still for a moment, his fists clenching and unclenching, his jaw set. He fought for control, his complexion reddening. He wavered, started to turn his head toward the reporter. He contemplated shouting back his humorous new FISH acronym, but anger so dominated his mind, he knew he dare not speak or try humor with the man. What he might say could turn out to be garbled, or vindictive, and the television cameras would show him losing control. Struggling with his hostility, Worthington swung open the door into the hotel corridor.

He saw Charlene. "Goddamnit, get me Henry D'Camp on the phone!" he commanded, tossing all politeness aside.

"Let's go to your room, Mr. Rhodes. You need privacy away from these reporters."

He looked around. He told himself he was a comet and they were his tail. He had to zip through some door and quickly slam it shut like the superstitious fellow who dashes across the road in front of a car, hoping the oncoming vehicle would wipe out the evil spirits who were after him. Grabbing Charlene's arm, he ducked into an elevator, looked for the DOOR CLOSE button, and pushed it hard. A hand reached in but withdrew just in time as the doors came together. "Jesus Christ!" was all he could say over and over again as they rose together through the floors of guest rooms. The doors opened on the 28th floor, and he said to her, "Where is this thing going to stop? Next they're going to blame me for the Watergate break-in. Why can't they simply stick to reporting the merits of our train? Isn't that supposed to be their job?"

"Now, now, Mr. Rhodes," Charlene consoled, "it's just a few of them. You saw the support from D'Camp's man. He closed it off."

"Yes, that's why I've got to talk to Henry. Get him on the phone."

Charlene dialed 8, 0, the area code, D'Camp's office number, waited and punched in her long credit card number and then her individual pin number. "He's left for the day. I'll try his home."

Worthington waited while Charlene repeated the procedure, fascinated as her long silver fingernails flew across the keys without breaking.

"Mr. D'Camp please." A pause. "And what's your name?" Another pause. She handed the phone to Worthington. "It's his son, Teddy."

Worthington spoke in his paternal voice. "Teddy, this is Mr. Rhodes, Emily's . . . Yes, thank you, I'm fine. Yes, Emily's fine. Is your father there?" Worthington whispered to Charlene, "Teddy's munching on something—for nine years old he must be twenty pounds overweight." "Oh, I see, your father's out West with the cowboys and Indians. Do you have his ranch number? Yes, I'm sure he will take you along with him some day to see the Wild West. You say I should call on his mobile phone? He's not in the ranch house? Thank you." Worthington wrote the number down, using the pencil and pad by the phone.

He handed the phone to Charlene. More politely this time, he asked, "Please try this number."

D'Camp's voice came across the miles, their connection weak. "You must be almost out of range," Worthington shouted into the phone. "Henry, you've got to stop these World News Syndicate reporters. They're trying to crucify me." He related the series of questions Johnny Redgrave had asked at the afternoon's press conference, and he told Henry about Barbara Waters at Scranton. Given their poor connection, Worthington repeated several of the questions, trying to make the media executive understand how distasteful the situation was becoming. After a pause, Worthington shrugged his shoulders. "Well, why can't you buy out their damn press service?" Worthington's voice was hoarse. "Henry, if you expect this project of ours to fly, you'd better issue instructions to your reporters to show up at our next public appearance in Indianapolis and start counteracting these ridiculous questions. Maybe they can yell out some catcalls, or throw some tomatoes at these renegade reporters. And you can also instruct your people to pay attention to reporting the truth. After all, that's what professional journalists are trained to do, isn't it?"

Worthington smiled at Charlene as he gently replaced the phone in its cradle. "That ought to do the trick with our media friends, don't you think?"

Chapter
Twenty-three

Henry D'Camp collapsed the antenna and folded his cellular phone, returning it to the inside pocket of his western jacket. "Worthington's mad as hell," he said to Brenda Turner, who was walking by his side. "Some guy from an outfit called World News Syndicate . . . ever heard of them?"

"It's the supermarket checkout rag. And I hear they've just launched the All-Gossip Television Network."

"They're pressing Worthington for his income tax returns, bank statements, audits—the works. I've got to do something. Beef up our spin doctors. Why is it, in this country when a man tries his damnedest to accomplish a great task, and when he achieves a little success toward his goal, some people immediately try to take him apart?"

"Some say, Henry, that in our society when a man holds a responsible position, both his public and private life should be open to scrutiny. They think they'll be able to anticipate how he'll perform for them if they can find out how he manages his personal affairs. When my father was alive and running the paper, he would always respect a public figure's privacy and not put into print their personal foibles, as he would call their indiscretions."

Henry reflected. "That was an era when society left shadows in which to hide." He walked a few more steps. "There was an unsaid gentlemen's agreement among newspapermen. Reporting was simpler then. Black was black and white was white, and gray hadn't been invented, and yellow jumped out at the reader like a screaming premonition of how the benchmarks of journalism would be eroded."

"Speaking of a bygone era, Henry, we're supposed to be looking for ancient ruins here on your ranch."

"Yes, that's why you dragged me out here." He laughed and put his arm around her. "I wanted to ride horses, but you said we had to be at one with the earth. And you assured me we'd only hike about four or five miles." He looked back and asked, "How far do you think we've come so far?"

"A half-mile at the most. Oh, look over there, Henry, wolfberry. That's a sure sign of ruins."

"Thank God, I thought for a moment you saw a member of the *canis lupus* family."

"Oh, I'm sorry I startled you, but it's so exciting. Remember, I told you wherever you find a wolfberry bush, chances are an Anasazi's hiding close by. I do believe they genetically engineered this member of the honeysuckle family so they could mark their civilization for all time, even in ruins."

"Wolves mark their territory, too."

"Just think, Henry, people were living right here on your ranch more than seven hundred years ago, and lots of them, too."

"You mean there were people before people. But, Brenda, they couldn't have been real people—I mean, like me and you. They were savages. And Walt Whitman disposed of them a hundred years ago in his poem:

On My way I pause here for America!
Still the present I raise aloft,
*   still the future I harbinge glad and sublime.*
And for the past I pronounce the knell of the red aborigine."

Brenda stopped. "Henry, for a literary man, you are misquoting our poet laureate to cover up your own unfamiliarity with American prehistory. Besides, Whitman knew nothing about the Anasazi." She reached down and picked up a pot shard. "See this black on white? Hard evidence Whitman never found in his *Leaves of Grass*." She put the shard down before walking on.

"Let's find some valuable pots intact."

"We might, but if we do—like that shard I just put back—everything stays where we find it."

"What's wrong with displaying one of their pots in my Washington office? It would impress visitors that I found it here on my ranch."

"The National Park Service insists it's wrong to take away any artifact."

"Jesus, I own the land. I can do whatever I want. I mean, that's my God-given right. I can build a house, graze my cattle, ride my horse . . ."

"But the pot belongs to the people."

He bristled. "What are you, a communist? Looks like I've bought the *Daily Worker of the West*, not the *Four Corners Tablet*."

"Henry, you don't understand."

"I understand perfectly." He kicked the wolfberry bush. "The premise of the American system is private property. You overrule those rights and you suppress the soul of this great nation." He looked down, trying to find a shard, did, promptly pocketed it, and glared at her.

"Would you like your eloquent statement set in forty-point type above my masthead?"

Henry grabbed her and took her into his arms. "To hell with these ruins, you're the one that excites me."

Snuggling in his embrace, Brenda whispered, "The Anasazi who lived here, Henry, were as human as you and I."

"Well then, how many of these ruins do I own?"

"It would take us a month of Sundays to walk across your entire spread. We'd need topographical maps, aerial photographs, and an extra pair of hiking boots. But I'm certain we'd end up with another map for your office wall dotted with lots of colorful pins."

"I'd go for that." He looked out over his ranch and asked, "Has anyone ever estimated the Anasazi population?"

"You can't get an archaeologist to come up with a count because there are so many unexcavated sites, like here on your ranch. But they will estimate for each known site, such as Goodman Point, Sand Canyon, Yellowjacket, Lowry, by taking the number of dwelling units and multiplying by two point five. The last figure I saw was a total of twenty thousand housing units—that means fifty thousand people. And since there are literally thousands of untouched sites, we should double our figure and then, well, probably double it again."

"Two hundred thousand Anasazi in the Four Corners area," he calculated. "That's a lot of newspaper subscriptions—eighty thousand households—and at a goodwill value of fifty dollars per subscriber that would place a market price on their local newspaper of four million dollars."

"The price for my rag just went up," Brenda teased. "But, Henry, the Anasazi had no written language."

"No alphabet? Can you imagine what these people missed in life? Those abstract expressions, those ideas that can only be set forth in writing. Those concepts only the written word, the sentence, the paragraph can convey."

"The deeper meaning of life, of ourselves, of our environment," Brenda suggested.

"Exactly. I mean, talk is talk, and then as quickly as it's spoken, it's gone, isn't it, lost to time." He wasn't asking a question.

"And also subject to misinterpretation."

"Yes, but writing is forever." Henry added with the pride derived from his choice of a lifetime career, "That's why I became a newspaperman."

They walked on a ways. "Say, I've an idea. I could name one of my ruins in your honor: Brenda's Bygone Borough."

"I'd put out a welcome sign on the Anasazi road."

"Oh, yes, the paradox of the roads you wrote about in your column. They were built by these people who didn't have the wheel. Would we have built the interstate highway system before Henry Ford came along? Hell no!"

Brenda laughed. "The road could have been an Anasazi WPA project—a community effort to keep the people focused on a productive goal—better than war parties."

"Brenda, you've just described the *Windjammer*! Worthington's project has the same great unifying force. And I say that's what this nation of ours needs today—an undertaking everyone can get behind, work on, and feel they're a part of."

"Great, you name one of your prehistoric sites for me and then bulldoze it out from under me for the right-of-way of the *Windjammer*. Henry, you're an Indian-giver."

He smiled. "I do own both sides of the argument. But I've changed my mind about one thing, Brenda, to me you're not some prehistoric site but a fascinating museum with shapely sculptures and challenges to my imagination."

Henry D'Camp pulled out his cellular phone and punched three digits. "Steve, bring the Rover out here and pick us up. And tell Alonzo to heat up the Jacuzzi. Ms. Turner and I have some more . . . ah . . . important business to discuss this afternoon."

He looked lustfully at Brenda. "We'll ride back to the house in comfort, and after we take our whirlpool bath, I'm going to dry your body with my tongue."

Chapter Twenty-four

Worthington reached for the notepad by the telephone in the sitting room of his hotel suite. "How do you spell his last name, Emily?" He wrote, Ernest L. Blumenschein. "How many postcards of this artist's work do you want me to buy for your collection while I'm at the Eiteljorg Museum gift shop?" He noted the number 3 and inquired if she wanted postcards of any other artists from the Taos School. "Three of each. Okay. Anything else while I'm here in Indianapolis?" He flipped to a fresh sheet of note paper, awaiting Emily's list. He jotted down, Danny—miniature race cars from the Indianapolis Motor Speedway, try to find the 1911 Marmon Wasp, yellow and black, number 82. "Driven by Ray who? Oh, he won the first Five-Hundred-Mile Race with a speed of seventy-five miles per hour. Spell his last name, too." Worthington wrote, Haroun. "And what does Elizabeth want?" On another sheet he noted, Sports Library at Butler University—interlibrary loan book tracing history of women in the Olympics. Worthington started to say good-bye, but hastily added, "Say hello to Françoise, and give Mommy a big kiss for me the moment she returns from her charity work with the homeless."

In the vacant silence of the hotel room, Worthington thought about little Emily in her expanding world of interests and Elizabeth and Danny in theirs. Their school's educational program was challenging them and the result would be a fine new generation coming along. He regretted being away and for a fleeting moment wanted to be home so he could listen to the three of them tell about their activities.

As he prepared for yet another of his public presentations on behalf of the *Windjammer* out here in the hinterland, there were few familiar faces, and certainly one less now that Charlene had been replaced by the two spin doctors from Henry D'Camp's empire. Charlene had been a little out of her league tossing powder puff rejoinders to the press. Good on the AV equipment, booking hotels, and sending out invitations, but given the growing barrage of hardball questions, more media experience was necessary. She was miffed when he had asked Henry for help and had left with barely a good-bye.

So now he must converse with Zoe and Edward, two twenty-somethings who spoke in the jargon of Generation X. Hadn't his own generation hidden in its special language? Worthington asked himself why all generations couldn't speak the same language. Getting things done in this country would be so much easier. He marveled at how Emily, now almost ten, was able to express herself with such directness. All day he had agonized about devising credible reasons for calling Anna. He admitted he was worried about rejection, or worse, making a fool of himself. Not so with Emily. If she met with a veto, she'd bounce right back with some other idea, some new request. Why couldn't he lay claim to the same buoyancy? Not only must he improve his *Windjammer* presentations, what with an increasingly hostile press, he must also improve his skills of articulation. But first he must round up the requested loot for his children.

Museums were usually housed in a Greek Parthenon-like building, so Worthington didn't expect to find the Eiteljorg Museum of American Indian and Western Art in such a contemporary form-equals-function building. This particular place of the muses manifested itself in a natural setting overlooking the city's White River. Running beside the river was a canal no longer in use, reminding him of the map of early transportation routes he had seen in Emily's classroom. The past was tucked away in its historic bed; the present was awake and hollering loud and strong, crying for attention; the future was promising, hoping, painting images of success. The museum which he was about to enter would document the past. The present was offering trouble enough. But the future was his to seek and explore. And he thought about Anna.

In the gift shop he purchased Emily's postcards, three each of Blumenschein, Bert Greer Phillips, and Joseph Henry Sharp. There were other Taos artists and, admiring their art on the postcards, Worthington wanted to look at the originals. He sought out the Southwestern Gallery.

The Wedding by E. Irving Couse drew his attention. An Indian husband stood beside his bride, each of them dressed in native costumes accessorized with feathers, beads, blankets, moccasins, and for her a silver concha belt. To Worthington, the young Indian maiden, with her hands clasped and her downcast eyes, concealed her thoughts in mystery. She was beautiful. With his arm around her, the groom endowed to his bride his protection and shelter. But was the artist warning the young couple they might not live happily ever after if they blindly followed their ceremonial functions and failed to powwow with one another?

Worthington thought about calling Anna. She was teaching everyone she could about the prehistory of the Southwest. The gallery gave him an idea. He would telephone her and ask if she knew a muralist who could glorify the Anasazi on the walls of the concourse of the *Windjammer*'s station in its new Four Corners city. Yes, he'd find a pay phone right away before he lost his courage to speak to her.

Loud voices from an adjacent gallery interrupted his plan. He heard someone say, "Quentin Ford IV." Worthington peered into the adjoining exhibit hall and noticed its collections were devoted to the Plains Indians. His eyes met those of the philanthropist. Ford recognized him and rushed over to shake his hand.

"Well, well, Mr. Rhodes, we meet again. Did you and your daughter enjoy Dr. Ardmore's presentation the other night in Georgetown?"

Worthington smiled politely. "Yes, we did, and Anna autographed Emily's book."

"A lovely child."

"As a matter of fact, I'm here buying some items to send home to her."

"You surprise me, Mr. Rhodes. I didn't know you had any interest in things of the past."

"Why, yes, I do. One can't have children these days without becoming involved at least to some extent with their studies."

"I wouldn't know. Mine attended boarding schools in Massachusetts and Connecticut." Ford observed the Southwestern Gallery. "Very nice paintings here—an oasis of art in an otherwise dry Midwestern environment. Hoosiers aren't noted for their art, apart from painting the vivid fall colors contrasting against those limestone cliffs down in Brown County."

"Literature and poetry instead," Worthington stated. "As a child I remember reading *Little Orphan Annie*."

"James Whitcomb Riley."

"Yes, and now every Halloween I read his folk poem to my children."

"'The gobblins'll getcha if you don't watch out,'" Ford quoted, and laughed heartily. "These days one never knows when the fantasy of authors will turn out to be life's reality." He smiled. "Well, my boy, I must be getting back to my group. I'm placing my private collection of native American dance masks on loan." The benefactor turned and walked back to the waiting patrons, their wine glasses raised in salute to him as he rejoined their circle.

Heading for the museum exit, Worthington puzzled over their conversation. He was surprised at how friendly the chairman of ILMA acted today in contrast to his demeanor in Washington. But hadn't his own posture slipped since that reception in the nation's capital? Outside in the parking lot, Worthington barely noticed the dark clouds overhead, nor did he mind the warm April rain. As he drove, peering ahead, the rain blurred both his vision and his thoughts. For alternating moments, images became clear with a sweep of the windshield wipers, only to besmear as more rain fell—photographs changing into abstract paintings.

Brushing aside his casual conversation with Ford, Worthington focused on his anticipated phone call to Anna. She and he shared an interest in art. So he would tell her about the museum's splendid collection of western landscapes, portraits, and still-life paintings. He would excite her with descriptions of Edward Weston's photographs of early settlers, Edward Sheriff Curtis' photographs of the Zuni and other Indians, as well as those Taos artists who had glorified her Indians. Then he would unveil his plan for the station murals, whose theme would pay homage to the great American West. Yes, Anna would endorse his idea.

Entering the hotel lobby, Worthington ran toward the bank of pay phones. He grasped the first instrument and punched out the long series of numbers that would ring Dusty's cellular phone. He remembered his pin number, and told himself he was silly to have allowed his mental block about talking to his father to dissuade him from calling Anna. Yet even as the phone rang, Worthington almost hung up.

Dusty answered.

Responding to his father's voice proved more difficult than Worthington expected.

"Who's there?" Dusty asked, and then repeated the question. "Speak up!"

Worthington managed, "It's me Worthington."

"So there is somebody there after all. I thought for a moment this phone had turned into some strange artifact."

Worthington's fingers clutched the instrument. Now he really wanted to hang up. Instead, he entertained an urge to yell at his father that his one and only son was calling, hoping his outburst would beget a paternal response. But could a son expect to change a parental mind-set? Not likely. Certainly an angry outburst wouldn't do it. Maybe he should follow Charlene's advice and try humor. "I want to add to my collection of antique wheels, and I read in the *Anasazi Nickel Ads* you found an old Toltec one. So may I please speak to the lady in charge? Actually I want to sell her something."

"You mean Anna?" Dusty's voice remained bland. "She's not here. I'm digging in some farming tract—she's put me out to pasture. Her square's back in the village plaza."

Worthington felt his nerve vanishing. "Well, never mind. I'll call for her later." He started to hang up, lamenting having made the call.

"Say, I've an idea for you." Dusty came to life. "You probably won't understand, but this archaeologist friend of mine over in Greece . . ." Christ! Worthington said to himself. ". . . rang me up here in the ruins—calling all the way from his apartment in the Plaka. He's winding up his Athens excavations—had a lot of experience there and in Mexico City, too. He's looking for his next project, and . . ."

"Sorry, sir, but I really have to go now. I'll call you back on your idea later. Maybe you could give your cellular phone to Anna tomorrow, because I've time in the morning to speak to her about my idea."

As he walked toward the hotel elevators, Worthington recognized Henry D'Camp's damage control duo—Edward with his long shaggy hair and Zoe with her short pixie-do.

"Mr. Rhodes," Zoe called out, "we've just enough time to review your evening's remarks. Edward and I must also brief you on how to deal with tonight's media questions about your past so you can give them honest, straightforward answers."

"Yes, I've been thinking about that, too, and I think that I should tell the hometown folks that their city was designed by the same team that laid out Washington, D.C.—Pierre Charles L'Enfant and his surveying assistant, Alexander Ralston." He winked at Zoe. "I could make up a tantalizing tale about their private lives that'd get the media off my back."

"No," Zoe advised, "we don't want you to fabricate anything and we don't want the media off your back. What we want is for these scribes who follow you around to portray you as being on the cutting edge of male honesty."

Edward looked at Zoe. "Especially now with his lawsuit."

"What are you talking about?" Worthington asked.

"He hasn't heard."

"Heard what? I've been driving around all day."

"You weren't listening to the car radio?" Zoe asked.

"No. What's going on?"

"Your news."

"What news?"

"Your lawsuit." Edward looked at Zoe. "He hasn't heard."

"I'm not suing anyone."

"No, it's you who's being sued," Zoe said.

"Sued for what, for Christ's sake?"

"Sexual harassment," Zoe told him.

Worthington exploded, "Sexual harassment? Of whom? I've not been served any papers."

"You will," Edward advised. "Her Washington attorney announced the charges to the media this morning. She's claiming you insisted she spend the night with you in Scranton or you'd fire her."

"Charlene?" Worthington exclaimed. "That's absurd! I never noticed anything about her except her long silver fingernails."

"She's scratching your eyes out with them," Zoe commented.

"What should I do?"

"My advice, since you have not been served, is to offer no comment. No sense in putting the issue in play until we have to." Edward leaned closer to Worthington. "Just so there's no more surprises, you'd better tell us if you've had, or are now having, any extramarital affairs."

Worthington dropped the kids' packages. Danny's miniature race car rolled across the lobby floor. As Zoe and Edward hastened to retrieve the little runaway, Worthington thought to himself, for the good of my family, for the good of the *Windjammer*, and yes, for Anna's sake, I must deny her existence altogether. "Absolutely not!" he replied out loud. "I'm not having an affair. There's no infidelity."

"'Methinks the gentleman doth protest too much,'" Zoe quoted, and laughed. Then she looked at him seriously. "Mr. Rhodes, our job is to get you off the defensive. By selling the merits of the *Windjammer*, we hope to do just that."

"But we may have to save his ass, as well," Edward confided to Zoe. "I've booked him into Club Nostalgia for a singing appearance later tonight."

"You did what?" Worthington asked in disbelief.

Edward continued to direct his comments to Zoe. "I hear he has a deep baritone voice and likes to sing those 1940s train songs."

"We'll draw the paparazzi with this booking," Zoe said. "And the local CNN stringer will cover it, too. I'll call her."

"Done. She'll be there. Said she wouldn't miss it. You know, Mr. Rhodes, if Zoe and I are going to sway public opinion—and that's what we're paid to do—then you've got to get with it. News today is also entertainment. Know what I mean?"

Zoe looked intently at Worthington. "Yes, a little darkening of the hair would give it more body, a touch of makeup and . . ."

Worthington didn't hear the rest of Zoe's cosmetic diagnosis. He thought only about his family—little Emily, and Elizabeth and Danny, too. He thought about Sara. Could he tell her the truth? He'd have to settle for these two young image makers who were experts in manufacturing male honesty.

Chapter Twenty-five

"Hey, Dusty, you on this dig, or are you just giving us the pleasure of your company?" Alex asked the bearded archaeologist as the seminarists gathered around the evening campfire. "All I've seen you do so far is talk on that cellular telephone of yours."

"Yes," Daisy agreed, "and we've yet to have our first bite of pizza, isn't that right, Greta?"

The school teacher nodded. "Those were his granddaughter's instructions."

"I haven't had that many calls. Besides, my square's out of town, so the ringing shouldn't bother any of you."

"It's just that we all came here seeking quiet from ringing phones and from people who are always wanting us to do something for them," Greta explained. "It didn't occur to me that I might want to place a call myself. My dear mother lives alone, and she might want me to do something for her."

"My number's gotten out," Dusty confessed. "But all the calls coming in have been quite necessary—my agent, my publicist, my editor, my publisher—they've all needed to confer with me about my next book. The launching date's in December. It's a Christmas book."

Alex harrumphed. "I thought this dig was a team effort. Last time I looked, your square was pretty shallow. At this rate, with you spending so much time on the phone, we'll never get out of here."

"What's a few phone calls? My colleague over in Greece has questions for me. And Emily's called several times, but no one else of any importance." He lowered his voice. "Oh, I guess my son called once."

"Then he's all right?" Anna exclaimed.

"Oh, sure," Dusty said. "Why wouldn't he be?"

"I mean . . . to me . . . ah . . . he didn't look all that well at my Washington reception."

"That's because he didn't feel comfortable with our scientific gathering."

Anna thought back about how, during her in-flight telephone conversation with Quentin Ford IV, she had acquiesced in the murder plan. "Do what you must," she had told the benefactor. Several weeks had passed, and Worthington was apparently still alive. How long would it be, she wondered, until Dusty's phone rang with news of Worthington's assassination?

Her thoughts were interrupted by George. "I've forgotten what it's like to talk on the phone. I'm suffering from telephone withdrawal. I dreamt about a telephone last night. It was one of those dreams where I just had to make a phone call. I kept reaching for it, but no matter how deeply I dug down into my one meter square . . ." He looked at Anna. " . . . carefully inserting my trowel, of course, the telephone remained buried. I could see its first row of numbers, but I couldn't get the damn thing out of the ground."

"Did you ever complete your call, George?" Martha wanted to know.

"No, and it's been bothering me all day. I think my wildcat drilling crew is sending me telepathic signals for me to call, but I don't have a phone."

"With my responsibilities at the bank, I'm always on the phone," Margaret said. "So, it's nice to get away from it for a while. On the other hand, there are these loans the bank president approved over my objections and I've been curious to know how many have defaulted."

Paul nodded. "I, too, figured I'd put the world of commerce behind me for the summer. But I've been wondering if my predictions about the current month's unemployment figures and our international trade deficit are on the mark."

"Yeah, and I'm supposed to schedule the filming of another product endorsement." Alex winked at Daisy. "They want me to demonstrate the new Dogpatch line of menthol rubs."

Martha looked questioningly at George. "Do you suppose Jennifer's had her baby yet?" She turned toward the others. "She's due any day now. It'll be our fifth grandchild."

Tony looked up from his camp stove where he was brewing cowboy coffee. "Yeah, and Dolly's entered her photo in the Miss

Llama contest. I think the judging was today. I'd sure like to find out the results so I could tell her."

"Okay, okay, I get the hint. Look, if any of you want to use my phone, then here it is." Dusty took the instrument from his jacket pocket and placed it on top of the low, crumbling wall encircling the Anasazi settlement. "Go ahead and make your calls. Just remember to ask the operator to call back with charges. You can each settle your account with me at the end of the dig."

"Daisy, you go first." Alex reached for the cellular phone.

"No, I'm first," George said with a determined look on his face as he rose.

Margaret advanced toward the instrument. "I've barely time to reach my office before they close."

Paul smiled. "I'm after you, Margaret."

But Greta was first to get her hands on the phone. Turning toward the others converging upon her, she warned, "Remember, *aikido* is basically nonviolent, but . . ."

◆　◆　◆　◆

By the time the cellular phone was passed around and handed to Anna, the instrument was warm from so many hands having held it. But Anna was suddenly cold. Who would she call? Worthington? To warn him? Quentin? To stop him? She couldn't let the others know of her reticence to make her phone call. For privacy she walked over to the ruins of the ancient stone tower.

Anna remembered the last time she was inside an Anasazi tower. Her graduate students had been asking whether these tall, round structures were intended simply as lookouts for each village, or had they served some higher purpose? Her class decided to experiment. At each site, at the prescribed hour, within either a still-standing tower or the rubble of one, she and her students lit bonfires. Throughout that dark Four Corners night, fires glowed within each Anasazi settlement, and were visible to neighboring pueblos, confirming a connection across space. By waving a wool blanket in front of their fires, the students were able to transmit a series of firelight dots and dashes—a Morse code dialect. These towers, she and her class had concluded, were the sending and receiving points of a Four Corners signaling nexus.

Finally Anna made her decision. She summoned her courage to place her telephone call. Quentin Ford IV's butler informed her his employer was traveling, so she dialed Stuart Wales at his Washington apartment.

"Anna! Good to hear from you. How's the dig going?"

"That's not why I'm calling, Stuart. I've got to know about Worthington Rhodes. Is it too late to stop the madness?"

"I'm afraid it is, Anna. Booth told me when I handed him the money that he would be setting his campaign into motion immediately."

"Oh, Stuart." Anna broke into tears. "You've got to stop him. I can't live with myself knowing I am the one who sentenced Worthington Rhodes. I'm an archaeologist, Stuart, an academic, not some awful conniving, plotting, scheming . . . murder has no justification, no logic, no reason. For God's sake, Stuart, you and I must own up to what we are permitting ourselves to become involved in. Since I talked with Quentin, I haven't been able to think straight. My God, Stuart, I feel just awful. I mean, you and I are educated, civilized people. We're not criminals, not murderers . . ." Anna choked up again. She sobbed uncontrollably.

Stuart spoke loudly into the phone. "Anna, please listen to me. Worthington Rhodes is not going to be shot, only discredited in the eyes of the public. Get hold of yourself. Mr. Ford knows Congress will have to withdraw their support for the *Windjammer* if Worthington's reputation is destroyed. Besides, your archaeological treasures will be preserved for all time. Getting rid of one man is a small price to pay. This man Booth, whom Mr. Ford hired, is a character assassin, an investigator, one who specializes in uncovering, or maybe even inventing smut about his victims and leaking it to the popular press. He's not your sinister assassin with the latest in telescopic sniper rifles." Stuart paused. "Anna, are you all right?"

Anna was bewildered. "How could I have misunderstood? You mean, all along Quentin was talking about hiring a dirty trickster?"

"Of course. And if one of Booth's stories explodes onto the tabloid pages, the hope is the legitimate media will pick up the exposé. And then one of those television network magazine shows will jump on the sordid details, and Worthington will have to run for cover."

"None of us can dodge an oncoming bullet, Stuart, but with this muckraking, a person can fight back. And I can assure you Worthington will. I know this man."

"I wish I could share your belief, Anna, but I can't help but feel that what Ford wants, Ford gets. And therefore I'm afraid a great leader will be silenced in our lifetime. But I truly believe history will say he was a legendary figure ahead of his time. We just have to go on with our lives."

Tony's fire and the aroma of his coffee beckoned a lightened Anna to rejoin the others. Telephone cravings having been satisfied, their conversations were less argumentative, their jokes whimsical, their laughter more sincere, their camaraderie more wholesome. Even the llamas, sensing they were in a special place, nuzzled Tony as he checked on them.

George saw Anna returning. "Anna, we're enchanted by the sunset this evening." In the western sky a formation of clouds kindled into bright orange bands tinged with deep crimson.

"Reminds me of a twilight baseball game when the stadium and the infield take on a magic glow," Alex said. "The baseball jumps right out in front of you like a full moon. And, gosh, you can really launch that hardball right into orbit."

As they watched, the sun hesitated only a moment before dropping behind Utah's Sleeping Ute Mountain. Its lingering rays outlined the form of a reclining Indian chief wearing a feathered headdress.

Looking pensively at the mountain, Anna accepted a cup of coffee from Tony, and turned toward the seminarists. "My friends, I'll share with you a wonderful legend about the origins and the destiny of the Anasazi."

The seminarists gathered around.

"In the beginning, the ancestors of the Anasazi traveled upward, rising out of their underworld estate, through the hole in the earth their modern-day descendants call the *sipapu*, to this world we now see reflected in our beautiful sunset. Here, a great chief told them that someday a fleet-footed animal with a flowing mane would arrive to carry them to their glorious future. But his people were afraid that the spirit of the chief's visionary animal might not respect their ancestors, so a shaman among them dusted the chief with slumber powder, and the chief lay down as you see him there . . . and fell sound asleep . . ." Anna pointed toward the mountain. ". . . stretched out across the southeastern corner of Utah. Someday, so the legend goes, the spermatozoa from the Sleeping Ute will propagate a brave new chief who will lead his people to rise up and reclaim these lands that, since the beginning of time, have rightfully been theirs."

Chapter Twenty-six

"Welcome, gentlemen, to Club Nostalgia," said the bouncer, muscles bulging through his double-breasted suit.

"Roosevelt, I want you to meet this evening's featured vocalist, the fabulous 1940s singing star of national radio, none other than Worthington Rhodes. Tonight's his stage debut right here at Club Nostalgia."

"This old place gonna jive tonight! Gimme some skin!" Roosevelt put one palm out for Edward and the other for Worthington.

Edward whispered to Worthington, "I should explain, the price of admission is dishing out a few words of 1940s lingo. That's why Roosevelt is wearing those tinted shades. At Club Nostalgia everybody enjoys a rose colored view of a past era."

Worthington smacked Roosevelt's hand. "Swell place ya got here. I dig your 1941 Oldsmobile parked out in front. I'll bet it's equipped with Hydramatic Drive."

Roosevelt smiled. "Yeah man. It's a real humdinger." He waved them inside.

Silhouettes of jitterbug dancers, their outlines traced in green neon, covered the walls. From a battery of ceiling track lights, moving beams of red and blue spotlights floated from table to table, highlighting first one party and then another of animated young patrons. Behind the stage a blown-up magazine advertisement of a 1948 vintage Chrysler Town and Country convertible with wooden trim affirmed the zenith of that era's automotive elegance. Behind the wheel, blonde hair ruffling in the breeze, arms outstretched as she grasped the steering wheel, a beautiful, smiling young American woman looked forward to her rightful legacy of happiness. By her side, a handsome clean-shaven man fixed his attention upon her.

The band, however, was definitely grounded in the digital 1990s. Electric cords connected the musicians and their instruments to a deafening power source. Green and red lights on their amplifiers flashed. Attired in 1940s baggy zoot suits, the group struck up with (*Get Your Kicks on*) *Route 66*. Pairs, holding hands, glided toward the dance floor. Those still sitting at tables swayed their bodies in recognition of the rhythm.

Observing their ages, Worthington commented to Edward, "Hey, there's nobody in this place who was even born in the 1940s—let alone the 50s."

"That's what gives Club Nostalgia its vitality."

Grabbing the microphone, even before the music stopped, the emcee shouted, "Are you ready to welcome our featured vocalist, the handsome and talented chief engineer of the nation's new maglev train?"

Cheers and whistles responded.

"Then let's bring Worthington Rhodes up here!"

More cheers and whistles.

Worthington jumped onto the stage, thanked the emcee who patted him on the back and handed him the microphone.

As the house lights dimmed, Worthington settled atop the tall stool and, with the spotlight focusing on him, began to croon a medley of pop ballads from the Hit Parade era. The applause from the enthusiastic audience rejuvenated him. Free to express himself through song, his self confidence surged. Responding to the young audience, Worthington came alive with exuberance. Together they partied in the melodies of yesteryear.

The CNN stringer filmed the swing-kids scene for the late night news.

Edward waited for Worthington to sing one more tune before running up on stage and grasping him by the arm. "Time to cut out. We've pulled off our media event for the evening."

Worthington held back. "But shouldn't I wait? Some in the audience might have questions they'd like to ask about the *Windjammer*."

"Forget it, we've made our hit. Let's get outa here."

They wove their way through a cheering crowd, many reaching to shake Worthington's hand or at least touch him as he passed by. Autograph seekers besieged him. At the door Roosevelt exclaimed, "Man, you've got a great voice! You could take the country by storm!"

Zoe drove up in a Chrysler LeBaron convertible, motioning for Worthington to climb in the rear seat next to his travel bag. "Zoe's packed your bag," Edward said.

"So I see. Where am I going?"

The airport. You're due for a little R and R back in Washington. Edward and I have revised your cross-country schedule. You need to be seen by the press and the public with your wife and kids. I've booked you as one of the singers at the upcoming summer solstice event at the Reflecting Pool in front of the Lincoln Memorial," Edward told him. "Television cameras and reporters'll be there. You know, your singing voice may save the *Windjammer* after all."

Zoe pressed her foot to the accelerator. "Now remember, Mr. Rhodes, always be ready—at any time you may be confronted by reporters firing questions. When you're in public always smile at your wife and when your children are with you, you want to be seen holding one of their little hands."

"Of course. Why wouldn't I?"

"Marriages and families are not easy to keep together these days—especially in Washington." Zoe turned onto the freeway ramp. "And then it's on to your meeting with Charlene."

"Charlene?"

"Yes," Edward said, "only you can talk her into withdrawing her lawsuit."

"Persuade her to withdraw it?" Worthington asked, incredulity in his voice. "But shouldn't I be hiring an attorney to defend myself?"

"No, your goal is for her to repudiate the suit, not exacerbate the problem," Zoe said. "Hiring an attorney will only draw the battle lines. That's why I've set up this rap session between the two of you. It took a great effort to get Charlene to agree, and then only if she could bring her girl friend along. I consented on your behalf, so long as the friend wasn't an attorney."

"Who's the friend?"

"C. C. Trinket."

Worthington was surprised. "The President's speech writer?"

"Yes," Edward said. "Look, you're a persuasive guy. Do anything—serenade her if you have to. Charlene works out at the spa in the Watergate complex along with a lot of other women in the District. There's a little coffee bar in the courtyard. She'll be expecting you first thing tomorrow." Edward turned around and patted Worthington on the knee. "Zoe and I've got the ducks in a row on this one. It's up to you now, man."

"What about Roybal's congressional hearing?" Worthington asked.

"With the Fourth of July coming up, he'll probably move for a postponement. Congressmen want to be seen back home, marching in a parade, cooking hamburgers at a barbecue and making patriotic speeches. Gives us time for all these fireworks from the press to blow over—allows Zoe and me an opportunity to recast your image."

"Before I return to the hustings?"

Zoe nodded as she pulled up to the unloading area.

"Oh, I better call Sara and the kids to let them know I'm coming."

"Done," Zoe said. "Sara's meeting your plane."

Boarding the late evening flight to Washington's National Airport, Worthington was feeling better about himself. Henry D'Camp's young spin doctors appeared knowledgeable and skilled. It would take a lot more than a few questions from headline-seeking journalists to stop him now. His feelings of buoyancy were magnified because he was going home. Sara would be waiting for him. He wanted their romantic reunion to play out perfectly. He would sweep her up in his arms, kiss her tenderly, and the two of them, arms around each other, would talk endlessly. Yes, things were going to work out nicely, after all.

Chapter Twenty-seven

Emerging from the jetway into the terminal's concourse, Worthington searched the crowd for Sara. She was standing off alone by a white pillar. Seeing her, he began to weave through the crowd of deplaning passengers, calling her name. Sara looked at him with a stoic expression, but did not move toward him.

Just then a television reporter and her cameraman stepped out in front of him, blocking his outreach for Sara. The reporter didn't bother to identify herself before she attacked him with a question, "Mr. Rhodes, what about your secretary's sexual harassment lawsuit?"

"It's all a misunderstanding. Now, if you'll excuse me, I'm meeting my wife." It was obvious Sara had already heard the news, for there was no welcoming smile on her perfect face. She only stared at him. He wanted desperately to reassure her the reports were groundless. Their lives could return to their idyllic state. Husband and wife would embrace and be off in the Volvo heading home where he would look in upon their three darling children who had been tucked in for the night.

Instead, the reporter fired another volley, her voice a mix of criticism and sarcasm. "How many other women have there been who've not yet had the courage to come forward and speak out publicly? Would you say men in positions of authority in Washington require sexual gratification from the women on their staffs? Isn't your little escapade, Mr. Rhodes, the tip of the iceberg in a scandal of sexual abuse by powerful Washington men?"

The cameraman moved closer, interfering with Worthington's view of Sara. The camcorder was practically in his face. Worthington tried to maneuver around the man, wanting desperately to reach Sara. To explain. To clear up for good this bizarre story. But the cameraman matched his every move, the camera's red light blinking.

Endeavoring to calm himself, Worthington looked into the lens and tried very hard to smile, but his lips remained set as if fixed in a sticky glue. Mentally he composed retort after retort, denial after denial, but try as he might he was unable to open his mouth and verbalize any of his responses. Worthington took his eyes off the camera and stared into the woman reporter's eyes. He saw a look, not of a journalist's inquiring curiosity, but rather the glare of antagonism. Moreover, the cameraman was preventing him from embracing Sara. Such interference, especially at this tender moment, was clearly unfair, contrary to family values, and certainly not in keeping with Edward's and Zoe's style and narrative.

Worthington tried to forge a passageway between the cameraman and the reporter. His move caught the cameraman by surprise. He lost his grip on the camera and it dropped to the floor, its lens exploding as if a bomb had been detonated.

Sara screamed.

Nearby deplaning passengers drew back in horror, their welcoming hugs and handshakes interrupted in mid-expression.

Worthington rushed to embrace Sara, but she held up her hand, palm outstretched, blocking him. "No," she yelled. "Don't come near me! I never want to see you again!"

"Sara, for heaven's sake, listen to me. We can't let these outsiders come between us. It's our lives, not theirs." He lowered his voice. "I love you, Sara. Please, let's just go home. I want to see Emily, Danny, and Elizabeth."

The sound of Worthington's intimate voice calmed Sara. He put his arm around her. "They don't have lobsters in Indiana, or I would have brought you a dozen."

Smiling in spite of herself, she fell in step with him as they turned to leave. Then he stopped, withdrew his arm from around Sara, bent over and helped up the cameraman. "I'm sorry," he said, "you're just doing your job."

Assessing the damage to his camera as he retrieved its broken parts, the man replied, "Fuck you."

With revenge and righteousness ringing in her voice, the reporter declared, "You'll see yourself on tonight's late news, and tomorrow you'll hear from our World News Syndicate attorneys."

Worthington took Sara's arm again. "There's nothing to the lawsuit, I assure you."

"If there's nothing to her suit, you should have simply denied the charge. Why on earth did you shove the cameraman?" Sara didn't wait for his reply. "It looked as if you were ready to slap that poor defenseless woman reporter, too."

Struggling with his emotions, hating himself, blaming himself, hating the media, blaming the media, Worthington wondered why he couldn't have controlled the airport fiasco. That reporter had really gotten to him. Why couldn't she have been civil with her questions instead of needling him, provoking him with her malicious attitude?

Worthington realized he must try again to explain to Sara about the lawsuit. And do something to soften its blow to Emily, Elizabeth, and Danny. His mission, first thing in the morning, would be to compose for them a succinct grade-school overview of the American legal system. Worse, he'd have to verbalize a simple explanation as to what sexual harassment meant when he wasn't sure himself.

He was stunned by how his mood, his life, his future had changed so abruptly, from walking up the Indianapolis jetway to walking down the Washington National jetway. His life was breaking into shards. The question he asked himself was whether or not he could put the pieces back together again. The answer he promptly heard himself say was that he must.

Chapter
Twenty-eight

The austere Watergate complex in Washington had been designed in the international style of Swiss-born architect Le Corbusier. Too bad, Worthington thought, for a magnificent turn-of-the-century railroad station would have been a developer's dream to restore and accommodate the many business and residential functions Watergate served. He hoped this cold, stark building wasn't a barometer for this morning's appointment with Charlene.

His assignment was to persuade Charlene to withdraw her lawsuit. He would also like to know the reasons she had trumped up her unjustified allegations. Even more important, her explanation would hopefully soothe Sara's suspicions. Winning back Sara's affection was paramount in his mind.

As Worthington entered the coffee bar, Ms. Trinket smiled sweetly, motioning for him to join them. She and Charlene were dressed in their exercise leotards. "Mr. Rhodes, there are two of us, so don't try anything funny," C. C. said with merriment.

Worthington smiled at Charlene. "Remember, in Pittsburgh you instructed me to put some humor into the plot."

Charlene's return smile was prompt, curt, and quickly gone. Only fleetingly did her eyes meet his.

"Confidentially, Mr. Rhodes, you were great last night at the airport," C. C. told him. "The President and I saw you on the Beltway Midnight Rumor Show. They filmed the entire episode."

"I thought he broke his camera."

"The All-Gossip Network travels with a second cameraman just in case. When the first cameraman hit the floor, all of us in the Oval

Office cheered. The President, in his great shadow boxing form, jabbed rights and lefts at the White House press corps."

Charlene looked at Worthington. "Reporters nowadays are abusive and disrespectful of people who hold responsible positions."

Ms. Trinket agreed. "You're right, Charlene, we're all fed up with the media and their probing questions. Last night, Mr. Rhodes, you became a national folk hero."

"I'm not looking for any personal notoriety, Ms. Trinket. I simply want our country to benefit from the best possible transportation system." He addressed Charlene. "That's why I can't understand you giving the press another opportunity to undermine the *Windjammer*. I know a woman today has every right to say no to unwelcome advances. And she certainly has the right to legal remedy when her voice is not heeded."

Ms. Trinket nodded. "Yes, in his speech last month to the National Organization for Women, the President said as much."

"But you wrote his speech," Charlene reminded her.

"Never mind. He still believes it."

Worthington looked serious. "And so do I. But, Charlene, you've got to tell me how you perceived any of my actions to be inappropriate."

Charlene raised her head, their eyes met, a tear formed and edged down her cheek. Suddenly she sprang up, spilling her coffee, and threw her arms around Worthington, kissing him.

Startled, he tried to draw back.

Charlene hung on. She sobbed, "Oh, Mr. Rhodes, I'm so terribly sorry. I've been just awful, and you're trying so hard to do your job." She sniffled. "Of course, Mr. Rhodes, I've dropped the suit. I couldn't possibly go on with it. I've already instructed my attorney."

Ms. Trinket said to Charlene, "I think you should tell Mr. Rhodes what happened—the whole story."

With Charlene still clinging to him, Worthington saw the flash from a camera. Too late, he urged Charlene to release him and draw back. "Mr. Rhodes, you've been like a father to me." She sobbed uncontrollably. As he put his arm around Charlene to comfort her, there were still more flashes, one after the other.

Pissed off, Worthington stood up, tipping over his ice cream chair. He looked around for the person with a camera and saw a fat little man pointing a lens toward him. The next flash was blinding. Rubbing his eyes with one hand, Worthington leaned over and grasped the chair leg with the other, his knuckles white.

"No, Mr. Rhodes, don't!" Ms. Trinket shrieked.

"Please put the chair down," Charlene pleaded. "We can go back inside the spa and get away from them."

Another flash and all Worthington could see was a total eclipse. By the time he regained his sight, the man had vanished. Righting the chair, Worthington tried to explain to the two women that he had no intention of attacking the man with the chair. "I'm not a man of violence. I'm not in the habit of hitting people. Last night wasn't my fault either. The cameraman was clumsy. I can tell you those pictures of theirs are not worth a thousand words."

Worthington sat down again and spoke directly to his former assistant. "Before we were interrupted, Charlene, you were about to tell me the story of this lawsuit of yours, and who pressured you into filing it."

"Well, I was going through my exercise routine here at the spa when this woman running on the treadmill next to me said she knew of a way I could earn enough money so I'd never have to work again. Naturally I was interested. She told me her name was Angela. All I had to do, Angela said, was to file a civil rights sexual harassment lawsuit against you and an attorney she knew could get me a big settlement. She assured me you'd pay rather than fight and endure the bad publicity of a trial. She told me I'd get rich quicker than she could do a 10K on her treadmill. I asked about the legal fees, and Angela told me it would be a contingency arrangement. If I won, my lawyer would get half; if I didn't win, he wouldn't get anything."

"And you went along with her," Ms. Trinket prompted.

Charlene nodded. "Yes, I needed money for my mother's therapy. She lost her medical insurance when she was let go by the CIA." Charlene choked up. "She has a substance abuse problem." Charlene dried her eyes. "This attorney Angela introduced me to drafted the detailed charges. He made up that accusation that you dropped jelly beans down my blouse. In fact, he used a special sexual harassment software package on his word processor designed to titillate a jury into awarding a sizable verdict. And then, to my surprise, he went ahead and announced the lawsuit to the press without my giving him the go ahead. It was as if he and Angela had the strategy all worked out and nobody cared about my feelings. I was being ignored. So I came to my senses and told them I was going to withdraw the charges. I had quite a difficult time doing so. The attorney at first refused. And Angela called several times urging me to continue with the suit, this time telling me all of sisterhood was relying on my exposing the sexual abuses of powerful Washington men. It was only when I threatened to go to the ethics committee of the District of Columbia Bar Association that the attorney and Angela complied with my demands and dropped the suit."

"Charlene, I'm proud of you," Worthington said. "Your assertiveness wins the day for all of us."

◆　◆　◆　◆

Unfortunately for Worthington the withdrawal of Charlene's lawsuit proved to be anticlimactic. For the photographs of the two of them, arms around each other, appeared on the front page of the next morning's *Washington Post*. Seeing the newspaper photographs of Charlene in her body-hugging outfit embracing him in the Watergate coffee bar, Sara launched into a tirade, accusing him of blatant infidelity. She demanded he immediately pack up and leave their Rock Creek home.

Homeless, Worthington booked a room in a Georgetown hotel. At first, in the early evenings, he would telephone Emily, Elizabeth, and Danny, but soon they went off to their summer camp in the Appalachian Mountains of Maryland and he found himself alone. He chided himself, for he should have anticipated the media would be constantly following him around. The thought suddenly struck him: my God! if they hadn't jumped on a Charlene story, they could well have uncovered an Anna Ardmore story. He must never call out her name again.

Chapter Twenty-nine

Worthington reclined in his first-class seat, accepted a glass of wine from the flight attendant and wondered how three weeks' worth of Washington R and R could have been any more stressful. Thinking he would try again to talk to Sara, he reached for the in-flight telephone in the seatback in front of him. As he ran his credit card through the magnetic slot, he changed his mind and instead punched out the number of Henry D'Camp's Bar 8 Ranch.

"Henry, just answer me one question. What ever happened to the truth?"

"Forget the word. Few of our writers mention it any more. And for good reason. Everyone's forgotten the purity the word once conveyed."

"When did truth go out of style, Henry?"

"I take it you haven't seen Webster's new Twenty-first Century Dictionary."

"No."

"Then buy one and turn to the back. They've a brand new section entitled, 'Obsolete Words of the Twentieth Century.' You'll find truth there under 'T'. Even in court, the oath today is 'Will you do your best to tell more or less what you think to be what happened?' Everybody has a different slant. It's no longer consequential to swear on a stack of Bibles. In this multi-religious world, you've got your Koran, the teachings of Buddha, your astrology, and your new age worshipers." Henry's laugh was hollow. "Listen, Diogenes, you're going to have to look to someone else for truth, because as you can see, I've become quite the cynic."

There was no question about it, Henry was down and having trouble bouncing back. After the fallout from Congressman Roybal's July third hearing, Henry himself had moved into the spotlight. Nasty rumors about him had spread after the head of the Appropriations Committee railroaded through approval of the *Windjammer* during a hastily-called session just before the Fourth of July. Roybal's mistake of trying to outmaneuver the media by transacting business during the three-day holiday weekend only raised a yardarm of red flags. When the editorial writers and television anchormen realized Roybal's trick, they scrutinized every aspect of the *Windjammer* for a news angle. Learning that D'Camp's Bar 8 Ranch was to be the location for the new Four Corners city, they acted as if they'd stumbled onto the scandal of the year. They screamed conflict of interest, pointing out that his newspapers editorially supported the project. Henry had intervened, hoping to cut off debate, but the more he tried to stifle the exposé, the more his efforts appeared as if he was orchestrating a massive cover-up. Henry realized he had no choice but to back off and remain silent, so he hastily beat a retreat to the peace and quiet of his Colorado ranch.

Not having Henry to kick around anymore, the media's questions spilled over into a laundry list of personal items having to do with himself. The press hounded him everywhere. He tried to dodge them among the evening rush hour crowds on the Metro after he left his office. But they tracked him down, even to his favorite Georgetown bistro on M Street. At first they queried him about alleged payoffs to certain Congressmen in return for their *Windjammer* votes. The most annoying was the implication that he was taking kickbacks from D'Camp, from contractors—actually from anyone and everyone. One columnist even suggested he was offering reporters bribes not to ask about his kickbacks.

His repeated denials and disclaimers brought no relief, for they expanded their probes to include members of his own family. His house and car in Maine kept popping up like perennial weeds. And some reporter somewhere was always resurrecting the Uncle Bill story. One absurd rumor was that Emily had accepted a payment from some contractor's offshore fund in order to pay the tuition for her summer camp.

In hindsight, the House Appropriation Committee's approval meant little, because now some members of Congress were promising their own investigations when the *Windjammer* legislation came up for debate on the House floor. No longer was its ultimate passage assured. And even if the legislation was finally passed and signed into law by the President, Worthington worried that "earmarking," the thinly-disguised practice of siphoning off appropriated funds into congressmen's pet projects, would take a lot of wind out of the *Windjammer*'s sails.

The steward set Worthington's lunch on his white linen-draped tray-table and refilled his wine glass.

The episode that made his leaking cup runneth over, Worthington recalled, was his singing engagement at the Reflecting Pool. He had stood beneath the bigger-than-life statue of Abraham Lincoln and shared the sixteenth President's view of the Washington Monument, atop which the spirit of the first President was thought to reside. The image of each monument reflected off the long pool in between. Worthington thought he might eavesdrop as these two leaders talked to one another on this magical sunrise of summer solstice. He listened, but heard only the tuning up of the band's musical instruments.

Worthington recalled how these two Presidents had suffered with their detractors, those who plotted against them, those who disparaged their every action, their every dream. Yet each man had persevered, addressed his tasks, plowed ahead, and planted the seeds that would grow the future of the nation.

When his turn at the microphone came, Worthington sang of Marian Anderson's *America*:

> *Oh beautiful for spacious skies,*
> *For amber waves of grain,*
> *For purple mountains majesties,*
> *Above the fruited plain.*

His voice reflected off the pool, north to the pair of polished granite walls, east to the obelisk for Washington, west to the listening Abraham Lincoln, and south to the cherry-tree-rimmed Tidal Basin. He sang beautifully on the dawning of this longest day of the year while the President in the nearby White House listened and applauded. The people lionized him in this mutually bonding summer solstice event.

Worthington wished he could carry a cheering audience along with him wherever he went. Without their support he felt vulnerable. As he did without Sara. Why is it, he asked himself, a man seeks Gothic buttressing? Given his strength, the male of the species should be able to stand alone. For, by definition, his masculinity formed the generative principle of the cosmos.

But the press corps had abbreviated the coverage of this summer solstice event, sending out only a negative reading. Silver Bell in the Night arrived leading a band of demonstrators.

Coincidentally the media appeared, filming the disruptive action. Waving placards and railing against the *Windjammer*, the Indians beat drums and chanted about preserving their sacred sites, their ruins, their heritage. The cameras filmed their footage and left. The departure of the media was the cue, for the protestors calmed down, tucked away their signs, and drove off in a fleet of new Fords.

Okay, Worthington thought as he finished his lunch, now for the good news. He sat in silence, thinking. Even after the jet landed in St. Louis, he was still trying to tally that first bit of positive news from his R and R in Washington. Walking up the jetway, he saw Edward and Zoe waiting in the concourse. He shook Edward's hand, kissed Zoe on the cheek. "How are we holding up on damage control?"

Their grim faces answered, suggesting the truth of the matter was that tougher days lay ahead west across Kansas, Colorado, and New Mexico—toward the Four Corners.

Chapter Thirty

Tony had left the ruins early morning, leading Dolly and Paco on another of his scheduled trips back to the Cross Cultural Trading Post to pick up supplies. For the seminarists, Tony's regular comings and goings marked time passages in their commitment to this ancient, unnamed settlement.

Then one day when Martha spied two desert tortoises, a pair of mule deer, followed by a vixen and her mate wandering through their dig site, George christened their pueblo ruins "Noah's Ark." Everyone agreed upon the name, and Anna said she would use it in her excavation field reports, rendering Noah's Ark an official site in the annals of American archaeology. She also promised to acknowledge them—Greta and Dusty, Margaret and Paul, Daisy and Alex, and Martha and George—as her able colleagues.

This evening around the campfire waiting for Tony to return, the seminarists were talking about what Paul had labeled "present-day marauders," those who, from time to time, had invaded their newly-named sanctuary.

Paul recalled the day a National Park Service ranger, leading a group of hikers, stopped by. "I cringed when he likened the cluster of Anasazi houseblocks to time-share condominiums and explained away the trace of the outlier road to Chaco Canyon as the genesis of Route 66."

"His trite metaphors exasperated all of us," Greta said.

"I was frustrated with him telling the story of John Wesley Powell who navigated the rapids of the Colorado River in 1869." Margaret frowned. "What was the point of him turning an historic event into a slapstick tale of a one-armed canoeist on a wild-river adventure?"

"This dig of ours is serious business," Dusty agreed.

Daisy laughed. "Wasn't that Arizona State professor, Jeremy Snow, sent by ILMA to entertain us?"

"Three nights of lectures—that's not what we call entertainment in Houston," Martha said.

"Don't you all agree that Snow was rather imprecise about the origins of the people who lived in our settlement?" Paul asked.

"Yes. I had trouble with his theories, too," Margaret replied. "But then, academics never do give you exact answers. Did you hear how he waffled on his dates?"

"That bothered me, too," Greta said. "First, he told us they came here some twelve thousand years ago, and then he said there's some evidence it may have twenty or thirty thousand. That's quite a range. Dusty, why was Professor Snow so ambiguous?"

"When there's no scientific proof or consensus, he wants to be vague—on purpose. It takes a strong-willed archaeologist like Anna to stick to her beliefs in the face of doubting Thomases. And I know from my experience, the field of archaeology is full of skeptics."

Martha looked at George. "But what I can't understand is how these people got here in the first place. George, didn't Professor Snow say they came by boat from Israel?"

"No, no dear, he told us that some authorities back in the late 1800s explained the presence of these early people with biblical references, saying they were descended from the lost tribes of Israel. But the professor pooh-poohed that idea and said today there's ample support for the theory they came across the Bering Straight on a land bridge from Siberia during the last Ice Age."

"I'd like to have collected the RT toll on that bridge," Margaret joked. "Just think of all those nomads wandering into the New World—ancestors of the Aztecs, Incas, Olmecs, Toltecs, as well as our Anasazi."

Paul placed another piñon log on the fire. "Snow's remarks about the trade that developed between the Toltecs and the Anasazi were really quite interesting. Not only goods but ideas traveled along those ancient roads."

"Anna would disagree with Snow's guess that our Anasazi roads were build as a result of influence from Mesoamerica," Margaret said. "She would say the roads were established by the Anasazi themselves to welcome the traders from the south."

"I'll bet those Toltecs walked all this way for the turquoise jewelry," Daisy speculated.

"Maybe," Paul replied. "But I wonder if they didn't view themselves as missionaries for their way of life. I mean, today we feel it's our God-given right to march into every Eastern European country and set up a fast food outlet."

"I agree with Snow that trade was important. It's like trading oil for . . . for . . ." George paused and said to Martha, "You know, I can't think why anybody would want oil if they didn't have a car."

"Maybe for lamps," she said.

"No, that's whale oil, dear."

"Anyway . . . they could have traded your oil for antler chandeliers." Martha looked around at the puzzled faces. "They're all the rage in Houston."

"I got traded once," Alex piped up, "from the Yankees to the Washington Sluggers. Spent the last three seasons in D.C.—three long, hot summers. Grew awfully restless. That's why I retired. Ready to start a new life." He looked lovingly at Daisy.

Daisy smiled at Alex. "You were a good catch for the Sluggers."

"Gosh, yes, I guess I was. The owners paid a heap of cash and threw in a shortstop, a southpaw, and a left fielder to boot."

Paul stood, and began to pace.

"That survey party that came through here last month certainly lacked in manners," Martha said. "Tony was really upset. His llamas were crying and spitting in frustration with that dog. Cute little thing, though."

"Yes, Martha, it took quite a while for Tony to quiet his friends down," Greta said.

"Have you noticed," Daisy asked, "how noisy it is around here early in the morning? Even Ranger Rick said our Anasazi didn't need alarm clocks for their wake-up call."

"Yeah, the birds and bees get me started before dawn. Daisy and I can't sleep any more after that."

Daisy hugged Alex. "This desert is teeming with life."

"Anyone seen Anna?"

Alex jumped up. "No, but Tony's back!"

Tony approached with Dolly and Paco in tow. Baguettes of French bread protruded from Dolly's loaded pannier, and a shiny new coffee pot dangled from the straps of one of Paco's wicker baskets.

Alex rushed over, grasped Tony's arm and whispered, "Did you bring the Trojans?"

"They were all sold out," Tony whispered back.

Alex looked at Daisy in despair.

"Now we can eat," Dusty announced.

"Anyone seen Anna?" Martha asked again.

George shook his head. "Not since I helped her light the camp-fire."

"Maybe she's gathering more firewood," Margaret said.

"No, I chopped a whole week's supply this morning." Greta pointed to a pile of wood.

"I'm sure she went off to meditate," Daisy surmised.

"Don't be silly, Daisy," Dusty said. "Anna's not one to meditate. She's a woman of action."

"You're all wrong," Paul said. "Anna wanted an escape from our discordant discussions."

◆　◆　◆　◆

The brilliant sunset of this long summer solstice eve had finally played out, and the moon—needing only a puff or two to become full—was rising by the time Anna reached the top of the mesa. She cleared away a few small stones, blew air into her thermal pad, and unrolled her sleeping bag. Enjoying her privacy on this warm night, she lay awake for a while. Mountains framed her night canvas: the Rockies to the east and north and, on the western horizon, the spires of Monument Valley. Occasionally a shooting star sped across the sky as if its mission was to rush breaking news to Earth's printing presses and television receiving dishes. Off somewhere a coyote howled, joined by a cohort, and soon the animal hotline was at work.

At one with the natural world, Anna eventually fell asleep. Sometime in the middle of the night the moonlight awakened her. Or was there something stirring? She sat up and looked around. She remembered her archaeological survey map showed the symbol for a small Anasazi site atop this mesa. Had she inadvertently placed her sleeping bag on top of their sacred kiva, and had she been awakened by their spirits? She listened for a long while, but on this night the voices from the past remained cryptic to her. And she fell asleep again.

Or had she? Amorphous figures gathered around her, joining hands in a circle. The ghostly apparitions spoke to her in their ancient language, and she to them. They led her to the edge of the mesa and bid her look down upon Noah's Ark—no longer a ruin but now a lively village. In the central plaza, flaming torches blazed, illuminating the red-rock walls of the four-story pueblo. She heard the gobbles of their turkeys and the barks of their domesticated dogs. The flickering firelight reflected off the precious water gurgling through their acequias from some far-off reservoir.

Fascinated, she watched as the inhabitants, decorated with body paint and wearing ornamented headdresses, began to move rhythmically to their wondrous strange music. Sliding their hand-held manos back and forth, the females ground corn in stone metates, keeping time with their males who had drawn together into a ring of dancing bodies. As the men pranced in the firelight, beads of perspiration competed with beads of turquoise strung around their necks. The rattle of animal bones tied to their legs with combed yucca strands accompanied their alien song. Anna was stirred by their chanting, and she tried with all her sleepy might to join in the beat of their drums, but her efforts failed to bring consonance to their erratic cadence.

Their muscles glistening in the firelight, the male dancers stepped up their undulations with bold, virile countermovements. Driving themselves into a frenzy, they encircled her, taking turns to reach out and touch her in curiosity. Some went further with their explorations of her body. She tried to back away, but the blue-eyed one, demonstrating his manhood, stepped forward and took command.

She was immobilized. She realized he was special among men. With pleasure she received him, and he impregnated her. He stayed inside her until the moon completed its elliptical arc. Only then did he free her, allowing her to return to the familiar rhythm of dawn now stepping onto the stage of the eastern sky.

Emulating the slow, relaxed stretching of a mountain lioness, Anna coaxed her body into an alert stance. With the first light of day, Anna pictured the ancient shaman who lived atop this mesa and whose duty, those centuries ago, after the dark of night, was to persuade the sun to return to their world and rise once again. Bestowed with his special powers, he would then lead the spirit of light across the sky on its daily mission of renewal.

And now unfurling before her was another beautiful Four Corners morning. Anna saw the eons of time play out in simulated fast-forward photography. Beginning with the Earth's creation, she saw the mountains form and then shift. Enormous dinosaurs romped and giant birds flew overhead. Lush trees grew, fell, and were buried by time. Prehistory people arrived on the scene and, as the millennia passed, developed from nomadic hunters and gatherers to agrarian planters and harvesters. The frames of time now flickered more slowly, the pace less hurried as these farmers built their pueblos, ceremonial kivas, and stone signal towers. Following their abandonment of the Four Corners, the rapid-fire frames of time picked up again and flew through seven centuries. Suddenly the images stopped as if the Master Projectionist had selected this particular sunrise on this particular morning to announce an imminent rebirth of humanity.

Watching the sound and light show, Anna puzzled, sensing unique feelings racing through her body. A deer grazed nearby. Seeing Anna, the doe looked up and observed her intently. Quizzically Anna returned the avatar's stare. An extraordinary communication ensued between females. And at that moment Anna knew. She understood the messages her body and the natural world were transmitting to her. Together in their sweet harmony, they proclaimed her immaculate conception. They told her the life growing within her was special because she was carrying the rebirth of the Anasazi spirit.

A baby, the innocence of a newborn, the perfect truth of a new life. A millennium ago in thousands of settlements like her Noah's Ark, her Anasazi practiced their new life of settling down in the Four Corners to live together in pueblos. Simple folk, loving their families, embracing their surroundings, building their kivas, their towers, their houseblocks. Their new lives, innocent of wars and assassinations, honest in their relationships with one another and unselfish. Their minds, their bodies, their souls flourishing in this natural womb of Mother Earth. As an archaeologist in search of scientific truth, she had always sought that coveted pure element which she could now define as the spiritual truth these ancient people enjoyed. At last, her search for this ultimate truth was fulfilled. Elated, Anna thought about the glorious future that her baby represented. And she was happy that she now understood that truth, ethics, and moral values were one; molecules of life connected together in a trinity that was surely as holy as that in any church, each with a basic obligation to protect and nourish the other. Her private and public life had merged into one. She was now a prospective mother carrying this Anasazi spirit. And so, from this moment on, Anna Ardmore's covenant to nurture the true spirit of her people was clearly defined for her.

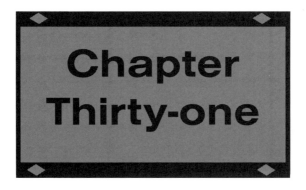

Chapter Thirty-one

When the sun rose at its farthest most point in the north and touched the Tropic of Cancer, marking the beginning of a rainy season, the shaman told the prehistory people to plant seeds that would bring forth their crops. Six months later, when the spirit of light fled south to the Tropic of Capricorn and the days shortened, they prayed he would not allow their world to end. The shaman invariably proved his mettle by making certain the sun not only rose but stayed in their sky a little longer each day so they could accomplish great deeds.

Starting down the return trail, Anna knew she would dedicate herself to her new mission in life. As Ethereal Mother, it was clear to her she now had an even more compelling reason to save her ruins—not only Noah's Ark, but all her settlements. She must do so for her spirit-baby.

While Quentin, Stuart, and their hired assassins were obsessed with stopping Worthington Rhodes, his successor could well prove to be even more destructive—a truism of history she had voiced to Quentin, but which he had chosen not to heed. Therefore, she realized, she must take matters into her own hands. The forces of Earth were commanding her to act.

She had hiked a ways before realizing she was no longer on the trail. Caught up in her thoughts and engulfed by the early morning shadows cast by needled branches, she had become confused and missed a turn. Trying to get her bearings, Anna stopped in the shade of a gnarled old juniper. Its thick, twisted trunk, bone-gray from centuries of a didactic sun, had spiraled itself into a corkscrew promising to decant vintage wisdom to Anna. She toyed with the idea of biting into one of its luscious berries. Out of the blue, the old juniper spoke to her, telling her to reveal to the world a story of an Anasazi wheel.

Stepping back into the more familiar sunlight of her science of archaeology, Anna resisted at first, knowing such a concocted story would be regarded by her colleagues as implausible, unfounded, and unproven. Yet, she believed, her Anasazi were smart enough to have invented the wheel, or the Toltecs, trading from the south, could have introduced the wheel to the Anasazi. "Yes," Anna said out loud to herself and to the tree. "That's why my people built those wide, straight roads leading to and from Chaco Canyon. Yes, the wheel has to be the explanation." She reminded herself there were thousands of unexcavated sites throughout the Four Corners. So, surely, someday, somewhere, some archaeologist would unearth a real wheel. Why not now?

Since no library housed a written record of the prehistory past, the information gathered so far could only be interpreted from academic platforms littered with the debris of personal biases, spoken in a clamor of politically correct opinions, and seen through the tinted glasses of gender-gaze. Indeed, if the truth were known, nearly every account of what had taken place in the American Southwest was little more than conjecture. Anna recalled little Emily telling everyone about the wheel. Out of the mouths of babes?

If there was an Anasazi wheel, the world would have to acknowledge her sites as important and protect them from wanton destruction. But to make her report believable she would have to cleverly document such a discovery and be as resourceful as the ancient shaman who recited his sunrise story. His scheme worked, and the people bought it. For the benefit of future generations she must engage in similar showmanship.

Yes, she would embellish the archaeological artifacts her group had found so far to point toward irrefutable evidence that the Anasazi had the wheel. As much as finding the Clovis projectile point buried in that mastodon a half century ago, her discovery would inspire the entire archaeological world to unite in a common cause of preservation. And only her seminarists, whom she would swear to secrecy, would know that she had to forsake the truth in order for truth to prevail.

Resolved to put her plan into action, Anna approached the camp, prepared to take charge. Before she could say anything, she heard Dusty's brusque voice call out, "Has anyone seen Alex and

Daisy this morning? First, Anna disappears, and now I can't find those two."

George answered. "Lil' Abner and Daisy Mae have eloped. They've left us a note."

Martha saw Anna and exclaimed, "Anna's back! Anna, we all missed you last night. Have you heard? Alex and Daisy have run off together. Can you imagine? A real romance on our dig. George and I were just about to share their note with everyone. Alex says he and Daisy were going to hike back to civilization to get married and start a family."

George nodded. "Daisy Mae must have thought it was Sadie Hawkins Day, not summer solstice. And I suspect Alex wanted to leave because the only find of importance to him on our dig was his discovery of Daisy."

"All our other finds, which have been so fascinating to the rest of us, were apparently of little consequence to him," Paul said.

Greta pouted. "Yes, Alex said the skull I unearthed in my square was just another dead Indian."

Anna seized her opportunity. "That skull is what I want to talk to all of you about. Greta, you've made a momentous find."

"I have?"

"Yes, your friend hails from Mesoamerica. In fact, he's probably Toltec." Anna cuddled the skull protectively in her arms.

Martha looked at its face. With its perfect white teeth it seemed to smile back at her. She shuddered. "But how can we tell where he's from?"

Anna pointed to the smile. "From the occlusion of the teeth."

"Occlusion?" Paul asked.

"Look at his bite. The upper teeth overlap the lowers, much like ours today." Everyone clenched their teeth and noted the space between their upper and lower front teeth. "If we were to find a skull with the teeth worn down and meeting directly together, we would have discovered an Anasazi corn eater because they ground their corn on sandstone metates and the sand particles wore away their teeth."

"The same as chewing sandpaper," Dusty said. "So Greta's guy can't be Anasazi."

Anna agreed. "Our man here is Toltec. Alex and Daisy should never have left. They're going to miss all the excitement. We're about to rock the archaeological ark right here in Noah's plaza."

Everyone looked surprised.

"What do you mean?" Paul asked.

"Today our wondrous archaeological ruins are as endangered as the Great Plains buffalo and the American golden eagle once were. We saved those icons from extinction and now, mounting the same emotional and patriotic campaign, we must save our Anasazi."

"But how?" Martha asked.

"We'll tell the world about Greta's discovery and its significance," Anna replied.

"What the hell is significant about finding this skull?" Dusty asked.

"Shut up and listen," Greta told him. "I'm sure Anna has something exciting in mind for us."

"Yes, I do. The news of your skull, together with an ancient wheel we are about to find, will draw the world's attention to the Four Corners."

"But there isn't any wheel," Margaret protested.

"I think it's Anna's imagination that we should pay attention to," Paul suggested. "Anna, are you asking us to invent the wheel for the Anasazi?"

"Exactly," Anna replied. "Remember that big flat, round stone Alex dug up?"

Everyone nodded.

"I said at the time it was used as a support base for one of the poles that held up the roof over the kiva . . . but I'm now convinced I overlooked it's real purpose. George, you take a stone augur and chip a hole through the middle of that round stone and smooth any rough edges with a sandstone rock. You'll have manufactured a wheel. Dusty, you take that roof viga you uncovered in your outlying square and taper the ends with a sharp lithic tool. Presto, you'll have crafted an axle for George's wheel."

"We could carbon date the wood," Dusty said, becoming caught up with the conspiracy. "That's the scientific technique I've used in Greece."

"Carbon dating doesn't work well in the dry Southwest," Anna said. "We've a better method here. At the dendrochronology laboratory in Tucson they've records of the different tree ring patterns formed during the wet years and the drought years. They can date logs back more than a thousand years. They'll substantiate the age of our axle."

"But what about my skull?" Greta asked.

"We're going to bash in the side of it to reveal an ancient, unsolved murder. This poor victim was, no doubt, the genius who invented the wheel. Now I ask you, was he killed because the shaman didn't want anyone superseding his omnipotent powers with a new technology that would advance their civilization?"

"I see." Paul looked at the others. "When the world finds out, every archaeologist from here to Greece will demand time to investigate. Our find will cause Congress to table the vote on the *Windjammer* bullet train and bury it in Roybal's committee."

"And to make sure the world finds out right away, I'll phone my journalist friend, Brenda Turner. She'll print the news in her *Four Corners Tablet*, plus get a dispatch onto the worldwide wire services. Television reporters will soon be swarming around our Noah's Ark honey of a story. Now promise me, my friends, none of you will ever tell anyone we fabricated our wheel."

The seminarists looked at each other.

"Martha and I are with you, Anna," George assured her.

"Me, too," Greta said enthusiastically.

"Well, okay, count me in," Margaret said.

"Sure," Dusty told Anna. "And I'll guarantee the international archaeological community will cite our find as momentous, just like they did with the Piltdown man. That old fossil fooled 'em for forty-two years."

Tony said, "Me and my friends'll never tell."

"I'll make it unanimous," Paul said.

"Thank you. I'm glad you're supportive. Now I'll give you another reason why it's so important for us to successfully carry out our mission."

Eyebrows rose.

"Our fable has yet another player-to-be."

"I just knew it!" Martha exclaimed. "You're going to have a baby, aren't you?"

Anna smiled. The women gathered around her, hugging her and wishing her well. Paul and George gave their congratulations.

"Yes, my baby is destined to be the rebirth of the Anasazi spirit."

◆   ◆   ◆   ◆

It can't be mine, Dusty thought. The truth of the matter is, that night in Georgetown I was faking it, and I've got a videotape to prove it.

Chapter Thirty-two

Whenever Brenda Turner wrote an important news story, she would recall her father's rules of reporting which he had learned while working his way up from cub reporter to the city desk at the old *New York Herald*. Even after he sought out the solitude of a weekly newspaper in the Four Corners, he stuck with the basics.

"People are busy," he would instruct her, "and don't have a lot of time. They expect to read the salient facts in the first paragraph and pick up the details in the rest of the story. And in that first paragraph," he would emphasize to her, "remember to answer the five W's: who, what, where, when, and why. And when appropriate, add the H: how." If his reporters didn't conform to this yardstick, he would crumple their copy and toss it into the large wastebasket beside his desk. And they would have to try again.

In her communication classes at the university, Brenda was introduced to a smorgasbord of reporting styles. As newspapers competed for readership in an expanding media world, different leads had come into fashion. Brenda liked the up-front hook which got the readers' attention so they would read the entire story. How much better, she reasoned, to write in a format in which she could include her own research, filling in background and placing the news in a broader perspective. As a result, Brenda believed, reporting the news had advanced from simply the five W's to an informative commentary.

This afternoon, trying to concentrate on writing the story of the discovery of the Anasazi wheel, Brenda struggled with her fifth draft. As she sat, legs dangling over the excavated kiva wall in the Noah's Ark site, Brenda savored her scoop. Now if she could only write the story on the portable computer on her lap, she could then transmit it via the internal modem out over Dusty's cellular telephone back to her newspaper. There the staff had been instructed to immediately fax her bylined story to Henry D'Camp's worldwide media headquarters.

The fact hat her exclusive would be printed in major newspapers across the country and around the world kept intruding on her thought process. Also distracting her from her efforts, Brenda knew the story was so important she would be interviewed by network television. This additional thought burdened her with worries of how she would appear on camera the first time. To make the best impression with her local readers and Southwest advertisers, she knew she must update her wardrobe. Appearance, after all, was as important in the West as in the rest of the country.

Anna had called her on the cellular phone the day before, stressing the importance of the find, saying excitedly, "Ours is the most important American archaeological discovery since the Clovis Point! You understand and love the Anasazi, so I want you to have the exclusive on this story. Do you realize what this means? For you? For the nation? For the world? Brenda, get out here as fast as you can!"

Anxious to be the Bob Woodward reporter on this story, Brenda had jogged the trail to the ruins. Now, having seen the wheel and the axle and having interviewed the members of Anna's team, including Dusty Rhodes, the bearded and eminent archaeologist from Greece, Brenda grappled with composing her story. Her sixth version read:

> The universally accepted axiom that prehistory Americans never had the wheel has been proven false by archaeologist Dr. Anna Ardmore who has unearthed an Anasazi wheel and axle deep in the Four Corners of the American Southwest. The extraordinary find was excavated inside a ceremonial kiva together with the clubbed skull of the person thought to be its inventor.
>
> "The Anasazi apparently rejected his new technology," Dr. Ardmore stated.

Brenda shook her head, saved that version onto a backup diskette along with her other attempts. Still trying to avoid her father's style, she began again:

Technology took it on the chin in ancient America. The wheel, long believed by archaeologists to be unknown to the Anasazi of the Southwest, has finally turned up. Along with the battered skull of its inventor.

Brenda discarded that attempt as well. Making matters worse, Anna and her group had gathered around and were watching her. The school teacher Greta was looking over her shoulder, reading her screen, critiquing her grammar and sentence structure. Abandoning the style of feature articles, Brenda reverted to her father's advice:

The wheel, thought to be nonexistent among prehistory Native Americans, was found two days ago by archaeologist Dr. Anna Ardmore deep within a sacred ceremonial room of an Anasazi ruins known as the Noah's Ark site in the Four Corners of the Southwest along with an axle and battered skull of its presumed inventor.

Dr. Ardmore said, "Our discovery is the most important ever in American archaeology. Up until now, accepted theory has been that the wheel, other than its use in small toys by the Toltecs in Mesoamerica, was unknown in the New World and was brought, along with the horse, by the conquering Spanish in the early sixteenth century."

In stressing the need for further excavations, Dr. Ardmore stated, "We must preserve and study all Anasazi ruins. Remember, these are the same people who designed and built at Chaco Canyon and Mesa Verde our country's largest multi-storied dwellings prior to the 1880s. So, heaven knows what other gems await us across the Southwest."

Anna hugged Brenda. "You and your story will have a real impact on the future of our country."

Tony read the words on the screen out loud so his llamas would know.

Dusty tossed his old hat in the air. "Every archaeologist I know will call, wanting to ask my personal opinion about this find."

Greta graded Brenda's story an "A-plus."

"It's a gusher all right," George declared.

"Yes," Martha agreed. "George, you and I will become the toast of the Houston social circuit."

"Now our bank president will listen to my opinions," Margaret said. "I'll have real credibility with him."

Paul looked at the others and gloated. "From now on my economic predictions will be widely quoted in the media and respected by colleagues."

Brenda connected her modem to Dusty's cellular telephone and punched in her paper's special number. "Your story is now being instantaneously printed out in Cortez on my new equipment as well as being fed into the D'Camp worldwide wire services," she told them. "And thanks to Anna, my byline will appear on the front pages of tomorrow morning's newspapers." Brenda beamed. "My father would be proud."

◆　◆　◆　◆

Later, Henry D'Camp's fax machine at his Bar 8 Ranch spewed out the story. "Oh, my God!" he exclaimed over the telephone to Brenda "You've killed the *Windjammer*."

"The truth never did any damage."

"Fuck the truth! You're fired."

"Henry, dear, remember the clause my attorney put in our contract? You fire me and I buy back my paper at one-fourth your purchase price."

◆　◆　◆　◆

Edward read the news out loud to Zoe. "Damn, now every environmental and academic group in the country will protest the *Windjammer*."

"As if we didn't have enough trouble with the press."

"But I'm not going to hand D'Camp my resignation letter yet," Edward said.

"Nor am I ready to cut and run. On this one, Edward, we've got to think globally."

◆　◆　◆　◆

On their honeymoon on Waikiki Beach, Alex said to Daisy, "Gosh, maybe we left too soon."

◆　◆　◆　◆

Quentin Ford IV rejoiced. He called Stuart. "Read the morning paper, my boy?"

"Yes, I have. And I've already talked to Anna. The entire story is true, Mr. Ford."

"Of course it's true. Her news'll do more than your assassin and his insidious group of journalists could ever do to stop the *Windjammer*. This woman is marvelous, let me tell you."

◆　◆　◆　◆

Silver Bell in the Night charged into Orlando DeBaca Roybal's private office, holding up the *Washington Post*. "Congressman, you've got to change your position now. Dr. Ardmore's found the wheel right in the path of the *Windjammer*."

"Whose wheel?"

"The Anasazi's. And Dr. Ardmore says there are still more treasures to be uncovered." Silver Bell pointed to the story as she laid the paper on his desk, covering his crayons. "The country won't support the bulldozers now."

"But I can't single-handedly reverse the committee's vote."

"No, but when the *Windjammer*'s final approval comes up on the floor of the House, you could tack on an amendment that would earmark the RT to preserve archaeological ruins. Don't you want to be on the winning side?"

◆　◆　◆　◆

In the privacy of his St. Louis hotel room, Worthington saw Brenda's story in the *Post-Dispatch*. Reading between the lines, he brushed away the drifting sands from his subconscious. Revealed to him were his thoughts of Anna. He wanted so desperately to see her, to hear her voice, to embrace her again. Yes, he would go to her as soon as his tour took him to the Four Corners.

◆　◆　◆　◆

A helicopter from one of the major networks hovered overhead, eventually settling down in a whirlwind of dust in the plaza of Noah's Ark. A team of reporters and cameramen emerged, led by Brenda Turner. She was attired in her new Southwest outfit: full red leather skirt, red shirt with its suede fringe, red and black tooled cowboy boots, and a red Stetson hat.

Leading her entourage to the ceremonial kiva, Brenda introduced Anna and Dusty. The silver bracelets on her wrists jingling, she gestured toward the wheel, the axle, and the battered skull of its inventor. She looked into the camera and began her rehearsed script. "I'm Brenda Turner, editor-in-chief of the *Four Corners Tablet*. Ever since my late father was editor, my newspaper has made a point of covering all the news about the prehistory Anasazi, but this find by Dr. Anna Ardmore is the most momentous we've ever reported . . ."

His face peering into the camera, Dusty interrupted. "Beats any discovery I ever made in Greece." He excused himself as he answered his ringing cellular telephone.

Brenda smiled at Dusty and then motioned for Anna to join her in front of the camera. "And here is the leader of the Institute and Living Museum of Archeology's expedition, Dr. Anna Ardmore. Can you tell us what your discovery means for all of us?"

Anna touched a white whooping crane feather to the brim of her safari hat and nodded into the camera. "The spirit of our ancient American Anasazi lives with us today."

Chapter Thirty-three

Fueled by the news of Anna's discovery of the wheel, Worthington's *Windjammer* presentations drew even larger crowds of both supporters and opposition demonstrators as his tour headed west from St. Louis across mid-America and on to the communities of Jefferson City, Columbia, Kansas City, Emporia, Wichita, Garden City, Trinidad, and Raton.

Past the 100th meridian, less rainfall meant a scattered population. Only a dozen or so folding chairs had been set up for Worthington's evening appearance in the gift shop of the old west depot of the Cumbres and Toltec Scenic Railroad in Antonito, Colorado.

With his customary charm, Worthington greeted train buffs from Grand Junction and Albuquerque, plus a lingering handful of tourists who had ridden the narrow-gauge steam train on its twisting all-day journey from its western terminus in Chama, New Mexico.

"That old relic poked along at five miles an hour, zigzagging almost a dozen times across the Colorado-New Mexico border," said a tourist, himself an old relic from Kokomo, Indiana. "I counted each state's hand-painted welcoming boards posted along the right-of-way."

"I wouldn't have wanted to go any faster, dear," his wife said. "We were just clinging to that canyon wall thousands of feet above that deep gorge. I was so frightened."

"I enjoyed the ride." A train enthusiast wearing an engineer's cap purchased in the gift shop spoke up. "Going back into the past is fun, but I do have to admit that after riding that train all day and covering only sixty-four miles, I'm ready to welcome tomorrow's high-speed magnetic train."

A shorter man came up to Worthington, extended his hand and smiled. He ignored the NO SMOKING sign as he put a lighted match to the cigar in his mouth. He was also oblivious to the NO DOGS ALLOWED sign. The animal by his side quietly surveyed the audience.

"Pleased to meet you at last, Mr. Rhodes. You may have heard of me. I'm Clarence Short, the man our governor put in charge of engineering your right-of-way. Without me and my pal Willie here . . ." he patted the dog's head until its tail wagged, ". . . your high-speed magnetic train would attract only paper clips back there in Washington." He guffawed.

"Good to meet you, Mr. Short," Worthington said warmly. "Getting to know members of our *Windjammer* crew is what this cross-country tour is all about. Tonight's show, though, is going to be pretty informal."

"We don't give a damn about putting on the dog out here in the West."

Willie barked.

Worthington laughed, connecting instantly with this surveyor. "Would you give me a hand with this route map?"

Together, the two men hoisted the large canvas up above a table offering railroad memorabilia for sale, and thumbtacked the map to the depot wall.

"And now for the artist's drawing of our train."

The surveyor helped lift the picture of the *Windjammer* above the counter displaying narrow-gauge railroad souvenirs.

Worthington was pleased with everyone's expression of admiration for his futuristic wide-bodied train. "Sleek, isn't she?" was Worthington's opening statement. Though his audience was small, the thought of how his train would expand their world was reward enough for him. He gestured toward his wheels of the future—their vehicle for enlightenment. "An equally thrilling ride, but quite different from the journey some of you took today. Allow me to bring you up to speed on America's twenty-first century railroad technology."

Outside, the parking lot gravel bubbled under tires coming to a quick stop. Truck doors slammed. Two men appeared at the old depot's 1880 vintage doorway. One hoisted a television camera which displayed the bold words ALL-GOSSIP TV NETWORK. The other exhibited the determined look of a reporter assigned to get quotes for an already composed story.

As the cameraman aimed the lens at Worthington, the reporter, whom Worthington recognized as Johnny Redgrave from World News Syndicate, boomed, "Mr. Rhodes, our readers and viewers want to know how much in personal commissions you are demanding from each land owner forced to sell their property for your train's right-of-way?"

Diverted from Worthington's presentation, the small audience turned their heads in unison toward the newcomers.

Before Worthington could reply, Redgrave continued with his side show. "Further, with the country entrusting so much of its money to this project of yours, Mr. Rhodes, how do you explain what happened the last time the government awarded you that grant for your lobstermen's association up there in Maine? According to stories three months ago—which have yet to be proven inaccurate—that same federal money paid for your house on the coast of Maine and your brand new Cadillac automobile."

Fuming, Worthington started to reply, but Redgrave fired again. "Now isn't there a passage in the Bible, Mr. Rhodes, about God asking us to be honest and faithful in smaller matters before awarding us with broader responsibilities?"

To Worthington's relief, Clarence Short stood, turned toward Redgrave and looked squarely into the camera. "Now wait just a damn minute. You can't go around making unsubstantiated allegations. It's not American, and besides, in this country a man's supposed to be innocent until he's proven guilty. By God, we've fought some wars to preserve that right!" Clarence's speech was intended to instruct the reporter in a principle of American jurisprudence.

Several others joined in with whistles and applause.

"Mr. Rhodes is one of us," a train buff told Redgrave.

"Yeah, you take that all-gossip crap back East where it belongs," another shouted.

A woman stood. Worthington recognized her costume as a 1920 Harvey Girl's uniform: black skirt eight inches off the floor, starched, high-collared white blouse, black shoes, and black stockings. "Go away, Mr. Reporter. We're not interested in the past. The future is ours to behold here tonight. You leave us and Mr. Rhodes alone."

Worthington was caught between a frown at the reporter and a smile for the woman when Clarence grasped his shoulder. "Come on, Mr. Rhodes, let's get outa here. You don't have to take this bullshit!" The surveyor led Worthington by the arm out a side door through the disused baggage room. Willie followed.

"You haven't answered my questions," Worthington heard Redgrave call out. In the next breath the reporter commanded his cameraman, "Back to the truck! We'll follow 'em!"

Outside, Clarence gestured toward his Range Rover. "Get in, Mr. Rhodes." He opened the vehicle's rear door, watching Willie make the leap into the back. Speeding away, he assured Worthington he'd lose that reporter on the back roads to Chama. Clarence turned off the paved state highway and accelerated, sending up a cloud of dust. "Have a beer. There's a cooler behind your seat."

"Don't mind if I do."

Clarence took a curve at high speed, looking in the rear view mirror. "I think we've lost the guys in the truck. They don't know the territory like I do. Say, toss me one of those brewskies."

Worthington handed a beer can to Clarence. "Here's to our *Windjammer*," he said happily, abandoning all inhibitions.

Clarence eyeballed Worthington. "You know, all work and no play makes Worthington a dull boy. Right?"

"Right."

"So, let's me and you see if we can loosen you up a bit."

Clarence soon steered the Range Rover into the parking lot of Klub Kokopelli. The parking lot was full of pickup trucks and motorcycles. Clarence pulled into a vacant blue-painted handicap space. The nightspot's bright yellow neon sign flashed a figure playing a flute and changing from one stance to another, giving the appearance of dancing. In one of the fleeting positions the figure appeared to have a neon erection.

Worthington laughed and stepped down into the club's den of iniquity. On stage a woman held onto a brass pole, moving her body in sync with the bump-and-grind music. Except for her engineer's cap and high-heeled shoes, she was naked.

Clarence chose a table by the stage. "I come here often." He stuffed a twenty dollar bill into the arch of the dancer's shoe. "A couple beers here in the evening, along with a show of tits and ass, and a man can feel like he's a man again." He ordered two draughts from the topless waitress.

"Any troubadours ever sing here?" Worthington asked as he took another swig from his frosty mug.

"Sing? Why sure, if you want to. This here's the Four Corners. You can do anything you want in these parts, so long as nobody gets killed."

"I've been known to knock 'em dead with a song."

"What song? I'll have Emiliano play it for you."

Worthington borrowed a cowboy hat and climbed up on stage as the combo struck up his tune. Booming out in his baritone voice, Worthington drew cheers from the ranch hands and train crews out for an evening on what there was of the town. Joined by another dancer, one now on each side of Worthington, the three of them cavorted on stage as he sang.

When Worthington finished, Clarence climbed up on the stage, took the microphone and announced, "Men, this here's Worthington Rhodes. He's head of the *Windjammer*, the fast new magnetic train and its giant city-station that'll bring good jobs and prosperity to the Four Corners." Clarence led the applause. "It'll be a new deal for all of us." The audience cheered. Cowboy hats flew in the air. Several shouted, "More, more." Emiliano directed the combo into *Happy Days Are Here Again*.

One man shouted, "We're with you, Mr. Rhodes. You're our kinda guy. We don't give a fuck about the wheel." Others whooped and whistled. One of the dancers threw her arms around Worthington and kissed him. A camera flash went off, blinding him momentarily. Then another. As his vision cleared, Worthington saw Redgrave standing in front of him.

Tipping his beer, Clarence called to Worthington. "They followed us. We better get the hell outa here."

"Aw now, Clarence, I'm just beginning to enjoy myself."

Clarence tugged at him. "Come on, you'll only give them more shit to write about." Carrying their beers, Clarence led Worthington out through the back door.

After driving fifteen or twenty minutes, Clarence pulled up to his boxcar home. "Come into my parlor car." Worthington followed the corrupting spider up the iron ladder. His host pulled the tabs from two beer cans, drank from each, and then poured a shot of whiskey into them. They fizzed over. He wiped off one with his sleeve and handed it to Worthington. "Boilermakers," he said. "A trainman's drink."

The surveyor slid the boxcar door open, welcomed Willie and, taking another swig of his boilermaker, reached into the twenty-five pound bag of dog chow and filled Willie's bowl. Slurring his words, Clarence said to Worthington, "You know what you need, old pal?"

Worthington slumped down on an army cot and looked up inquiringly at Clarence.

"You need a good piece of ass. Not like one of those dance hall whores. But one who'll treat ya right."

Worthington downed his boilermaker. "That was good. I'd like another."

Clarence stumbled over to his refrigerator. He opened a can of beer and tossed it across the room at Worthington. Suds spewed out of the missile—cosmic debris trailing a comet. Watching the foaming projectile, Worthington roared with laughter. Clarence held his belly and guffawed so loud the dirty plates in the sink rattled. Willie ran for cover underneath Worthington's cot. Clarence tossed the whiskey bottle. Worthington barely made the catch.

"Iss okay, Willie," Worthington assured the dog as he added the amber fluid to his can. "Your dog's acting like he's the one who needs company tonight."

"Out here there's only coyote bitches. And they're tough mothers." Clarence guffawed.

Worthington suddenly felt Clarence's boxcar rolling down the tracks, its speed increasing, its rocking motion nauseating him. His words now came haltingly. "Clarence, where's this freight of yours headed?"

Clarence drank again. "I know just the woman for you. She's out here on one of those archaeological digs, and you should dig her chassis." He cupped his hands and held them out from his chest. "Yeah, and you know what else."

Worthington shook his head, the boxcar tilting to take a curve. He heard the engineer blow a warning blast.

"You wouldn't have to worry about the consequences, neither. Me 'n Dillon were taking some linear and angular measurements, and we passed through their camp the other day. Tony—he's the guy with the llamas—told me she's already been knocked up."

The boxcar stopped with a screech. Worthington couldn't believe what he was hearing. He put down his can. He stared at Clarence. "What's this woman's name?"

Clarence looked surprised. "You don't need to know her name. She's a good lay, and then you're on your way." He guffawed again.

Worthington stood up, at first unsteadily. Then as his adrenaline took control of his body, he planted both feet firmly on the boxcar floor. "What is her name?" he demanded.

Willie poked his head out from under the cot and watched. Clarence answered apprehensively, "Anna. Anna something or other. What difference does her name make? Put women between the sheets and they'll know what to do for you. They'll beg you for more with one of their seductive looks, you know what I mean." Clarence let out another guffaw.

Worthington's clenched fist hit squarely on the arachnid's jaw, silencing his guffaws. For good measure his other fist punched deeply into the abdominal spinnerets of Clarence's gut. The look of surprise on Clarence's face faded as he reeled backward, stumbled and fell, passing out on the old wooden plank floor of his boxcar.

Willie whined.

Watching Clarence collapse, Worthington felt great. This time his violent temper had been properly directed at a coarse, sexist, unfeeling lout. Men who degrade women with their macho talk deserve to be floored. He made up his mind he wouldn't stay around here any longer; he'd make his escape from this web and start his journey back to sanity.

Anna. His Anna. She was going to have his baby. He would stand by her. He wouldn't abandon her like his father had his mother, left alone in the wilds of Maine, no hospital, the doctor on his way through the snow. No sir, he knew his obligation, and he would honor it, regardless of the consequences to his own life. But why hadn't Anna told him she was going to have his baby? To a goddess like Anna, he may be only a mere mortal, but she must understand he was a responsible man.

Outside, in the light of the full moon, Worthington asked himself if he, an adulterous man, was any better than Clarence? Only if he made amends. Sara. His Sara. He'd have to win her back by being honest with her. And not that male honesty manufactured by Zoe and Edward, either. He would tell her that, in a weak moment, he had tasted the forbidden fruit. He would profess his true love to Sara and ask her to forgive him for fathering Anna's baby. But he must make her understand that he would assume responsibility for supporting this child. Certainly there was enough love in his family to embrace an innocent newborn.

Worthington followed the winding, twisting gravel road. He walked past a fence strung with barbed wire. The pasture beyond was punctuated with sage. He smelled its pungent aroma. Clumps of this bitter bush crowded around a darkened house. Its dependent outbuildings were also engulfed by these invading shrubs. He grieved for the entire farm.

The continuing physical and mental exercise sobered his mind. The only intrusions on his thoughts were the night sounds. Off in the distance a nocturnal creature answered a screech owl. At the edge of a white water stream two raccoons cleansed the finds of their night's hunt. He heard the soft breeze whisper through the cottonwoods and wondered what insights might be derived from this sweet voice.

The road crossed the stream. On the wooden bridge Worthington stopped and watched the changing reflections of the moonlight on the water. He tried to recall which side of the

Continental Divide he was on, the Atlantic or the Pacific. Was this water intent on joining the Rio Grande and flowing successfully to the Gulf of Mexico, or was its destination the Colorado River where it would disappear into the endless sands of Baja California?

Suddenly a bull walked onto the road and stood there looking at him. The bull seemed bent on blocking his path. "Christ," Worthington said out loud. "I've got to pay more attention to the night. I can't be wandering out here without anticipating the dangers." His adversary's stance presented a major problem. He asked, "How am I going to outwit this huge animal?" He reasoned that if he was to continue his night walk, he'd have to come up with some sort of a plan—quick. He could grab a fence post and try to chase the bull away. But the bull might charge him instead. He could distract the bull by singing. On the other hand that might only antagonize the animal, so he ruled that out, too. Maybe a plan of compromise might work better with the beast. He would gather some dried grasses and offer them as a token of their meeting half way. At that moment the bull seemed to sense Worthington's determination to overcome the impasse, and he voluntarily moved off the road.

Worthington walked for the rest of the night, his thoughts focusing with a clarity he welcomed. In the silvery moonlight he began to filter the messages the press was sending. With each new bend in the road, he tried to sort out their hidden motives. Their attacks, he was now certain, had not been coincidental. Their questions had been designed to discredit him. Moreover, their queries sounded as though they had been orchestrated by a master impresario, timed to disrupt each of his presentations. Yes, he was now sure someone had been organizing a campaign to denounce the *Windjammer*.

He thought again about his chance meeting in Indianapolis with Quentin Ford IV. Could Quentin be the bull in the middle of the road? "The gobblins'll getcha . . ." Of course. He needn't re-examine the chairman's remarks at the Eiteljorg Museum for their double meaning. Quentin must be acting on his own, or perhaps on behalf of ILMA to save the archaeological sites. Yes, that was what was going on. Quentin had hired his own media mercenaries. For this once, being paranoid was healthy. Quentin was out to get him. And like the bull, he must now offer him a compromise solution, for what he wanted most in all the world was to see his *Windjammer* built.

But a handful of grass just wouldn't do it this time. And Quentin wasn't going to move out of the way. Why hadn't Quentin come to him in the first place? Communication is not easy when emotions get in the way. He was guilty of the same inhibitions when he tried to talk to his own father. Nevertheless he must try to communicate some plan of compromise to Quentin Ford IV. But what could it be?

Walking along, he came upon the eroding walls of an old adobe church. Rising from the one remaining roof beam, a white wooden cross reflected the moonlight. He envisioned the 1940s movie star, Jennifer Jones, playing the role of Saint Bernadette. He entered the adobe ruins to find his vision. Above where the alter had once been, someone had piled up rocks, creating a small grotto. They had placed a carved wooden santos, a bunch of artificial flowers, and a prayer candle in the shrine. Bending over and lighting the wick, Worthington suddenly saw the whole picture. He would work to save the prehistoric sacred sites of America and not destroy them during construction of the *Windjammer*. Yes, and Anna would like that; she'd admire him and his resourceful efforts, and her baby, when it grew up, would be proud of him for preserving the Anasazi ruins for its generation to see and to touch. The details, of course, were still to be worked out, but thanks to Jennifer Jones, he did have a plan—a compromise he could offer Quentin Ford IV.

Worthington resumed his walk. Off in the distance he heard a rooster crow. As the eastern sky brightened with the promise of a new day, his pace quickened. Song birds punctuated the early morning stillness with their nostalgic selections. He scuffed the gravel, bent over, picked up a flat rock and skipped it across the stream. With delight he noticed a plethora of wildflowers, their colors recognizable in the swelling daylight. Their fragrances were as welcome as early morning bacon on a campfire griddle.

The sun was rising over the distant Rockies as Worthington walked into Chama. Down the road from Klub Kokopelli, the old log building now sober and silent in the light of morning, he saw the Gandy Dancer Diner. He looked at his watch. Yes, he was on time for his breakfast meeting.

Inside, scanning the crowd, Worthington picked out Edward and Zoe sitting at the counter. He climbed up on the vacant stool between his disconsolate spin doctors, simultaneously slapping them on their backs. "Good morning, guys. Thanks for saving me a seat. Have you cleaned up last night's news reports yet?" Worthington laughed heartily. "Wait 'till you hear about my revelation."

Chapter Thirty-four

The Farmington Community Band concluded its opening arrangement of John Philip Sousa's *Semper Fidelis March*. The concertmaster turned to the cheering crowd gathered in the plaza of the eleventh century Anasazi stone city. "Welcome to our Tenth Annual Greek-American Friendship Day. Thanks to the Salmon family and the San Juan County Archaeological Research Center, our summer series this year is taking place here in the Salmon ruins at the terminus of the ancient Chaco Great Northern Road. Perhaps next year we could meet on the Acropolis in Athens. As your local travel agent, I could get you a special round trip ticket and tour of classical Greece plus a cruise of the Aegean islands for less than a thousand dollars. Cheaper than a week in Dallas." There was a murmur of laughter.

"Here in the Four Corners, community bands made up of volunteer musicians have been playing for more than a hundred and forty years," he informed the audience. "Later on in this afternoon's program you're in store for a real treat. Anthony Andros, owner of our world-famous local eatery, The Taverna Apollo, will play Mikis Theodorakis' memorable score from *Zorba the Greek* on his bouzouki." There was polite applause.

Along with Zoe, Edward, and a host of townspeople, Worthington relaxed on his day off. Old people, young people, Hispanics, Indians, Anglos, and visiting tourists from Europe and Asia munched on picnic lunches. Men carried ice chests to the chained-down picnic tables. A baby cried. Program vendors called out. A troop of Girl Scouts marched around waving the blue and white Greek flags they had made especially for the occasion.

Worthington lazily stretched his arms high in the air and awaited the next musical selection.

The conductor raised his baton and the crowd quieted for a medley of *New York, New York,* followed by *St. Louis Blues* and *I Left my Heart in San Francisco.* Matching the beat, Worthington's mind tapped out how to structure the bits and pieces of his compromise plan that he hoped would persuade Quentin Ford IV to call off his journalistic wolf pack. He realized this was a tough assignment, and not one he could address solely by himself. He'd need the sounding board of several qualified experts who could critique the effectiveness of his plan and also voice their professional endorsements.

"When do we get to the Greek music?" Zoe whispered to Worthington. "That's the reason I came. My maternal great-great-grandmother was from Mykonos."

"She was? I'll bet you got your lovely dark eyes from her."

"No, she taught Zoe to belly dance, and later in the program we're in for a real treat." Edward turned his baseball cap around so its bill pointed backwards.

Zoe laughed. "Everyone can learn a lot from their family. We've always been close. My father sees to it—reunions every year and we send each other E-mail."

Worthington thought about his father. A lifetime apart. He didn't like the bearded old man. Yet he really didn't know him. So why did he hold him in contempt? Dusty was a gruff old man. Yes. But so was his friend Henry D'Camp. Why couldn't Dusty be his friend, too? Maybe that was too much to ask. But couldn't he put Dusty into the category of advisor, someone qualified with whom he could discuss his plan to placate Quentin Ford IV?

What had his father said about his archaeologist friend in Greece? Wasn't Dusty trying to find him his next assignment? Wasn't Athens building a subway through layers of Greek and Roman ruins? Surely they were having to cope with the same problems he must face here. And hadn't he read about the Mexico City subway? Ruins in the way. Burial sites. Sacred places. Each country's ethos crying out for preservation. Yes, Worthington concluded, if the Greeks and the Mexicans could somehow construct their rail lines over, under, around, or through their ancient cities while being sensitive to archaeological interests, he must do the same for this country. Worthington stood up. "It's imperative I find a phone and call my father," he said to Edward and Zoe.

"Here, use mine." Zoe reached into her daypack and handed him her cellular phone. To make his call Worthington sought the quiet of the stone ruins. Once inside this cloister, his head almost touched the juniper poles of the low ceiling. The smoke-marred walls seemed to press in on him. Through a doorway in the opposite wall he could see another room. Beyond was another doorway and room, at the end of which yet another doorway led to still another room where light from a clerestory window illuminated the trilogy of passageways.

He punched in Dusty's number. A busy signal. Continuing to press the instrument's redial button, he entered the second room and sat on a ledge. Finally, over the sound of the distant band music, Worthington heard a ring.

"Dusty Rhodes."

"Congratulations," Worthington said to his father. "You've made a major discovery on your sabbatical."

"Are you someone calling from the American Archaeological Society?"

"No, no," Worthington said and laughed. "It's me Worthington."

"Oh." Dusty sounded disappointed.

"Actually I'm calling from a tiny room inside the Salmon Ruins." Worthington laughed. "It's the oldest phone booth I've ever been in."

"You in a ruins? Hard to believe. I've been taking calls for days now from all over the world. The entire archaeological community wants my opinion. The press, too." Dusty paused. "Even my little Emily called."

"She did?"

"Yes. To congratulate me. She said she knew I'd find her wheel. She's told her classmates it was her grandfather who found the wheel."

"That's why I called you, sir."

"Yes. Well, ah, thanks."

"No, I mean I want to ask for your advice. In addition to offering my congratulations, of course."

"What are you trying to say? Speak up. I'm expecting several important calls from authorities wanting my scientific verification. We only have one line out here."

Worthington began to fume at his father's impatience. Christ, he swore to himself. Why doesn't he give me a chance to express myself? But why should I even have to ask his permission to speak? He realized, difficult as it might be, he must wend his way through this conversation if he was to achieve his objective. He tried, "Today is Greek-America Friendship Day here." He held the phone so Dusty could hear the music.

"That's Greek music!" his father exclaimed. "Where'd you say you were calling from?"

Worthington told him again.

"You in a ruins? Don't you think it's pretty late for you to become an archaeologist?"

Worthington moved into the third room. Here the ceiling was higher. He laughed. "I hope it's not too late to join the archaeological march. But I'll need your help to get in step."

"What sort of help can I possibly give you?" Dusty asked warily.

Attracted by the light in the fourth room, Worthington ducked his head and entered. The room was much brighter. His tone of voice was positive. "When I called before, you mentioned your friend in Greece . . ."

"Angelo Angelopolous? My archaeologist friend who is looking for a new assignment?"

"Yes."

"My advice is the same as I was about to tell you last time. He's someone you should consult with. He's highly qualified. He has degrees in both transit engineering and archaeology." Dusty was enthusiastic. "The archaeological community is overjoyed with the discoveries he turns up and how he allows them time for scientific study—photographing, cataloging, and laboratory work—before the bulldozers arrive."

"With the help of your friend, the *Windjammer*'s excavations could provide enough grist for doctoral dissertations for the next hundred years," Worthington was quick to reply. "But let's hope he would temper his archaeological passion with the pragmatic approach of an engineer."

"He will. I guarantee it. You want to hire him?"

"Yes, right away! He has the know-how I need for the *Windjammer*. How can I get in touch with him?"

"Why don't you call him. I'll give you his telephone number."

"I'd rather discuss my plan with him in person. Could you call him and set up a meeting in Athens as soon as possible?"

"I can't get away from our dig, but I'll contact Angelo and tell him that you want to see him. Let's say, at the Grand Bretagne Hotel on Constitution Square—tomorrow evening at the end of siesta."

Worthington looked at his watch. "Yes. There must be an airport around here somewhere. This is great, Father. We'll be marching shoulder to shoulder on this one." Worthington began to pace back and forth across the earthen floor of this Anasazi room. After all these years of being estranged from his father, he now felt a feeling of kinship. Worthington choked up. "Father, now you and I will be working together to save the nation's illustrious past and to build its glorious future."

Chapter Thirty-five

When Worthington told Zoe and Edward he must leave immediately for Greece, the news took them by surprise. But when he related his conversation with Dusty, Edward's imagination went into high gear. While Zoe drove to the Four Corners Regional Airport, Edward verbally composed media news releases about Worthington's dynamic new tack of navigating through the winds of compromise, and Zoe voiced her edits. Their combined youthful enthusiasm added to Worthington's exhilaration.

"When you've got Zorba hired, we'll stage a news conference right there in front of the Parthenon on the Acropolis overlooking Athens," Edward declared. "A prime time, front page photo-op for the media."

"Don't you think he's been photographed with enough naked caryatides already?"

They all laughed as they arrived at the tiny terminal building. Edward jumped out of the car to shake Worthington's hand. "Call us as soon as you arrive in Athens. Zoe and I'll have a slew of ideas for you by then."

Worthington grabbed his travel bag and started to run for the ticket counter.

"Wait," Edward shouted, "I have a story for you to tell the media." He raced after Worthington.

"What story?" Worthington called over his shoulder.

"The Great American Compromise. The media'll love it. And so will the bull in Washington—the one who's been out to stop you and the *Windjammer*."

"Your flight's in the final boarding stage, Mr. Rhodes," the airline attendant advised.

Edward ran with Worthington toward the gate. "According to history texts, President James K. Polk pulled it off back in 1846."

Worthington handed his ticket and bag to the flight attendant at the foot of the plane's fold-down stairs.

"'54° 40' or Fight' was the battle cry of the Manifest Destiny crowd in the Oregon Territory," Edward recited. "But the fur trappers up in British Columbia claimed all the land south of the Columbia River."

Worthington turned and called from the top of the stairs, "They compromised!"

"You're right," Edward shouted as the plane's second motor started. "Compromise is the currency of smart politicians. They agreed to extend westward the 49th parallel bordering the northern reaches of Montana. Everyone agreed on the new US-Canadian border."

Worthington nodded at Edward and waved. The flight attendant retracted the stairs and shut the door.

Later, on the long overseas flight from JFK to Athens, Worthington reflected about compromise and what he would say to Quentin Ford IV. From his study of political science at Bowdoin, he had come to believe that compromise denoted strength, not weakness. The willingness to modify one's position on an issue in order to achieve one's ultimate objective had enabled the American political experiment to flourish. Otherwise, with so many economic and political interests at play among its many ethnic groups, the United States would have been Balkanized into countless enclaves, each committed to do battle in unbending advocacy of their positions.

❖ ❖ ❖ ❖

"Welcome to Greece, Mr. Rhodes. I'm sure you noticed our Metro station construction in Constitution Square." The man with bushy eyebrows, holding a trowel in one hand and a railroad spike in the other, introduced himself. "I'm Angelo Angelopolous. Wherever you see our five interlacing Olympic rings of red, orange, blue, green, and yellow on those construction barricades, you can be sure progress is taking place."

"That's what I want to talk to you about," Worthington said. "Progress for my country is number one on my agenda, and I'm looking forward to our interview." He led Angelo into the hotel lounge.

Angelo handed Worthington his resumé and ordered two glasses of ouzo. "To your health," he said as Worthington began to read.

"What do you consider your strong points to be?" Worthington asked.

"I can down five of these without flinching."

"What are your weaknesses?"

"I love my car and I can't save any money. I've spent tomorrow's rent money gassing it up. Two hundred drachmas per liter, you know."

"What would you do if a Greek bull stepped in front of your car?"

"I'd honk my horn."

"What's been the biggest challenge in your life?"

"Talking to you right now."

"Do you want to help me build a magnetic train across North America, preserving our archaeological wonders?"

"More than anything else."

"Good, you're hired."

The two men clinked their glasses and drank the clear anise-flavored, unsweetened liqueur.

"We must have a toast to the Olympic spirit," Angelo proposed as he signaled the waiter.

A smile of inspiration lit up Worthington's face. "Angelo, I have just this instant renamed our maglev train The *Anasazi Spirit*."

"May your train have the energy of a whispering arrow."

"I couldn't have said it better."

Chapter Thirty-six

The Rocky Mountain maples had turned a brilliant red, the white-barked aspen were quaking their gold, the dwarf gamble oaks had leatherized their leaves, and the piñon had brought forth their bounty of pine nuts. The Four Corners landscape had been transformed into the fall season.

Anna's appearance had turned just as gradually and just as certainly. She had Tony bring her bolts of cotton cloth from the Cross Cultural Trading Post so she could make her own maternity skirts. From spun llama wool, she wove brown, black, and gray squares which she sewed together, fashioning a native serape. And from the tanned hide of a deer which Tony shot, she crafted sandals and lined them with rabbit fur. She discarded her makeup in favor of painting symbolic designs on her face with red ochre and black charcoal. One day she showed up with her hair wound tightly on each side of her head in wheel-like bobs, reminiscent of the ancient Hopi women.

The seminarists witnessed Anna's metamorphosis. Although they talked among themselves about her bizarre turn, either out of respect or in fear of offending, no one commented to Anna. Yet all of them were concerned how her marked change had transformed her slowly, but surely, into a prospective Anasazi mother.

Anna's perspective about archaeology, which had already shifted, took on a winter's cold of rationalizing that the end justified the means. She felt she no longer had the time to pursue the traditional scientific method of advancing a theory, digging up evidence, and establishing proof. But why this premonition of time running out? As the days grew shorter, Anna vowed no longer to bury herself in the past, but instead to look to the immediate future. And that meant preparations for the birth of her child.

"Anna, we are all so excited about your new baby. Have you thought of a name?" Martha asked her one day.

A mystical look came into Anna's eyes. "He shall be called Popé."

"After the inspirational Indian leader who united all the New Mexico pueblos?" Margaret asked. She explained to the others, "He's the one who, in 1680, led his brothers in the only successful revolt in North America against the tyranny of the Spanish invaders."

"Anna, we should think about getting you to the hospital in Farmington," Tony urged. "In your delicate condition, we'll have to travel the trail slowly."

"No, up on my sacred mesa is where I am to give birth. I shall call Silver Bell in the Night to come and be my midwife." Anna looked at Tony. "You will meet her at the Cross Cultural Trading Post and show her the way to Noah's Ark."

Chapter Thirty-seven

Worthington paused at the Propylaia, the monumental gates leading to the Acropolis, and stared up at the Parthenon. The twenty-five-hundred-year-old Doric temple, dedicated to the goddess Athena, dominated the rock plateau.

"From these portals you have the best view of ancient Athens." The tone of Angelo Angelopolous's voice was reverent. "To really appreciate this special place, we must not allow ourselves to be disturbed by all these tourists. Here a man must ponder his own thoughts."

At last Worthington could finally dismiss his humiliating boyhood trip to Greece, for his father had now become an ally, and he, Worthington, was taking a new look at the science of archaeology. Anna's archaeology. For her sake, he was anxious to share his new outlook with his principle adversary, Quentin Ford IV. He hoped to get him off his back so he could build *The Anasazi Spirit*. He also yearned to make amends to Sara by asking for her forgiveness. His plate was full.

The two men walked to the corner of the Parthenon where Worthington's press conference was to take place. They were followed by reporters and cameramen. Worthington's opening statement was simultaneously translated into Greek for the local media, "I am Worthington Rhodes, architect of a preservation train that will soon span America. It is fitting that we have the Parthenon as our backdrop this morning, because this magnificent structure rose as a tribute to your Olympic spirit. It transmits a message to the world telling of the importance of the mind, of the body, and of the soul.

"The Acropolis in the fifth century B.C. was a city on the edge. It was the birthplace not of architecture, for the megalithic monument of Stonehenge was built two thousand years earlier; nor of art, for outstanding examples of Aurignacian cave paintings were drawn by the Lauscaux artists sixteen thousand years earlier; nor of literature, for the Sumerians, with their cuneiform writing, recorded their ideas in the fourth millennium B.C. No, the Acropolis was the cradle of democracy. During this golden age, man was free at last to express himself in words, in deeds, and in skills. Today, as we strive to advance even further, progress can only be thwarted by narrow-mindedness, fanaticism, prejudice, intolerance, and discrimination.

"Now, across the oceans in America, I will personally make sure your Olympic message is actively championed, for we will respect all accomplishments of man while at the same time, through advances in technology, strive to improve our modern society. Honoring our original Americans and their achievements, the official name of our magnetic train will henceforth be *The Anasazi Spirit.*

"Now I want to introduce your own Angelo Angelopolous. He has graciously consented to undertake the new position of Director of Routes and Preserver of the American Legacy, a title I have shortened to DR. PAL."

The two men answered question after question about their plans for *The Anasazi Spirit.* Eventually a little girl stepped forward and looked up at Worthington. "In your country do you build temples to your goddesses?"

"Please excuse my daughter, Merika," said a woman holding a CNN television camera. "She's taken the day off from school, Mr. Rhodes. She wanted so much to see you in person so she could tell her class."

"In my country, Merika, we idolize our goddesses in private ways, and on very special occasions a goddess may visit us."

◆　◆　◆　◆

After the press conference Worthington walked back to his hotel through the narrow, winding streets of the old Plaka, lost in thought. Back in his hotel, he rode a Lilliputian-size elevator to the third floor and walked down the hall to his room. He opened the door. A woman was in his bed. "Oops, sorry, wrong room," he apologized. Embarrassed, he turned and started to shut the door.

"Come back here, you dashing scoundrel," a female voice commanded.

"Sara!" Worthington exclaimed, his voice choking with emotion and surprise. He leapt across the room. Sara sat up, the covers falling away from her. A sheer negligee draped her shapely body. He embraced her. Their lips re-introduced themselves. "How'd you find me?"

"It was your photograph in the *Washington Post* with those two sirens in engineer caps dancing arm in arm with you."

"Oh, my God! Klub Kokopelli."

"You looked as if you were going to be led astray."

"I'm afraid I was a little tipsy."

"You looked so vulnerable. I called your press aide. She told me you'd flown to Athens, so I decided to catch the next nonstop out of Dulles. She related your plan to hire Mr. Angelopolous, told me where you were staying, and about your news conference at the Parthenon. So here I am. I watched you on TV. You were wonderful."

"I'm so glad you've come, Sara."

"All the way across the Atlantic I kept saying to myself, 'Worthington, husband of mine, you're a very interesting, exciting, and adventuresome man.' I know most women would react negatively to such a provocative photograph. But I'm not 'most women,' and you're not 'most men,' and heaven knows, our children are not 'most children.' It's just that . . ."

"What, Sara?"

"You've excluded me from your life. I guess you've been so busy, but I've felt so left out of your plans . . . I guess the expression would be 'shunted to a siding' . . . I mean, you and I used to talk about everything . . . our hopes, our dreams, life in the District . . ." She looked searchingly at him. "Worthington, I want us to reconcile—to enjoy the relationship we treasured before you became so engrossed in your project, but I don't want you to abandon *The Anasazi Spirit* . . . I want to be a part of your life again."

Worthington hugged her with a passion that surprised her. "You forgive me?" he asked.

"Do you forgive me?"

"But, Sara, there's something else I must tell you."

"Worthington, I don't care about your Uncle Bill, about Charlene, about your past income tax returns, your old house in Maine, or about anyone else." Sara smiled tenderly. "We forgive each other, and will stand by each other, no matter what."

The telephone rang.

"Probably Angelo with another idea," Worthington said, picking up the phone. "Mr. Ford! How nice of you to call." He whispered to Sara, "He saw the news conference and he's bubbling with excitement."

"My boy, how wonderful. I'm so happy and, of course, Stuart is, too. Everyone at ILMA will want to be on your train from here on out. I love the new name."

"I'm glad to have your support."

"Yes, I'm passing the word to . . . ah . . . my boys in the media. I do believe you and I have reconciled our differences." Ford continued breathlessly. "Now here's what I want you to do. You bring that Angelo Angelopolous back to Washington with you and I'll tell Stuart to stage the grandest social event of the season in Georgetown. Every benefactor on the East Coast will have to attend the reception and contribute to our united causes, that is, if they want to maintain their social status among the altruistic of America."

Chapter
Thirty-eight

Silver Bell in the Night found both the store and the cantina at the Cross Cultural Trading Post invaded by the media. From the many languages being spoken and the flags of various countries displayed on backpacks and camera bags, it was apparent Anna's discovery of the Anasazi wheel had drawn worldwide attention. The journalists were joshing among themselves about which of them would write the exposé revealing the real murderer of the inventor of the wheel. Leon, the proprietor, was all smiles as he sold the last of his stuffed armadillos to a Japanese photographer. Contributing to the circus atmosphere, the local people were selling T-shirts with a silk-screened caricature of Anna driving a Stone Age chariot.

Anxious to reach Anna's side, Silver Bell was happy to see Tony, but dismayed when he warned her about the rain storm headed their way from out of the Southern Rockies. She told him he was an alarmist and suggested that by evening the sun would come out and they would have another magnificent sunset. But Tony disagreed. "With clouds as black as those, we could be in for forty days and forty nights of rain."

Since she had counted on his llamas to carry her supplies, she became even more distraught when he explained that his animal friends were so skittish about the impending storm, they wouldn't go anywhere, and he'd had to lodge them in the barn out back for the night. When she insisted they must get underway immediately, he told her to pack those items she absolutely had to take with her into her backpack. She did, and a few minutes later they set out, following the now well-beaten trail toward Noah's Ark.

After an hour of hiking, Tony announced, "I felt a drop of rain."

A distant lightning bolt zigzagged across dark clouds in the western sky. Thunder rumbled. Silver Bell paused atop a small mesa, took out her rain poncho, and assessed the storm. On the western horizon those dark clouds were releasing sheets of rain. Yet the sky was not entirely overcast. In the south the sun shone, highlighting distant mesas in a polychromatic light. The landscape waited for the storm to decide upon its course. Perhaps, on a day such as this, thousands of years earlier, an Anasazi leader had first set eyes on the Four Corners. Silver Bell could hear the elder counseling with Spider Woman and his subsequent pronouncement to his followers, "This is the place. We are home now." Silver Bell, too, felt at home. The air was electric and, sensing the energy about her, she felt a communion with the spirits of her ancient people. She dismissed the idea that a far-off storm could prevent her from fulfilling her midwifery mission.

But when they descended into the next arroyo, to her shock, she saw water gushing along the stream bed and covering the trail. A media person ahead of them was trying to cross the stream, but found himself waist-deep in muddy water. He called to his two partners for help, but seeing him struggle, they panicked. Abandoning him, they ran past Silver Bell and Tony back toward a known civilization. Tony adeptly lassoed the drowning man with his rope and pulled him to safety. The man nodded his thanks and took off down the trail after his cowardly companions.

"We'd better turn around, too," Tony advised.

"No! We must press on. We'll use your rope to ford the stream. Come on!"

Tony tied the rope to himself and then around Silver Bell's waist and waded into the quickening current. She followed, plunging into the rising, bubbling waters, with her arms up, holding her pack high. She dodged drifting branches and other forest debris swirling past her in the swollen stream. Once she almost lost her footing. By the time she reached the opposite shore, the water had risen chest high. Scrambling up the bank, she looked back. Somewhere upstream the force of the water had uprooted a young cottonwood tree and now whipped it along in its clutches. They had made it just in time.

Silver Bell recalled Worthington Rhodes telling Congressman Roybal that he had ordered his engineers to design bridges along the *Windjammer*'s route that would withstand a hundred-year flood. "A wall of water," he had said, "can do as much damage as a California earthquake."

Rain now pummeled them. Heavy drops struck the rocks like bullets being fired. She had forgotten how noisy the rain could be. In Washington, precipitation was misty. But out here the rain attacked the land. Silver Bell pulled up the hood of her poncho. As she struggled to keep her balance on the slippery trail, water cascaded around her feet and mud splattered her legs.

She and Tony reached the top of the next rise. Down below they saw an awesome divide, a deep, narrow corkscrew canyon.

"The trail's going to be slippery going down, and we'll have to maneuver around those petrified sandstone spirals in the bottom of the canyon," Tony said apprehensively.

"And even more treacherous going up the other side." Silver Bell dried her face. "We must be getting ten inches of rain in this storm."

They started down. Ahead of her, Tony slipped on a wet rock and fell onto the muddy trail. Suddenly Silver Bell felt the hair rise on the back of her neck. Lightning illuminated the canyon below where she could see water, deep water, rushing through the narrow gorge. Simultaneously thunder roared around them and overhead a loud crack terrified her.

"Look out!" Tony yelled. A giant ponderosa pine, struck by the lightning bolt, was falling toward them. Tony clamored onto his feet, grabbed Silver Bell and together they dove for the protection of a rock outcropping as the giant tree fell with a swoosh of air across the canyon, its reddish trunk bridging the chasm and its green-needled branches splashing mud as it hit the opposite bank.

"That was close." Silver Bell's voice was weak.

"Yes," Tony agreed, "but don't you see, the tree has become a short cut planned for us by the heavens. We'll walk right across." He gestured into the gorge. "We'd never have made it down there."

"Let's go then, Tony." Silver Bell took several steps onto the trunk and stopped. "It's slippery," she called back. "And it's a long way down," she said with fright as she saw the raging stream churning around the smooth spires of sandstone and tumbling and washing loads of dirty tree limbs as it awaited the rinse cycle.

"Wait," Tony yelled, "let's leave our packs under those rocks and come back for them in the morning." He retrieved his rope and tied the twisted hemp around Silver Bell and himself, securing the line to a healthy descendant of the fallen ponderosa. This time Tony led the way. Instead of walking, they crawled on their hands and knees.

"Oh, Tony, look up there!" Silver Bell screamed as they passed the midway point. A mountain of water was rushing down the canyon and descending upon them. A tidal wave of doom.

"Goldarn! That wave must be thirty feet tall. I've heard stories about these flash floods, but in all my years in the back country I've never been in one."

"It'll swamp us," Silver Bell screamed as she straddled the log.

"We've got to get across and up to the top of that rise," Tony called out. "Can you stand up and run the rest of the way? That's our only hope."

The roar of wind struck them first, followed quickly by a rush of air whipping around them. Neither Tony nor Silver Bell found they were able to stand, for the force of the rushing air pinned them to the log. There they sat in terror, amazement, and awe—halfway across the gaping canyon. They watched in horror as the wall of water approached. The wave hit with such force the Earth shook and their bridge quivered. As the water splashed around and over them, Silver Bell feared she would be swept off her precarious perch. She hoped Tony's rope would hold. She felt the log buck beneath her. As she pitched forward she saw Tony wrap his long legs around the trunk. Silver Bell followed his lead and tried to hold onto an imaginary saddle horn and balance with her outstretched arm. As quickly as it had come, the wall of water passed.

Tony turned and saw her. "I see you're still in the saddle, Ms. Bell."

Silver Bell nodded. "We've beat the eight-second bell. But if that wave had been another foot or two . . ."

"Let's get the rest of the way across before this Brahma bull comes alive again."

They inched their way through the branches at the top of the fallen ponderosa. The opposite bank was wet and glistened with billions of quartz crystals impregnated in the sandstone. Slowly they made their way up the sparkling rise.

"We must get to Anna," Silver Bell said with determination.

Reaching the top of the bank, she grabbed Tony's arm as they stared ahead into the flooded valley. She saw only the top of a round tower and several rock walls of the ruins protruding above the turbid water. "Tony, we're too late."

"No, Ms. Bell, I just know our people are safe. Before I left Noah's Ark they were making two litters out of aspen poles and preparing to move their camp up to Anna's sacred mesa. We'll take that ridge trail over there and meet them."

"Look at this devastation." Silver Bell shivered at the horror of several bodies bobbing, face down, arms outstretched, bumping up against the tops of rock walls. Electronic gear floated everywhere. She saw an arm and hand clinging to the edge of a satellite dish, its antenna pointing upward toward the heavens attempting one last desperate communication. A camera with the letters ALL-GOSSIP TV NETWORK sank in the murky waters.

Sloshing through puddles, Silver Bell followed Tony in silence. Before he could turn and offer his hand, she leapt across the gaps in the places where the rain had washed away the cliffside trail . As the path connected with the one leading to the mesa top, her thoughts focused on a place for birth, not death.

On top of the mesa, Silver Bell saw a camp in the twilight. Three men sat on canvas chairs under a tarpaulin stretched between four aspen poles. A portable table stacked with supplies of food was also protected from the rain. Off to one side, a campfire smoked inside a ring of confining rocks. And in the other direction three tents had been erected so that they faced the East.

"Thank God! Here they come," George said to Dusty and Paul.

"I told you they'd make it," Paul said. "You must be Silver Bell in the Night. I've never been so happy to meet someone."

"How's Anna?" Silver Bell asked.

"The women are with her in the middle tent," George replied. "She went into labor about an hour ago, and Martha told us the contractions are coming every twenty minutes now."

"No, she said every twenty-five," Paul corrected.

"You'd better go to her," Dusty instructed Silver Bell. "Let us know if you need any boiling water."

Margaret and Greta came out of the tent when they heard the voices. "I'm so relieved you're here, Silver Bell," Margaret whispered. Then in a louder voice she called, "Martha, tell Anna Silver Bell's arrived."

"She's having a hard time—she's exhausted," Greta confided to Silver Bell. "I'm afraid the sudden storm caused us to move our camp sooner than we had planned—and much faster, too, to beat the flood. It was a difficult climb for her. Margaret and Martha tried their best to support her. Dusty and I carried one of the litters with the food lashed to it, and George and Paul carried the heavier one with the tents and camping equipment. The trail was so treacherous in the torrential rain that each of us fell at least once."

"Ms. Bell and I are thanking our lucky stars, too," Tony said. "If we'd been washed off our wild ponderosa, we'd be surfing Lake Powell by now."

"Now, now, why don't you people help Tony get some dinner on the table while Anna and I find out when this baby wants to come." Silver Bell disappeared into the folds of Anna's tent.

Anna was propped up with pillows and lying on top of a sleeping bag. She was in a buckskin nightdress fringed at the bottom. Each hanging thread was strung with tiny beads. The bodice of the dress was also decorated with attached beaded threads. Silver Bell was surprised at Anna's bizarre makeup and hairdo, but before she could comment, Martha spoke in a worried tone of voice. "I've never helped another woman give birth before." She cradled Anna's head in her arms.

"Love is what's needed most at this precious time," Silver Bell said.

Anna looked up, saw Silver Bell, and smiled faintly. "There's always love at a sacred place. That's why I asked the men to place my tent right over this Anasazi kiva." Anna's eyes closed. She grimaced with another contraction.

"Breathe deeply, Anna," Silver Bell counseled. "Try to make your abdomen rise as you inhale and fall as you exhale."

Anna nodded as Silver Bell tucked a pillow under her knees.

"I'll count for you when your contractions become stronger, and then I'll want you to switch to a pant with shallow chest breathing to get you through the first stage."

The rain continued to beat down on their canvas roof—as determined in its mission as a school children tormenting their teacher. There was, however, no recess for the storm nor was there a respite for Anna's labors throughout the dark night. When Anna's cervical dilation was complete and Silver Bell could see the baby's head in the birth canal, she sent Martha out to announce to the others that the birth was imminent. Silver Bell was now alone with Anna, experiencing the unique bond between midwife and mother. "You can bear down and help push your baby out to join this special world of ours," she told her in a soothing voice. "Now comes the joyous part, because you can use all your strength for your baby's benefit."

In the ensuing hour Anna did her best to comply with Silver's Bell's guidance. At one point in her weakened condition she grasped Silver Bell's arm. Her voice was unsteady. "If I leave this world, then I want you to . . ." Anna cried out in her struggle.

"Anna, Anna," Silver Bell said, trying to calm her as she bent over her, instructing her and encouraging her. "You're going to be all right. Women give birth every day."

But Anna whispered, her voice barely audible, "I want you to give my baby to Worthington Rhodes. He'll raise the child to realize its full potential." Anna paused. "The Anasazi will rejoice."

"Of course, of course," Silver Bell said. "But, Anna, you're going to be just fine."

The birth of the baby was slow—head first, then shoulders, then the body. With Anna's last push the baby was free, took a breath, and cried robustly.

"It's a boy, Anna!" Silver Bell exclaimed. She cut the umbilical cord, clamped it, wrapped the baby in a blanket, and turned to give Anna her newborn child.

Anna's face was ashen.

Dawn was beginning to lighten the eastern sky when, from inside the tent, the others heard Silver Bell scream. "Anna, Anna! Come back!" Her voice broadcast her despair across the mesa top.

Silver Bell emerged from the tent, carrying a baby bundle. The storm had passed and the rays from the rising sun illuminated the baby's face. She looked down at the newborn Popé and spoke his name softly. She turned and looked toward the Sleeping Ute. Framed by a rainbow, the mountain seemed to stir.

Epilogue

"Dear, sweet Popé," Emily cooed as she cuddled the child seated on her lap, making sure he was comfortable and could see the pictures. "This is my favorite storybook." She opened the cover and pointed to the handwritten inscription penned on the title page. She read out loud: "'Dear Emily, may the spirit of the past be the prologue to your future. As you go through life, protect and nurture this spirit. But you must also welcome the sunrise into your life. With love, Anna.'"

Emily looked up at Worthington. "Daddy, the beautiful lady loved us, didn't she?"

Before he could reply, Emily looked at the little child in her lap. "Popé, you're part of our family now, and we love you."

Popé nodded.